EVEN STEVEN

Chris Sherrill

Copyright © 2024 Joseph C Sherrill
Library of Congress Registration #TXu002461784
All rights reserved.

Hardback with Dust Jacket ISBN: 9798992526738
Paperback ISBN: 9798992526707
eBook ISBN: 9798992526745

evenstevenbook.com

DISCLAIMER

No part of this book may be reproduced in any form or by any electronic or mechanical means including information storage and retrieval systems, without permission in writing from the author. This is a work of fiction. Names, characters, places, and incidents are either the product of the author's imagination or are used fictitiously. Any resemblance to actual persons (living or dead), events, or locales is entirely coincidental.

1

The man slapped five crisp twenty-dollar bills on the table. He watched with a sneer as another man dumped a bag of ice into the steel tub, which was now filled with frigid water.

"Looks good to me," the first man said. He turned to Sara Durant. "Well, little lady, are you ready?"

Sara gave him a hard look. Then slowly, as if she had all the time in the world, she undid the belt of her terrycloth robe, slipped it from her shoulders, and casually held it out.

"Here Carl, hold this, will you?"

Carl took the robe while keeping his eyes rudely and obviously glued to Sara's stunning physique, ordinarily hidden under typical jeans and baggy shirts, but now revealed to view in a one-piece black swimsuit. Her lithe body was athletic, with supple muscles like a Greek statue. She was sensual but not vulnerable. Self-assured but not conceited. The type of woman who was easily underestimated—by both men and women.

EVEN STEVEN

Others joined the circle around the ice tub. They were at Sylvan's Gym, where word had spread that Sara Durant, a homicide detective with the Nashville Police Department, was going to try to break the club record for immersion in the ice tub. The previous record of eleven minutes was held by none other than Rudy Kennesaw, the burly club manager who had put up one hundred dollars as a challenge.

"You say you can last eleven minutes," said Rudy with a lascivious smile. "Remember what you promised to give me when you lost the bet."

"Dream on," replied Sara.

The assembled crowd snickered and nodded.

A man wearing a yellow hat pointed his phone at the surface of the water. "Thirty-four degrees Fahrenheit," he announced.

Sara paused by the side of the tub.

"You don't have to do this," said Carl.

"Correct," replied Sara, as she boldly stepped into the tub and stood with the icy water lapping at the middle of her smooth thighs. "Is the clock running?" she asked.

"Starting now," said the man with the yellow hat, while looking at his phone.

Without hesitation, Sara slid into the tub. The slushy water rose to her neck, and little ice cubes bumped against her chin. After one sharp intake of breath through pursed lips, her facial muscles relaxed and she half-closed her eyes. Casually, she rested her hands on the sides of the tub, as if

EVEN STEVEN

taking a comfortable Sunday soak at home.

The assembled group peered down at her.

"I'm sorry," she said, "But you're going to find this awfully boring. I should have brought a book or a magazine to read. Oh, well." She shifted her legs under the water, creating ripples in the floating frozen chunks.

One woman whispered to another, "I'll bet she studied with what's-his-name. The Iceman."

Her friend nodded. "Wim Hof."

Sara glanced at the pair. "Willpower and breathing. That's it. And practice, of course."

"I'm freezing just *looking* at her," said a man with bulging muscles that looked as if they had been inflated with a bicycle pump.

Time ticked by as the crowd slowed their breathing, nearly in sync with Sara.

"Five minutes elapsed," announced the man with the yellow hat.

Rudy folded his arms in annoyance.

Carl said, "I see a hundred bucks leaving your pocket, my friend."

The group watched attentively. Some took videos and photos for social media. Sara made no indication she cared. She sat with her eyes closed, as if meditating. Much to the disappointment of many, she was not turning blue.

EVEN STEVEN

"Seven minutes," said the man with the yellow hat. "Four more to go. Rudy, she's got you beat."

"Bonkers," someone said.

Sara opened her eyes. Slowly, she took both hands and splashed some ice water on her face with a teasing air of confidence. "It's good for the complexion. You probably saw *Mommie Dearest*, right? Joan Crawford was a bitch on wheels, but she knew about skincare."

"Nine minutes elapsed," said the man with the yellow hat. "Two minutes and change to go."

Sara had put her phone on the table next to the cash. Suddenly, it buzzed. She looked over at it. "Shit!" she muttered. "That ringtone is headquarters. Official business. I need to get that." She pointed to a petite woman with wavy blonde hair and neon green nails standing next to the table. "You! Pick up my phone. Say I'll be right there."

"Me?" asked the petite woman.

"Yes, you! Just pick it up!"

"One minute left," said the man with the yellow hat.

The petite woman picked up Sara's phone and tapped it onto speakerphone. "Sara will be here in a few seconds," she said.

"Who is this?" a voice demanded.

"Just a friend. She'll be right with you."

"Thirty seconds!" announced the man with the yellow hat.

An urgent voice from the speakerphone shouted, "Tell

EVEN STEVEN

Detective Durant this is official police business!"

"Captain Riggs!" shouted Sara. "I'm at the gym! Getting dressed!"

"She'll be here in a moment," said the petite woman.

"Ten, nine, eight," began the man with the yellow hat. "Seven, six, five..."

The group picked up the chant, "Four, three, two, one... Sara wins!"

11:31 appeared on the stopwatch as the man with the yellow hat held it out for everyone to see.

Amid the clapping and general joviality, Sara hoisted herself from the tub and, dripping wet, took the phone. Someone handed her a towel. The petite woman took Sara's robe from Carl and draped it over her shoulders.

"One second, Captain," said Sara into her phone. With her free hand she scooped up the twenties and shoved them into the fleecy pocket of the robe. Covering the phone, she said to Rudy Kennesaw, "Nice doing business with you." She turned and hurried to the entrance of the women's locker room. She quickly found a quiet corner and said, "Sorry about that, Captain. What's up?

"What's up, Detective Durant, is a homicide. If you're not otherwise engaged"—his voice dripped with sarcasm— "we need you at the scene. Your partner is on his way."

2

Sara drove her Ford Mustang Dark Horse—the one personal indulgence she allowed herself—across the Cumberland River to Bell's Bend, a rural enclave half an hour west of town. On Old Hickory Boulevard, there was a driveway you could easily miss because of the overhanging trees, but on that day, it was marked by a gaggle of TV news trucks. Waved through by the uniformed cop, Sara eased a hundred yards down the hard gravel drive and pulled up behind one of the dozen patrol cars and EMT vehicles massed in front of a handsome brick house with a tidy lawn, flanked by large walnut trees, their limbs bare in the January cold. The high walls and sharply angled gables of the house made it look like a modern version of a medieval fortress, giving the property an air of grand isolation.

She got out of her car and approached the screens hastily erected around a section of the driveway near the garage door.

There she saw Detective Jake Patterson, standing with his head down in intense focus. Aged forty-two going on thirty,

EVEN STEVEN

Jake possessed a cunning yet demure disposition and always looked the part of the professional police detective—grey wool business suit complimented by a crisp white button-down shirt with a smartly knotted blue necktie. Straight out of central casting.

"Hey, partner," she said.

Jake looked up. He smiled and gave her a nod, "We've got a nasty one here." Although a Nashville native, his voice sounded like a radio announcer reading the weather report. A little too self-important. He motioned for her to follow him behind the screen.

Lying on the driveway in a pool of sticky blood was the body of a middle-aged woman. Sara instantly saw that her head had been crushed, with bits of brain and cranium oozing out from where the skin had been ripped apart. Her matted hair was dark brown. Otherwise, the body was intact—two hands, two feet, no obvious wounds. She wore navy stretch pants, an old baggy and tattered white Vanderbilt sweatshirt (now mostly red from blood), and camouflage Croc sandals, one of which was lying a few feet away.

The medical examiner, a man about fifty with a shock of white hair that made him look a bit like Einstein, saw Sara and came over.

"Detective Durant, you're looking quite professional today," said Dr. Pieter Yeager in his distinctive Eastern European accent. He was an immigrant from Romania who had attended medical school at Vanderbilt and, after graduation, had never gone home.

Sara never quite knew how to take Dr. Yeager's backhanded

compliments. He seemed like he might be flirting, but she wasn't sure. Or maybe he was being sarcastic, but in a really subtle way? He was inscrutable, and Sara had no interest in digging deeper.

"Who's our lucky winner?" said Sara, ignoring his ambiguous comment.

"Don't know yet," said Jake. "No identification on her. And her face is pretty well flattened."

"Time of death?"

"Rigor mortis is just setting in now," said Dr. Yeager. "The body has some residual warmth. Moderate lividity. So, I'd say she's been deceased for about four hours. That puts time of death at noon today."

"Who discovered the body?"

"FedEx guy," said Jake. "Totally freaked him out."

"Is he a suspect?"

"We haven't ruled him out, but his truck"—he nodded in the direction of the FedEx vehicle still parked in the driveway circle, curving around the front of the house—"is clean. Nothing on his tires. Driver has no criminal record. Seems really shook up. And besides, the victim's Cadillac is in the garage. The right front tire has blood and brain matter on it. I'm sure testing will confirm it's the victim's."

"Anything in the car?"

"We're dusting for fingerprints and trace DNA. Nothing yet. My guess is that the perp ran her over with her own car and then parked it back in the garage. Left the key fob lying on the center console. But like I said, no prints."

"Of course," nodded Sara. "That would be too easy, wouldn't it? No, our perp is smarter than that. How about neighbors? Witnesses?"

"The nearest house is through that forest of trees," said Jake, pointing to the east. "You can see it through the bare branches. No one home. We'll check again later. In the other direction is an open field, and then a creek overgrown with kudzu and hackberry trees, and then a house. About a quarter mile away. The hackberries and overgrowth block the view all year."

"Pretty isolated out here," nodded Sara. "Burglary?"

"No evidence of forced entry. Nothing appears to be disturbed inside. No signs of the place being ransacked or even searched. On the kitchen table is one place setting with a half-eaten sandwich and salad. The television was turned on. Looks as if the victim was interrupted during her lunch, perhaps by a visitor. And before you ask, there's no surveillance camera. Just the usual alarm system on the door, which was not activated."

After talking to some of the uniformed officers, Sara returned to her car and drove downtown to the gleaming, glass-clad box that was the Metro Nashville Police Department Headquarters, on Murfreesboro Pike, on the southeast side of the city, halfway to the Nashville International Airport. She went to her office and sat behind her desk.

Her phone rang. It was Jake. "We got identification on the

victim. Her name is Edna Shriver. She owns the home. Retired school administrator at Hillcreek Academy, an elite private school. Has a son living in Denver. We're contacting him. She was married, but her husband died a few months ago. They both lived in this house. That's all we know."

"Thanks," said Sara.

Edna Shriver! Sara recognized the name—as well as the manner of death.

From the pile of cold cases in her filing cabinet, Sara took a thick folder. It was labelled "Janie Smalls." She opened it. Three years earlier, the body of Janie Smalls, age thirty, had been found in her own driveway at her home in rural Goodlettsville. She had been run over by a vehicle, and among other injuries, her skull had been horribly fractured. Her own truck had been the murder weapon, although the medical examiner thought she had been knocked unconscious by some other object before being run over. Nothing had been disturbed in the house. There was no video surveillance. In the truck, a single hair was found. It was long and brown, and female. Smalls was a redhead.

Sara had been the lead investigator. Janie Smalls was a divorced woman, living on a generous one-time settlement from her ex-husband, a healthcare executive. They had no children, so there was no child support to pay. On the day of the murder, her ex-husband was in Europe on business. He was engaged to his new girlfriend and did not financially profit from Janie's death, so Sara crossed him off the list.

Emails and text messages revealed that Janie Smalls was having an affair with a married man named Paul Shriver. The affair had been going on for over a year, with trysts at fancy

EVEN STEVEN

hotels in the afternoon. Shriver was a traveling salesman who set his own hours, while Smalls had plenty of free time as a wealthy divorcee.

Paul Shriver also had an airtight alibi: on the day of the murder, he was in the hospital for a colonoscopy.

The single strand of hair was the only solid clue. It was analyzed. Female, age about fifty. Bore traces of Aqua Net hairspray. Very old school. It all came back to her. As part of the routine investigation, Sara had interviewed Edna Shriver, Paul Shriver's wife, at the couple's "other house," a luxury condo in downtown Nashville. Edna invited Sara inside, and they sat down at the kitchen table, where she served coffee in antique cups. She was cool, polite, seemingly forthcoming, but rather stiff in her demeanor. Yes, she knew that her husband had an affair with Janie Smalls. She had discovered it when she had "accidentally" (her word) seen messages on his phone. This was several months ago, she said, and Paul had sworn to her that he had ended it. Case closed.

This was curious to Sara because she knew for a fact that evidence on Janie's phone, and a credit card charge at The Hermitage Hotel, indicated that Paul and Janie had canoodled just a week before Janie's death. Either Edna was lying or she was ignorant. Sara guessed it was the former— the woman was sharp as an eagle.

During their conversation, Sara leaned close, and into her nostrils came the unmistakable scent of Aqua Net hairspray.

"Just for the record," said Sara, "where were you on the morning of Wednesday, the eighth of June?"

"As I recall," she said, "I was here, at home, confined to my bed with a terrible migraine headache. I've been suffering with ocular migraines for several years. They can be triggered by the blue light from screens, like my computer. A modern malady, I suppose! Very frustrating. Anyway, I was secluded in my darkened bedroom all morning until about three in the afternoon, when the pain finally faded away. I left the house around five to go shopping. Pretty sure I also went to the Produce Place in Sylvan Park that day. I prefer the produce there. Always fresh, never wilted. I'm sure I have the receipt—it's probably still in the bag in the recycling bin or I can pull it up on my bank app."

Sara asked her about the strand of her hair found in Janie's truck.

Edna shrugged. "Yeah, I was in the truck months ago. I saw her at the mall and wanted to make sure she got the message to leave Paul alone. She let me sit in her truck while we talked—just five minutes. She apologized, promised it was over, and that was it. She was kind, and I left feeling at peace. My fingerprints might still be in the front seat, unless Janie cleaned it, but keeping a spotless truck didn't seem her priority".

Edna was correct about that, noted Sara—the inside of the truck cabin was covered in a fine layer of dust and grime, with empty miniature bottles of wine and cans of Red Bull on the floorboards. Sara strongly suspected Edna Shriver but had too little evidence.

A few days later, a man came forward. His name was Ed Dawson. He was a homeless guy who had a makeshift camp in the woods behind the Walmart along the Cumberland

River, about a mile from the Smalls' house. The cops had picked him up for vagrancy, and while at the station, he told a story of watching from the woods when the police and EMTs had arrived at the Smalls' house. Seeing the activity and learning that it was a murder investigation, Dawson recalled that, a few hours earlier, he had seen two women in the driveway, and they were arguing. One woman struck the other, sending her to the ground. She then got in a pickup truck and drove up and down the driveway before parking the truck in the garage. Dawson couldn't see any more than that. The woman got out of the truck and into a white car and drove away.

"A white car?" Sara had asked.

Dawson nodded. "Yeah. It was a big sedan—maybe a Cadillac."

Sara checked her notes. Edna Shriver, the wife of the cheating husband, drove a white Cadillac.

She took all the evidence to her boss, Captain Riggs. He was an old-school cop with a square jaw, thick eyebrows, and a hawkish nose. His buzz-cut hair gave him the look of a Marine drill sergeant, which he actually was before retiring and joining the force as a police lieutenant.

"Looks like a strong case against Edna Shriver," he nodded.

But when the assistant district attorney reviewed the case, she disagreed. Ed Dawson, their witness, had a record of alcoholism and drug abuse, along with a string of petty crimes, stripping him of any credibility. "Any good defense attorney will rip him to pieces," said the ADA. "Get better evidence."

EVEN STEVEN

But there was no better evidence. Edna Shriver was never arrested. Neither was anyone else, and the Janie Smalls murder investigation went cold.

And now Edna Shriver was dead—viciously murdered.

3

While Sara was at her desk, mulling over the killing of Edna Shriver, her phone rang. It was the medical examiner. She picked up the call.

"I've got an interesting development in the Shriver case," said the medical examiner.

"What would that be?"

"While examining the body, I found that her tongue has been mutilated. Specifically, the mark of an eye has been carved into it with a sharp knife or scalpel. I'm sending you the image now."

Sara's police intranet pinged with a new message. She opened it. Sure enough, it was a photo of a bloody tongue. Carved into it was a football-shaped ellipse. In the center was a circle, and within the circle was a small and precise puncture reflecting a perfectly centered pupil of an eye.

"Thanks," she said as she hung up the phone.

EVEN STEVEN

Her blood ran cold.

This grotesque mark was the unmistakable secret signature of a notorious vigilante killer. Unknown to anyone outside of a small circle of trusted investigators, it was his personal calling card.

Sara pulled up another thick case file. The name on the cover was "Even Steven." She put it on her desk and opened it.

The vigilante's real name was Earl Steven Pollard. His nickname—or crime name—was self-appointed during a year-long killing spree in which he followed a strict pattern or plan. He murdered, viciously and without regret. But if it's possible to qualify his pathological narcissism and sociopathy, he killed only people who police detectives and district attorneys were convinced had committed murder. He took the law into his own hands and meted out painful justice to those who, in his judgment, had avoided their day in court. In his mind, he was "getting even" with people who had committed heinous crimes but had done no time.

While most cops were genuinely horrified, there were more than a few who tacitly approved of Even Steven's campaign to rid the world of unpunished murderers.

The first of his victims had been Johnny Wallace. The Nashville Police had suspected Wallace of killing his business associate, Rob Chantly, who was found hanged in his bedroom. His death gave Wallace control of a billion-dollar hedge fund, and he used his newfound wealth to buy a mansion in Belle Meade and a two-hundred-foot yacht, which he kept down in Key West. Nashville detectives had a pile of circumstantial evidence pointing to Wallace, but the medical examiner insisted the death was a suicide, and the

EVEN STEVEN

ADA said the case was too weak. The clincher was when Wallace told a friend at a drunken party on his yacht that he had "terminated" Chantly—but then the friend recanted.

One morning, a housekeeper at Wallace's mansion arrived and found him hanging by the neck in his palatial bedroom. There were no clues. The security system had been disabled. No witnesses came forward. The case looked like a suicide, except for one bizarre detail: when the body was discovered, blood was dripping from the mouth, which the medical examiner assumed was from an internal injury to the neck or throat. But when the coroner hauled the corpse downtown, put it on the stainless-steel autopsy table, and began a close examination, he made a shocking discovery. Cut into the victim's tongue was the figure of an eye—a football-shaped ellipse with a circle in the widest part, and a small puncture in the center. In theory, this death-mark could have been self-inflicted except for one problem: it was made after death. And the coroner then discovered that death was not caused by hanging from the thick rope found on the body, but by a thin wire used as a garrote.

Wallace had been murdered by manual strangulation, then his tongue had been inscribed. Only after these tasks had been completed did the killer put the rope around Wallace's neck and string him up from the heavy bronze and crystal chandelier in his bedroom. The rope had been neatly tied off on one of the big mahogany bedposts. There were no other clues.

The public had not been told the gruesome details. The police wanted to reserve the tongue mutilation in case they got a confession from some crazy person who didn't know that key piece of evidence. Sara had noted the parallel between the deaths of Wallace and Chantly—the apparent death by hanging—but could find no connection, no other person in common. Was the murder of Wallace done in revenge for that of Chantly? And what did the eye carving mean?

A few days later, a letter arrived at Nashville Metropolitan Police Department Homicide Section. It was one sheet of paper, printed on a common printer, probably at a public library. There were no fingerprints, no DNA on it. It was postmarked Bowling Green, Kentucky. The letter said this:

Thank me for sending Johnny Wallace to the Hell he deserves. Lex Talionis! Your Friend, Even Steven.

They quickly learned "Lex Talionis" meant "eye for an eye" in Latin, and Sara and the other detectives would have consigned the letter to the "quack" file were it not for one additional detail: a drawing, in pen, of an eye, which exactly matched the eye carved into the tongue of the victim.

This was something only the killer could know.

To be taunted was infuriating, but the detectives had no choice but to wait for more evidence to surface. None did.

Two months later, another body was found. Frank Sinclair had been dumped into a bathtub after being shot with a .22 pistol at close range in the back of the head. The small bullet is perfect for such executions because it has enough momentum to enter the skull, but then it ricochets around inside the cranium, tearing up the brain and causing instant death. Very tidy, with little bleeding. The symbol of the eye had been cut into Sinclair's tongue before, or while, his corpse was in the water in the bathtub. He lived alone; he was discovered by police performing a wellness check after he didn't show up for work for two days and didn't answer his phone.

Sara knew who Frank Sinclair was. He had been the prime suspect in the drowning death of his girlfriend, Ashana Wright, who was found in her bathtub. Sinclair claimed he had been camping alone that week, but no one could confirm his whereabouts. He smelled guilty as hell, but Sara couldn't prove it.

Sure enough, a few days after the murder of Frank Sinclair, a printed letter arrived at headquarters. This one was addressed to Detective Sara Durant, who had been identified in the press as the lead investigator of the Wallace case. It had been mailed from Cookeville, about a hundred miles east of Nashville.

The letter said:

It feels good to even the score! Keep an eye out for more to come! Your friend, Even Steven.

And there was the crude eye drawing.

In the following months, there were three more revenge killings—gruesome executions—of murderers who had escaped the long arm of the law. Some of the cases dated back many years. One victim, number 5, had been suspected of killing a prostitute a decade earlier. Fittingly, he was found bound and gagged, with his severed penis stuffed into his mouth, along with the requisite eye carving on the tongue. The letter from Even Steven had read:

Number 5 was particularly sweet! Live by the sword, die by the sword. Your friend, Even Steven.

EVEN STEVEN

Which brought Detective Sara Durant to the case of Edna Shriver. The inscribed eye on the tongue of the victim was the unmistakable hallmark and signature of the vigilante killer, Even Steven. This made it number 7 in his self-appointed campaign of public retribution.

There was just one problem.

At that moment, Earl Steven Pollard was incarcerated at Riverbend Maximum Security Institution (RMSI) in Nashville, one of the toughest prisons in the United States. Number 4244-0871 had been there for over a year. Despite the efforts of Pollard's high-powered defense attorney hired by his very wealthy and very misguided uncle, his execution date was approaching. Since executions had resumed in Tennessee in 2000, over a dozen inmates had been dispatched at Riverbend, and Pollard had no expectation of clemency. He was not leaving until they carried him out in a box.

Victim number 6—a man named Greg Hammock—had been his last known victim.

4

Earl Steven Pollard was a guest of the state because he had made just one career mistake. But one was all it took to bring his reign of terror to an end.

Two years earlier, the body of Greg Hammock had been found buried in a shallow grave in Radnor Park, a natural area located in Davidson County about ten miles southeast of downtown Nashville. The medical examiner determined he had been electrocuted by the placement of one electrode in his mouth and another shoved up his rectum. The usual eye design had been carved into his tongue. The voltage had more or less fried his guts, but it had taken time—probably five or ten minutes. Bruises on his wrists and ankles indicated he had been restrained. It would have been an excruciating way to die.

Like Johnny Wallace, Frank Sinclair, and three others before him, Greg Hammock had been the prime suspect in a murder. In each case, there had been no other suspects, but the ADA had declined to file charges due to a "lack of evidence." Hammock had been accused of viciously electrocuting his wife, Regina, in a remote, abandoned cabin in Long Hunter State Park, on Percy Priest Lake, east of Nashville. Weeks later, her decomposing body was found by hikers in a shallow grave. At the time of her disappearance, Hammock had claimed Regina had gotten lost while on a hike in the park and, when her body was found, he insisted some "crazed killer" must have kidnapped her and taken her to the cabin. Sara and the other detectives thought Hammock's story was preposterous, but they could find no evidence to arrest him.

Because he was her husband, he stood to inherit her estate. Indeed, after his wife's death, he received everything; but instead of moving away to a different state or buying a sailboat and cruising the Caribbean, he had chosen to stay in Nashville and flaunt his new wealth. Many thought this attitude was cold, if not pathological.

After Hammock's body had been dug up, the usual letter had arrived:

Number 6! Another piece of scum erased! The voltage was too high. Killed him too quickly. I'll do better next time. Your Friend, Even Steven.

The postmark was from Tullahoma, a small town southeast of Nashville. It was so small, in fact, that it had just one post office. And that post office had a camera in its little lobby.

Sara went there and pulled the surveillance footage. The postmaster knew every person who came in that day, save one: a man who placed a single letter into the mail slot. This man had a record, and he was quickly identified as Earl Steven Pollard, age thirty-two, resident of North Nashville. He was arrested, charged, and convicted of the deaths of

EVEN STEVEN

Johnny Wallace, Frank Sinclair, and Greg Hammock.

"I'm disappointed," Pollard had said to Sara just after his sentencing. "I was just getting started. I have a long list of people who need to face justice. But of course, you know who they are! You have the same list as I do. The only difference is that I'm acting on my list. You are not. You let killers go free. And yet you judge me."

"Yes, I do judge you," Sara had replied. "You're worse than the people you kill. You do it for pleasure."

"Nothing wrong with enjoying your work," he had replied with a lustful smile as he was led away.

On the day—heck, the entire *year*—of the Shriver murder, Earl Steven Pollard was behind bars. A quick call to the warden confirmed that Pollard was in his cell and had been present for all the twice-a-day headcounts in the maximum security wing of Riverbend. He could not possibly have murdered Edna Shriver. And yet his trademark eye had been carved into her tongue, and the method of death perfectly fit the pattern he had established.

She was number 7.

Clearly, as Sara saw it, there had to be some sort of copycat killer on the loose, trying to carry on Even Steven's campaign of vengeance.

But how could the copycat know about the death mark on the tongue? During Pollard's interrogation—which was mostly characterized by his boasting about his exploits and expecting the cops to thank him—Pollard had revealed how he had used public records to pinpoint suspects for targeting. But he had insisted that his trademark calling card was known only to himself.

Perhaps it was. Or perhaps he was lying. Always a possibility! The other scenario was that there was an informant within the NMPD Homicide Section who was sympathetic to Pollard and had leaked the trademark tongue mutilation to someone who was inspired to continue the serial killings, so long as there were cold cases with strong suspects.

Sara had no choice. As much as she loathed the idea, she would have to go to Riverbend and interview Pollard. If he had any involvement, the odds were good he would be happy to boast about it. After all, he was already on death row, and what did he have to lose by being truthful?

She glanced at the clock on her computer. It was a few minutes before 6:00 p.m. Visiting hours at Riverbend were Monday through Wednesday 8:00 a.m. until 4:00 p.m. and Thursday 8:00 a.m. until 11:00 a.m. It was too late to see Pollard today, even for a Nashville police detective. She called the prison and ordered Pollard be made available at 8:00 a.m. the next morning.

She turned on the local news. The TV trucks had been at the scene of the Shriver murder, and the reporters were eager for a hot story to boost humdrum ratings. Let's see, she thought, what will they say about it?

She scanned the channels. It was the lead story everywhere. Gruesome murder in Bell's Bend! Woman run over by her own car! Shots of reporters, microphones in hand, umbrellas shielding them from the evening drizzle, talking in front of the death house. The cops and investigators were gone now, the screens taken away, and generator-powered halogen lights mounted on aluminum stands and yellow police tape marked the busy scene of just a few hours earlier.

Pre-taped interviews with neighbors followed. Sallie Corley, who lived a mile away, said she was shocked. The area was peaceful, remote. She had neither seen nor heard anything unusual. Was the killer still on the loose?

Police Commissioner Joe Gaines and Mayor Susan Noles made statements for the hungry cameras, just in time to hit the evening news cycle. *Residents should lock their doors. Be aware of any strangers in the neighborhood. Don't go outside alone—always have a buddy. Practice an abundance of caution. The perpetrator could be anywhere.*

Sara scoffed. Sure, be afraid—but only if you happen to have gotten away with murder in Nashville sometime in the last couple decades. Otherwise, you could do whatever you wanted. If you were innocent, Even Steven—or rather, his sudden imitator—had no interest in you.

Jake stuck his head into her office. "Enjoying the show?" he said with a grin.

She turned off the television. "Seems like the higher up you go in the department hierarchy, the further your head gets driven up your ass."

"So, if you made captain, you'd be different?"

"You bet. I wouldn't forget where I came from."

"Sweet home Alabama."

She nodded. "But I don't get home very often. Of course, there's nothing for me there since my childish ex-husband destroyed our marriage. Just bad memories."

EVEN STEVEN

"Yeah, I get it. You hungry? Let's go to Brewhouse and get some dinner and a few drinks."

"I guess that's one advantage of being single," she said as she put on her jacket, shut off her computer, and went to the door. "You can go wherever the hell you want at night without a testosterone tyrant giving you the third degree."

On a Tuesday night, Brewhouse Bar & Grill was half-full, primarily because it was one of the very few neighborhood joints in downtown Nashville that did not feature live music. It wasn't that Sara had anything against singers and pickers, but sometimes after a long day at work, it was nice to just drink quietly. This was one of those nights.

They sat at the bar, looking across the bartender's alley at the shelves of bottles illuminated by colored lights. The video screen—muted—showed a basketball game. Sara ordered a cheeseburger and a beer. Jake did wings and a double bourbon. They sat in silence.

After loosening his necktie, Jake asked, "When does your brother's trial start?"

"Opening arguments are this week. I'll need to spend some time in court. You know, moral support."

"Sure. I'll cover for you. No problem. Seems like a weak case the DA brought."

"Very weak. Ricky was making money hand over fist buying and managing apartment buildings with his partner. Then one night—you remember the police report—the partner, guy named Brett Millar, was found dead in Centennial Park. Struck in the head, fell into the pond, and drowned. A witness said she saw a man running from the scene. Just because Ricky and Millar were having a business dispute, the prick detective running the investigation—Foster—zeroed in on Ricky. He got the witness to say the assailant was Ricky. It's all bullshit."

"What's Ricky's alibi?"

"He was mountain biking in Percy Warner Park, south of town. But he was alone. No one to verify his story. To make it worse, Millar's wife went on the warpath, demanding they put Ricky on trial. She says Ricky stood to make millions from the death of her husband. And that was true. After Millar died, Ricky became sole owner of the company but transferred a meaningful sum to the Millar family."

"Well, good luck to him. You couldn't meet a nicer guy than your brother."

"Thanks."

Sara liked Jake because he was the ideal wingman. He was content to simply *be there*, a dependable friend, undemanding, inwardly content. A dedicated company man who lived by the book. In at 9:00 a.m. sharp, out at 5:00 p.m. Reports always typed and submitted on time. As long as the rules were being followed, nothing seemed to annoy him. He had an equally straightlaced girlfriend named Rhonda, who apparently wasn't bothered by Jake's commitment to his job. The perfect cop wife! Sara had learned not to question Jake's old-school persona. It was what it was, and as long as he was a good cop, it didn't bother her. She wasn't going to rock the boat.

But still, she had asked herself: Could Jake be the one who leaked the information about the Even Steven tongue mutilations? Perhaps unwittingly tipped off the wrong person about a vital piece of hidden evidence? Given license to a copycat killer?

Suddenly Sara felt very lonely—the kind of lonesomeness you feel when you have no one in your life with whom you can share your every secret desire. Friends and colleagues? Yes, she had many. But a true confidante? None.

Jake got up to use the men's room. No sooner had he disappeared than Sara felt a presence at her side. She glanced over. A man had sidled up next to her and was leaning with one elbow on the bar, facing her, not two feet away. There were plenty of empty stools at the bar, and Sara instantly knew the guy had deliberately entered her space. He was big, maybe six-foot-four, wearing a red plaid shirt and jeans with a big silver belt buckle in the shape of a bronco rider. His hand rested on the bar, inches from her elbow.

"So, darlin', what brings you here tonight?" he said in a syrupy Florida drawl.

"My desire to be left alone," she replied without looking up at him.

"Aw, come on, let's be friendly," he said as he slid an inch closer. His physical presence was disconcerting. It disturbed her personal energy field.

"No, thanks." Still no eye contact. But, in her mind, she knew the exact distance from her hands and feet to his vital body parts.

"I got money. I'll show you a good time. You ever had a real man before? I'll bet you haven't." Out of the corner of her eye, she saw him motion to the bartender. "Give the little

EVEN STEVEN

lady whatever she wants," he called.

Sara looked up and caught the eye of the bartender. "No, thanks. I'm good."

"I'm just trying to be nice," the man said.

"Then be nice and move away."

The big shape next to her was motionless. He was thinking. Sara waited for the escalation.

"Listen, bitch, I don't know where you get off being so high and mighty!"

Sara sighed to herself. She didn't want this. Not tonight. But she had no choice.

Sure enough, she felt a beefy hand on her shoulder. "Someone needs to teach you a lesson in bein' polite."

She shrugged off the hand. "I said, 'no'." Still looking straight ahead. Out of the corner of her eye she saw the bartender down at the end of the bar, not paying attention.

And then it came. The move she had been expecting. These goons were all alike. So predictable.

The hand slid onto the inside of her thigh, above her knee. She glanced down, just to make sure her senses weren't deceiving her. Yep. There it was, all beefy and hairy. Fingertips making slight indentations in her joggers. She felt her stomach churn with disgust.

Do it quick or slow? That was the only question. I'm in no mood to play games, she thought. I'll make this quick.

EVEN STEVEN

With lightning speed, her right hand shot across her lap and grabbed the guy's wrist. As she stood up, she violently twisted the hand around the guy's back while, with her left hand, she took a fistful of hair and slammed his face down onto the lacquered wood bar. The man groaned, his face bleeding from a broken nose. Dazed, he teetered on his feet.

The bartender looked over, startled by the sudden commotion.

Sara turned the guy around and marched him through scattered tables and astonished patrons to the front door. She shoved him through the door onto the sidewalk, where he fell in a heap. He got up on his hands and knees and wiped his mouth with the back of his sleeve.

"You dumb bitch," he muttered.

Sara stepped close to him. She opened her coat and showed him her badge. "That's *Detective Dumb Bitch* to you, buddy. You should learn some manners. Trust me, you'll get more action."

She turned and, under the astonished eyes of passers-by, went back into Brewhouse. Threading her way through the tables, she resumed her seat at the bar. To calm her nerves, she took a deep slow breath. Violence was not her favorite thing, but sometimes it was necessary. She waited for the adrenaline surging through her veins to subside.

Jake reappeared and took his seat next to her. "Sorry I took so long. Rhonda called. She wanted to know how to stop the toilet from running, so I had to walk her through it." He looked at Sara. "Say, are you okay? You look a little flushed."

Sara turned to him, "She needed your help with a plumbing

problem?"

"Yeah," he shrugged. "Silly, isn't it? But that's life, I guess. Little things."

"You're a very lucky person," said Sara. "A very lucky person."

5

At 8:50 a.m., Detective Sara Durant walked through the front entrance of the sprawling RMSI, along the Cumberland River five miles northwest of downtown Nashville. The prison opened in 1989 to replace its century-old neighbor, the Tennessee State Penitentiary. Made up of twenty different buildings, the complex was designed to hold over 700 of the state's most dangerous and vicious criminals. All Tennessee male death row prisoners are housed at Riverbend, which is home to the state's electric chair and lethal injection gurney.

Officers checked her in and then escorted her to the visiting center reserved for attorneys and law enforcement officers. She took a seat in a drab, windowless cinderblock room with one table and three aluminum chairs, all bolted to the floor. She waited.

At exactly 8:00, the door opened, and a guard entered, followed by an inmate and another guard. Earl Steven Pollard wore the ubiquitous orange shirt and pants. His wrists and ankles were loosely shackled with thin chains, affording him limited mobility. The leading guard sat him in the inmate's chair and secured him with a padlock. Then the two guards withdrew, leaving the door open.

Pollard shifted his thin, wiry body on the unyielding chair. With a shock of black hair contrasting with his pasty complexion, he seemed physically younger than his thirty-four years but, at the same time, spiritually much older. He regarded Detective Sara Durant with a peculiar mixture of contempt and fascination, as his pinpoint eyes—gray, almost silver—burned with animal intensity.

His thin lips curled into a sneer. "Good to see you again, Detective Durant. Is this a social call? Have you brought me some cookies? Or a hacksaw planted in a fruitcake?"

"No cookies, Earl. No fruitcake. How are you getting along in your new home?"

"Very nicely, thank you. Uncle Leonard keeps my account at the prison commissary topped up. I can get the things I want."

Of course, thought Sara. Uncle Leonard. Lived on a crumbling soybean plantation out on Old Charlotte Pike. A multi-millionaire. Earl was his only living relative, so he lavished money on him. Paid for his white-shoe lawyers. But he couldn't keep his wayward nephew from being convicted and sentenced to death. Sara wondered how else he helped him.

"Good to hear," she said. "Let's get down to business."

"Okay," said Pollard. "Have you found him?"

"Who?"

EVEN STEVEN

He sighed. "You think I'm stupid. You know who I'm talking about."

Sara clenched her jaw in surprise, realizing Pollard already knew why she was there, but she made sure his taunt didn't affect her. "I didn't realize the paperboy delivered this far."

"Paperboy? You are behind the times, Detective. Or may I call you Sara? Yes—how about, 'Sara Smile.' Just like the famous song on the radio when I was a kid. How did it go? *All alone with me... watching in the night...* Something like that."

Sara skipped forward, "What can you tell me about Edna Shriver?"

"Who?"

"Now you think *I'm* stupid. You know. The woman whom we suspected of killing her husband's lover, Janie Smalls. Shriver was found dead yesterday in her driveway. Her head had been crushed, driven over by her own car. Same as Janie Smalls."

"Do tell!" exclaimed Pollard in an exaggerated southern drawl.

"And I think you know of one other detail about the victim."

"What would that be?"

"The eye. You know what I mean."

Pollard leaned forward so that his chest was pressed against edge of the table. Sara could smell his rank breath.

"On the tongue?" he whispered.

EVEN STEVEN

Sara nodded.

Pollard smiled and leaned back. Then he shrugged. "So, what do you want from me?"

"No one in my department would leak that piece of evidence to the killer. It had to have come from you."

"You flatter me!" laughed Pollard.

"No, I'm not flattering you. To the contrary, I think you bragged about it to one of your cellmates or to a guard. Now you've got some idiot out there trying to cash in on your fame. A new Even Steven is taking over your brand. A cheap knockoff trying to fill your shoes."

"I don't think so," sneered Pollard.

"I think so. The city thinks so. Everyone thinks so." Sara shook her head sadly. "Here you are, rotting in prison, while your appeals drag on for years. The average inmate on death row in Tennessee survives twenty years of appeals and delays. Then it's the electric chair. Or lethal injection. Or some other method of horrible slow death they'll invent by that time. My guess is that you'll be gone by the age of sixty. Forgotten. Another faceless, nameless prisoner eliminated by the system. And to think that some hayseed amateur is taking over your franchise just because you couldn't keep your stupid mouth shut."

Pollard stiffened in his chair and glared at Sara. Expecting him to lunge at her, Sara braced herself.

"You think you're so wise," he hissed. His eyes narrowed. "You think I'd tell just anyone my secrets? Let me tell you something: The person who killed Edna Shriver is very smart. Very smart and very cunning. Entirely worthy of carrying on the name of Even Steven. Until, that is, until I get out of this place."

"You? Get out? Dream on."

"I make dreams come true, my dear," he smiled.

Sara felt the sexual innuendo. While repulsed, she decided to play along. "So do I."

"I'll bet you do."

"Let's get back to business, shall we?" she said. "Here's how we see it: You were caught, and now, some bozo is cashing in on your notoriety. We even received a letter from him."

Pollard's eyes narrowed to reptilian slits. "A letter?"

"Sure. Just like the ones you sent us. Just like the one you sent from the post office in Tullahoma. Remember? You should have smiled for the camera." While Pollard glared at her, she reached into her briefcase and pulled out a sheet of paper and read it aloud:

"*It's good to be back! Number 7 was nostalgic, and the Caddy did a nice job on her pretty face. Your Friend, Even Steven.*"

She slid it across the table to Pollard. "See for yourself. It's a copy—you may touch it."

With his fingertips, he picked up the paper as if it were toxic. He studied it. With a shrug he pushed it back to her.

"Very interesting," he said.

"That's all?"

EVEN STEVEN

"Was it mailed to you?"

"Yes. The post office thinks it was put into a letter box at Nashville International Airport."

"And?"

"There's no way this guy could know these details unless you, or a partner of yours, trained him."

"Him?" said Pollard with a sly smile. "Aren't you making an assumption?"

"This new killer is a woman?"

Pollard laughed, showing yellowed stumpy teeth and red gums. "Just messing with you. Trying to discourage gender discrimination. This is the twenty-first century, you know. Come to think of it, I'm not aware of any female serial killers. Perhaps it's time we had one. You know, to break the glass ceiling. Anyway, a moment ago you said some 'bozo' was imitating me and now you suggest that I trained this person. Which is it, Sara? Bozo or carefully coached protégé?"

"I'm thinking a combination of both. Let's move on, shall we? Tell me about your uncle, Leonard Givens. He pays for your attorney, Kelly Thrasher of Thrasher & Rogers in Nashville. Everyone knows that prisoner phone calls may be monitored and recorded by prison authorities in Tennessee, and all mail may be opened and inspected. There are only three ways to send a message or communicate with the outside. The first is by recruiting an inmate who is about to be released, someone who could leave with valuable information or instructions. The second is by befriending or bribing a guard, guys who are underpaid and open to an unscrupulous second stream of income. The third way is through your attorney, with whom you are entitled to have confidential conversations."

Pollard frowned. "Be careful, Sara, or you won't be smiling long. Accusing my attorney, an officer of the court, of criminal malfeasance is a serious charge that I'm sure she will not take lightly."

"Then you tell me, Mr. Pollard—how did you teach the killer of Edna Shriver your system?"

He fixed his sharp eyes on her before turning away. "I'm retired," he replied. "This is your problem." He sat with his arms crossed.

"No comment?"

"I'm done."

Sara knew she would get nothing more out of him. She called for the guard to take Pollard back to his cell. The time was 8:30 a.m.

When Sara returned to the station, she found a message from Captain Riggs, summoning her to his office. She found him behind his big oak desk.

"Close the door, Detective," he said as he peered at her from over his reading glasses. She did so. "Sit down." With one meaty hand, he vaguely waved in the direction of the chair facing him. She took a seat.

"You wanted to see me, Captain?"

"Does the name Rodney Billinger ring a bell?"

She shook her head. "No. Should it?"

EVEN STEVEN

"You sent him to the hospital last night. Broken nose."

"Too bad."

"Is that all you have to say?"

"He put his hand on me. It was self-defense."

"He put his hand on you? Where?"

"The inside of my leg as I was sitting at the bar at Brewhouse. He was extremely aggressive."

"So, you smashed his face?"

Sara did not answer.

Captain Riggs held up the palms of his hands. "Okay. Let's cut to the chase. Are you familiar with the Billinger Building at the corner of Commerce Street and Third Avenue?"

"Yes, of course. It's one of the tallest buildings in Nashville. Retail stores, offices."

"Okay. Well, Rodney Billinger is part of the family. His father is Dwight Billinger. His uncle is Edward Billinger. These people have big money and big clout in this town."

"So why is young Rodney Billinger such a jackass?"

"I don't know," sighed Captain Riggs. "Families can be weird. The point is that they've got lawyers and money enough to make our lives miserable. I've already gotten a subpoena for the security video at Brewhouse, and officers are serving it now. Hopefully it will be enough to get the Billingers to back off. In the meantime, Detective Durant, I want you to think about the fact that the primary responsibility of a law enforcement officer is not escalation but *de-escalation* whenever possible. Your job is to stay cool and objective—above the heat of the moment. In short, while you may *represent* the law, you cannot let your emotions take over and take the law into your own hands. Am I clear?"

"Yes sir," she nodded.

"Now then." He leaned back and regained his poise. "Earl Steven Pollard. You saw him today?"

"Yes. He denied any knowledge of a copycat killer. He denied disclosing the details of the tongue carvings and the letters to anyone. But of course, he could be lying. We have no leverage over him. He's on death row, and his rich uncle sends him money, so unless the governor commutes his sentence, he's got nothing to lose."

"Who is this rich uncle?"

"Leonard Givens. Has a pile of old soybean money."

"Yes, I'm familiar. Time to pay *him* a visit," instructed Captain Riggs.

6

Half an hour east of downtown on Old Charlotte Pike, a set of stone gates, mossy and crumbling, came into view. Sara drove her Mustang onto the long gravel driveway, shaded by gloomy oaks and large magnolias, that led straight as an arrow past rolling fields to its destination: a weatherbeaten but still grand mansion. Its most dramatic features were its six white columns framing the broad front porch and the perfectly rectangular façade enclosing five windows on the second floor and four on the first. It was topped by a low gabled roof that gave the desired effect of an ancient Greek temple.

As she stepped out of her car and stood in front of the solemn structure, she could practically hear the low song of enslaved people in the soybean fields and the crack of the overseer's whip.

Never mind. That was yesterday. Today is for business. She went to the big front door with its peeling paint and pressed the softly glowing button.

EVEN STEVEN

Presently, a man appeared and pulled open the door. His black hair was hard and neatly combed, and he wore a white jacket and white pants. He said nothing.

"Detective Durant, from the Nashville Police Department, here to see Mr. Givens."

"He's expecting you," the man said as he stepped aside, allowing her to cross the threshold.

The air was startlingly warm, like the inside of a greenhouse.

"Please follow me," said the man. He led Sara through a living room with white plastered walls and a ceiling showing hairline cracks, a threadbare Persian carpet, Empire-style furniture, and most strikingly, a mural-sized painting of the estate itself. It featured this very house shown at the top of a low hill, with lush and productive fields and forests surrounding it. In the picture, the sky was blue, and all was at peace with the world.

She noticed a young woman sitting in a far corner of the room, curled up in a wingback chair, reading a book. There was something odd about her appearance—her hair seemed greasy and her posture contorted. But Sara thought it was none of her concern, and the man said nothing as he marched briskly forward.

He led her through a set of French doors, and suddenly, Sara found herself in an enclosed sunroom, with big windows overlooking a field with pale violet hills in the distance. The air there was even warmer than the house, almost like a sauna. They approached a man sitting in a recliner looking at a laptop. The man in white then beckoned Sara to come closer.

EVEN STEVEN

"Leonard Givens?" she said. "I'm Detective Sara Durant."

The man in the recliner looked about eighty or ninety and was dressed in a linen shirt and baggy khaki pants that had fit him better twenty years earlier. His rolled-up sleeves exposed parchment skin, and thin grey wisps of hair lay askew on his bony head. After closing his laptop, which the man in white removed, he extended a skeletal hand, "Please sit down."

Sara took a seat on an old wicker chair.

"Would you care for a drink?" he said.

"Just water, thank you," she said. "As you know, I'm here on police business."

"So you are," replied Givens. "Marcos, please bring our guest some water, and I'll have a cosmo," he said with a quick wink.

Sara watched as Marcos disappeared into the house.

"Do you have any children?" Givens asked abruptly. His keen grey eyes fixed on her.

"No, I can't say that I do," she replied.

"Hmph," he nodded his head. "Too bad. So, we find ourselves in the same boat. I had a daughter, but she died of lung cancer many years ago."

"I'm sorry to hear that."

He said nothing for a moment. From somewhere in the house, Sara could hear the solemn tick-tock of a grandfather clock.

EVEN STEVEN

"You're here about Earl," said Givens.

"Yes."

"He was a good kid. An outstanding student. Earned his degree in computer science at MIT. Got a job with a tech company in Nashville. Was on his way to a bright career. Then you know what happened, right?"

"Remind me."

"His parents—my sister, Judith, and her husband, Mark Pollard—were murdered in a home invasion. They were both shot to death. Awful, terrible thing. It was terrible for me, and I cannot imagine what Earl went through. The police investigated, and they accused Earl of doing it! He was arrested and put on trial, but there was insufficient evidence, and Earl's girlfriend provided an alibi. Still, his reputation was destroyed. He lost his job and had to make a living by devising various internet businesses that he could operate without having a public presence."

"And then new evidence emerged," said Sara. She knew the story but wanted to let him talk. Perhaps he'd add a new insight.

"Yes, new evidence," said Givens. "Two years after the murders, and long after Earl's life had been destroyed, a bullet casing in the evidence file was tested for DNA, and a match was found. It was no one in the system, and it was not Earl. It was someone else. The police said they hit a stone wall, and the case went cold again, but Earl kept digging on his own. Doing the job of the cops, you might say. He found the match. The print belonged to a guy whose wife had been killed in an auto accident. His name was Tony Lafoy. Earl's

EVEN STEVEN

father, Mark Pollard, owned an automobile dealership, and Lafoy was convinced his wife died because of negligence by the car company. It was some problem with the ignition switch abruptly turning off while the car was on the highway, causing it to lose control. Lafoy, who had a history of violent crime, blamed Mark Pollard for the accident. This was preposterous, but some people get ideas in their head, and you cannot reason with them.

"Upon learning about Lafoy, Earl made a fateful decision. He didn't trust the police or the district attorney. I can't say what he should have done. I suppose he should have gone to them and demanded they reopen the case. But for whatever reason, he took matters into his own hands. He told me he made a bomb and put it in the guy's car. *Bang!* That was the end of Tony Lafoy."

Marcos appeared with a tray holding a lusciously pink cosmopolitan martini and a pitcher of ice water with lemon slices floating in it. He poured Sara a glass and handed it to her.

"Thank you," she said.

Then Marcos gently handed the martini to Givens.

The old man looked at Sara. "I'll drink for both of us. My ration of grog, twice a day." Then he turned to Marcos. "Thank you. You may go now."

Sara waited for Marcos to leave. "I remember one of our detectives investigating the Lafoy murder. We thought it was organized crime, since Lafoy was a shady character."

"Well, no gang killed him. Earl did."

EVEN STEVEN

"Why did he tell you?"

Givens shrugged. "I suppose he wanted me to know the truth about my brother-in-law's murder. My wife had passed away. He wants people to know what he does. Maybe he likes to brag and believed I would never betray him."

"So Tony Lafoy was Earl's first vigilante killing. He was judge, jury, and executioner."

"As the months and years passed," continued Givens, "Earl told me there were others just like Lafoy. People who had gotten away with murder. Their victims had never gotten justice. Earl wanted to be the instrument of their retribution. But rather than kill them secretly, he wanted to devise a way for the police to know why these people were being eliminated, that it wasn't just random innocents who were being killed, but deserving criminals. You know, when someone gets murdered in their home, there's a great hue and cry, and all the people are afraid and they lock their doors because they think a killer is on the loose. But that was not the case with Earl. If you were innocent, you had nothing to fear."

"But why the savagery?" asked Sara. "The sadism?"

Leonard Givens fell silent. His eyes focused on the distant hills. Then he spoke in a tired but determined voice, "I don't know the answer to that. Anyway, Earl is all I have. He tried to do the right thing. Maybe he took it too far, but those people deserved what they got. And now he's in prison, with a death sentence. I try to do whatever I can to make his life more comfortable."

"You know that we should have you charged as an accessory

to murder," said Sara. "Your nephew told you these things and you did nothing. You were—and still are—complicit."

Givens shrugged. "I'm an old man. I suppose you could haul me into court, and I'd go there in a wheelchair with a big matronly nurse, an oxygen tube shoved up my nose, and a doctor telling the judge how sick and close to death I am. And I would deny everything."

"Okay. Let's cut to the chase. You may have heard on the news about another murder. A woman named Edna Shriver was run over by her own car in her driveway."

"Yes," he nodded. "Why?"

"Edna Shriver was mutilated. Her tongue was - - um she was killed, we suspect, because she had been implicated in the death of her husband's girlfriend, a woman named Janie Smalls. Just like Shriver, Janie was found in her driveway, with her head crushed by a vehicle."

"You need a scorecard to keep track of these unfortunate events," said Givens. With a trembling hand, he took a sip of his martini.

"Our problem is that, at the time of her murder, your nephew was safely behind bars," said Sara. "He could not have done it. It may have been a copycat, but that seems impossible because there are details of the Even Steven crimes known only to the police and to Earl himself. The other possibility is a protégé. Someone recruited and trained by Earl from behind bars, tasked with continuing the Even Steven crusade against unprosecuted killers. This person could be an inmate due to be released, a prison guard he bribed, or his lawyer, Kelly Thrasher. You pay Ms. Thrasher,

EVEN STEVEN

don't you? Does she perform special services for your nephew?"

For the first time during their visit, Leonard Givens raised his voice and became agitated. "How dare you suggest such a thing? I pay the firm Thrasher & Rogers to provide ethical and vigorous representation for Earl. He deserves a competent defense attorney, just like any other citizen. And may I remind you, Kelly Thrasher is no magician. Despite her efforts, Earl was found guilty and sentenced to death. If I did anything, I should have fired her."

"Well, *someone* is carrying on the work of Even Steven."

Leonard Givens drained the last of his grog and set the glass on the table next to his chaise. "Well, so much for today's ration," he said. "Damn doctors. They tell me what to eat, what to drink, how often to take a crap, when to piss. I feel like a lab rat. What's the use of living if you can't take any pleasure from it?" He suddenly cast a salacious eye at Sara. "Young lady, if I were twenty years younger, I'd give your sweet little skirt just what it deserves."

Sara caught her breath. This sudden flash of sexual aggression was interesting! Was this indicative of some sort of family trait? Normal one moment, and then the mask comes off and the animal is revealed? Such crude come-ons were nothing new to her. She smiled. "Well, life can be cruel, can't it?" she said. "I suppose I'll never know."

As a shadow crossed his face, Givens looked away. He seemed to become smaller in his chaise. "I've had a good run," he said quietly. "Now my focus is on helping Earl before he gets crushed by the system."

7

In her office at NMPD Homicide Section, Sara huddled with Jake. But she was distracted by an elaborate spread of catered lox and bagels he had placed between their desks. It stood out like a sore thumb under the cheap fluorescent light. She watched him meticulously assemble a plate and was unnerved by how much it annoyed her.

"Why do you bring these ridiculous snacks?" asked Sara. "Shouldn't a doughnut suffice?"

Jake smiled. "Gross." He nibbled at a caper. "I worked a summer as a donut fryer at Daily Donuts. High school dream job. Until I became disgusted by the clientele."

"Okay, well, it smells. Just keep it over there. Let's focus on business. Back to Leonard Givens. He struck me as a typical overprotective uncle who's ready to forgive every transgression by his nephew because he's got no one else in the world. He's blind to his nephew's sins. He's got lots of money and he shovels it to Earl.

"Our problem is that murder number 7—Edna Shriver—was

committed by someone other than Earl Steven Pollard, most likely a protégé. They knew things that only Pollard would know, so I think we have to reasonably assume that this protégé was trained by Pollard after he was arrested and convicted of murder number 6, Greg Hammock. From the moment of Pollard's arrest, he was held without bail at Riverbend with his private contact limited to other prisoners, the guards, his lawyer. His mail and phone calls were monitored, so he could not have made plans through those methods of communication. And though we know that Leonard Givens pays his nephew's legal bills and sends money to the prison commissary for his account, we cannot know if Givens sends money to anyone else."

"You mean, like, directly to the protégé?" asked Jake as he carefully organized the catering spread on his side of the desk.

"Yes. Why not? Givens might think that, if he subsidized the protégé, there might be some basis for arguing that Earl Steven Pollard was wrongly convicted."

She drummed her fingers on the arm of her chair as she pondered the thought. "Let's get down to business," she said. "We need lists. We need a list of the guards and staff working at Riverbend—the people who could have direct contact with prisoners. We also need a list of prisoners who have been released in the past month who served hard time with Pollard."

Jake nodded in the direction of her computer screen. "Have you checked your inbox since you came back from visiting Leonard Givens?"

"No, why?"

EVEN STEVEN

"Well, you might want to look for my message."

She opened her inbox and clicked on a message from Jake. It contained two attachments. She opened them. One was a list of the staff at Riverbend. The other was a list of recently released inmates.

"I'm one step ahead of you," smiled Jake.

"Very impressive," said Sara.

The Riverbend staff list showed over 400 names, from the warden to administrative workers, correctional officers, unit managers, custodians, and medical personnel.

The list of recently released prisoners was only thirty-five.

"We need to find the intersection between Pollard, a corrupt prison staffer, and a recently released prisoner," said Sara as she scanned the lists. After a moment, she said, "Look at this. The staff list includes a person named Daniel T. Smalls. Like Janie. He works in the prison kitchen as a cook. See what you can find online about him."

After a few minutes of searching, Jake shouted, "Bingo! Look, here's an article from *The Tennessean* about the Janie Smalls' murder. It mentions her brother, Danny Smalls, who was a short-order cook at a local diner. Danny says his sister was a beautiful person, much loved, and so forth."

"Edna Shriver was our top suspect in her murder, but we didn't have enough evidence to put her away. That would give Janie's brother, Danny, plenty of reason to support the subsequent revenge murder of Edna. There are a lot of coincidences here."

EVEN STEVEN

"Could Danny Smalls be the actual protégé?" asked Jake.

"No," replied Sara. "Our records show he was working that day. Pulled a double shift. No way he could have snuck out for that long a period of time. Someone else had to have killed Edna Shriver."

While Sara and Jake were meeting, six miles to the west, at the Riverbend prison, Danny Smalls was at work in the vast kitchen. Feeding over 700 inmates and 400 staff three meals a day was no small task, and Smalls was just one of two dozen cooks and other food workers working the day shift. Today was like any other day. Nothing special about it. The lunch order consisted of 300 slices of pepperoni pizza, 300 cheeseburgers, a dozen pans of "vegetarian meat loaf," 500 chicken fingers, and 150 pounds of green salad, all made and consumed within a four-hour window.

After wheeling a case of frozen pizzas from the freezer into the kitchen prep area, Danny took his fifteen-minute break. He sat down on a pile of potato sacks and took out his phone. There was a text notification from his bank.

Ten thousand dollars had been deposited into his checking account. The sender was Timber Lane Ventures, LLC.

Smalls smiled. Old man Givens had made his second of three payments. With thirty thousand dollars in the bank, Danny could afford to sell his house, buy the RV he had been saving for, quit his stinking job at Riverbend, and hit the road.

He got up and walked nonchalantly through the bustling kitchen and down a hallway leading to the food storage areas and the big freezer units. At the end of the hall was the loading dock, where the trucks delivered food and supplies from the outside world. Danny didn't enter the dock, which was always guarded; instead, he headed down a set of stairs to an unmarked door. He pushed it open. Before him was a section of the yard reserved for death row inmates. It was used only a few hours each day, and at the moment, it was deserted.

Wearing his latex kitchen gloves, Smalls took a key from his pocket. He turned back to the door that was now closed behind him and tested it on the lock. It worked. Satisfied, he reached down and gently pressed the key into the soft soil next to the door, went back inside, and closed the door behind him.

Hurrying back up the stairs, he found an empty potato sack in the hall and went to his locker. Into the sack he stuffed a pair of civilian pants, a shirt, windbreaker jacket, and finally, a wallet with one hundred dollars cash and a forged Riverbend Maximum Security Institution laminated identification card. The photo was of Earl Steven Pollard. The name read *Tim Fogarty*.

He returned to the stairwell by the outside door and jammed the potato sack under the concrete stairs. He stripped off his kitchen gloves and stuffed them into his pocket.

8

In the maximum-security wing, Earl Steven Pollard was in his cell. It was 10:00 a.m. He was normally confined to his cell for twenty-three hours of the day, with one hour out for exercise and showering. He noted to himself that, today, his one-hour exercise period was at 11:00 a.m., just before the plastic tray with his lunch was slid through the slot in the steel door of his cell.

Perhaps this would be the day his life would change. The plan had been devised and funded, and the only question was when.

At exactly 11:00 a.m., two guards came to his door and unlocked it. The door swung open.

"Okay, Pollard, let's go," said the guard. "Shower today?"

"No, I'll just go out in the yard and get some fresh air," he replied.

"Suit yourself."

EVEN STEVEN

The guards—one in front and one behind—walked Pollard along the row of steel cell doors to another door, a double set that required the trio to be buzzed through under the watchful eye of a guard behind a bulletproof window. They went down a hall into a small room with another door. The door closed behind them, and yet another door opened, and the sudden glare from the sun made Pollard squint. Even on a cloudy day in January, natural sunlight burned compared the weak glare of the flickering overhead lights in his cell.

Pollard walked through the door into the exercise yard. It was not a large space—perhaps fifty yards on each side—mostly dirt and, in less worn areas, a sort of tough, scrubby grass. No trees. Some metal benches were placed here and there, bolted to concrete foundations. The plain cinderblock walls were thirty feet high and topped with razor wire. About a dozen other inmates loitered about. A few were playing basketball using an old hoop with a tattered net, but it was better than nothing. Pollard avoided the basketball area—it was the territory of the gangs, and he didn't need the aggravation. He had bigger business to conduct.

The guards left him alone. He looked up at the guard tower. It was manned, but the guy was facing in the other direction, the barrel of his long gun pointed at the grey sky.

Pollard casually strolled around the corner to the steel door with its peeling green paint. After glancing around, he bent down and probed into the earth.

A jolt went through his body as his fingertips touched the hard metal of a key. He quickly pried it out of the dirt and, without looking at it, put it into his pocket.

This was the moment he had been waiting for. Freedom was

at hand! He felt his heart racing. *Be calm*, he told himself. *Be cool.*

He felt the key in his pocket. Its jagged teeth and smooth sides. He looked around again. No eyes were on him. He swiftly took the key and slid it in the keyhole. He tried to turn it. What the hell? It wouldn't turn! A wave of panic and anger flooded over him. *Okay, relax.* He jiggled the key in the lock. Suddenly, it turned. He pulled open the door and slipped inside.

It was dark. He paused while his eyes adjusted. Just as Danny Smalls had told him, he was at the bottom of a concrete stairwell. He searched under the stairs and felt a large potato sack. He gently pulled it out. Civilian clothing and a laminated ID card. In the gloom, he squinted at the name. *Tim Fogarty*. He repeated it silently to himself. *I'm Tim Fogarty. Tim Fogarty.*

He changed and stashed the sack and his prison clothes under the stairs. Then, with nervous expectation, he climbed the steps. At the top, down a short hallway, he found himself at the edge of the loading dock. A big box truck was backed up, with its doors open. On the side of the box was painted a logo of a medieval coat of arms and the name "Estes & Sons Produce." Two kitchen workers were unloading big plastic bins from the truck. The driver stood on the pavement, leaning against the cab, smoking a cigarette.

Taking a deep breath, Pollard sauntered up to the two workers.

"Hey you guys, how's it going?" he said. They paused and looked at him. Without waiting, Pollard said, "I'm Tim Fogarty. First day on the job. Can you believe it? I don't

EVEN STEVEN

know what the fuck I'm doing. But I'm supposed to catch the van out of here. It leaves at 11:30, right?"

"You ain't got no car?" asked one of the men, a big burly guy with a beard.

"Nah. Saving up for one. I rode the bus here. From the John C. Tune Airport."

"The prison van don't leave for another hour," said the other man, a skinny guy with wire-rimmed eyeglasses.

Pollard's blood ran cold. *In forty minutes, the guards will know I'm missing. The whole damn prison will go into lockdown. I'll be screwed. They'll send me to the hole.*

The driver—an old man wearing a Carhartt jacket and jeans—glanced up at them. "I'm leaving as soon as these guys get done unloading the truck. I'll give you a lift into town."

"Ain't that against union rules?" said the burly guy as he hoisted a bin.

The driver shrugged. "I don't care. Just helping out a fellow human being. What's wrong with that?"

"Thanks," said Pollard. He saw a dozen bins still in the truck. Wanting to play his part convincingly and not draw attention, he said, "I'll give you a hand." He went into the truck and lifted a bin of apples. "Where do you want it?"

"In the cooler, inside," replied the skinny guy.

Pollard hefted the bin onto a two-wheeler and then piled up two more. He pushed the loaded hand truck through the big door leading down the hallway into the kitchen. The cooler was off to the left, so he went in and parked his load. He slid the bins onto the floor and turned to leave.

"Don't just leave them there, you dumbass," said a man in a white cook's outfit. "Put them with the others, over there." He pointed to a stack of similar bins.

"Uh, sure," replied Pollard. He picked up the bins, one by one, and stacked them where they belonged.

Again, he turned to leave.

"While you're at it," said the cook, "we need to move these onions to the back. See? There." He pointed.

"I gotta get back to the loading dock," said Pollard.

"This will just take you a minute. Say, are you new here? What's your name?"

Pollard drew a blank. *Shit—what's my name?* He gave the cook a blank stare. A drip of sweat trickled down his temple.

The cook's eyes were steady and his face a blank mask.

Suddenly Pollard blurted out, "Fogarty. Tim Fogarty."

"Well, Mr. Fogarty, if you want to last more than a day here, you'd better learn to keep moving."

"Yes, sir." Pollard hastily moved the bins of onions.

By the time he was finished, the cook had vanished. Pollard left the cooler and, keeping his gaze lowered to avoid eye

EVEN STEVEN

contact, hurried to the loading dock.

The rear doors of the truck were closed, and the engine was running. Pollard jumped down from the elevated platform and went to the passenger side door of the truck. The truck began to roll forward. He knocked on the side panel. The truck stopped. Pollard opened the door.

"I figured you weren't coming," said the driver.

"Sorry—I got tied up for a minute," said Pollard as he climbed up onto the seat.

"Okay," nodded the driver. "Get in. I'm headed back to the warehouse on Harding Pike. Near the Krogers and Publix. I'll drop you off anywhere along the way."

Pollard made a mental map. The driver would take the Briley Parkway south, cross I-40, and continue down White Bridge Pike or Route 155 to Harding Pike. Perfect.

"There's a car wash just before the Community College," Pollard said. "I'll get off there."

"Okay," said the driver. "By the way, my name's Rupert. But my friends call me Jimbo."

This seemed weirdly random to Pollard, but he just smiled. "Pleased to meet you, Jimbo."

"So, you're new at the prison?"

"Uh, yes."

"Work in the kitchen?"

"Yes."

EVEN STEVEN

"I'm not being nosy or nothing. Just making conversation. You don't mind, do you?"

"No."

They rode in silence for a few minutes. Pollard glanced at the clock on the dashboard. The time was 11:45a.m. In exactly fifteen minutes, all hell would break loose at Riverbend.

Traffic slowed down to a crawl. "Must be an accident," said Jimbo. He checked his phone. "Yep. Solid red for the next two miles. But if we get off, we'll waste even more time on the back roads. We're better off staying where we are. Mind if I turn on the radio?"

"No, go ahead."

Jimbo pressed the button. The radio was tuned to Super Talk 99.7 "The News on the Fives."

Pollard sat quietly as the truck crept slowly ahead. The minutes ticked by. It was nearly noon, and they were not yet even to I-40, where the traffic was expected to break.

The news from Riverbend would come, if not during this cycle, then the next one in five minutes or the one after that. If the prison break was the big story, Pollard would have to kill Jimbo. But how? He glanced around for a weapon. None. This was going to be nasty.

Then Pollard said, "The news is a bummer. Always bad stuff. Mind if we turn to music? Do you like country, Jimbo?"

"Personally, I'm partial to classic rock. Led Zeppelin and the Stones. Let's see…" He pushed a button. "105.9 The Rock," he said with satisfaction as the sound of "Whipping Post"

EVEN STEVEN

filled the cabin.

The clock said noon. Pollard imagined the shock waves reverberating through the prison wing at that very moment, as the guards realized he was gone. The lockdown would happen within seconds. Every corner searched. How long would it take them to find his clothes stashed under the stairs by the loading dock? To interrogate the kitchen workers? To learn about the phony "new guy"—what was his name, again? Tom Flannigan? No, Tim Fogarty. And the truck from Estes & Sons Produce?

Mercifully, the traffic broke open after I-40, and they made the speed limit the next half-mile. To the sound of Travis Tritt's "T-R-O-U-B-L-E," Jimbo pulled over at the White Bridge Car Wash.

Pollard opened the door and got out. He turned to Jimbo. "Thanks, buddy. Have a great day."

He watched as the truck merged into southbound traffic.

9

Earl Steven Pollard walked at a brisk pace along White Bridge to Knob Road, where he turned east and strolled, with a nonchalant attitude, until he arrived at a tidy brick house with blue shutters and a Toyota Camry in the driveway. He went to the front door and boldly rang the bell.

A woman answered the door. "Get in here," she hissed while looking around. "Anybody see you?"

Pollard ducked inside, and the woman closed the door. Pollard found himself standing in a nondescript living room with a faux leather sofa, hooked rug, and a wide-screen TV hung on the wall.

"Your uncle told me you might be coming," said the woman. She was middle-aged, dressed in mom jeans and a Tennessee Titans sweatshirt. Her bleach-blonde hair was cut in a seventies shag. "I don't want to get mixed up in nothin'."

"Nice to see you, too, Debbie," smiled Pollard. "We're just going for a little drive. No more than an hour. Then I'll come back here. I won't be Earl Pollard. I'll be your distant cousin.

EVEN STEVEN

In a week or so, I'll be gone for good."

Debbie nodded. "I guess I owe your uncle a favor. When I was his bookkeeper, he was always very kind to me. When my husband Arthur died, it was generous of him to pay for a nice funeral. I'll never forget that."

"Do you have my things?"

"Yes—right here. Mr. Givens had them sent over." She handed Pollard an envelope. Inside was a driver's license and a Visa card, both in the name of Charles Kaplan, and a prepaid burner phone.

Pollard inspected the license. "The guy who made this did a nice job." He pocketed the items. "Let's get going." He saw a Cleveland Indians baseball cap hanging on a clothes tree by the door. He picked it up and put it on his head. "Mind if I borrow this?" he asked.

"No, go ahead." Debbie picked up her purse, and they went out the door. She paused to punch in the alarm code. "Can't be too cautious these days," she said. "There have been break-ins in the neighborhood. Too much crime."

Pollard smiled and nodded. "Yeah. You need to be careful."

They went to the car. "You drive," he said. "Don't speed. Just relax. I'll hunker down."

They got into the Camry. Debbie backed out of the driveway and drove west, back toward White Bridge Road. But instead of turning, they continued straight on Knob Road to Charlotte Pike, where they turned south.

Pollard, who slumped in his seat with his cap pulled low and his eyes just above the level of the door, tuned the radio to SuperTalk 99.7.

"Breaking news," said the announcer with professional urgency. "We have a report from the Riverbend Maximum Security Institution here in Nashville that a death row inmate has apparently escaped. Earl Steven Pollard, who was convicted of multiple murders in the so-called Even Steven serial killing spree, was found missing after a regular headcount today at noon. Authorities are tight-lipped, but sources say he may have escaped through the kitchen and then onto a delivery truck. It's not known if he has any accomplices. Pollard is described as a white male, average height and weight, dark hair, with a tattoo of an eye on his upper right arm. He is considered extremely dangerous, and if you should encounter him, do not interact with him and immediately call police."

"Extremely dangerous?" scoffed Pollard. "That's a damned lie. I never touched anyone who didn't have it coming to them."

Debbie said nothing, but her knuckles were ghost white on the steering wheel. They crossed under I-40 and soon came to a sign that read, *Oak Hills Medical Office Park*. They turned in, and Debbie parked in front of one of the offices. Pollard, still slouching, took his phone and tapped in a number.

After two rings, an sweet but bossy country lady answered, "This Shirley, Dr, Winston's office, what you need honey?"

"Please tell the doctor that Charles Kaplan has arrived," said Pollard.

"Does Charles Kaplan have an appointment?"

EVEN STEVEN

"Yes. But please inform Dr. Winston. He will know what it's about. It's an emergency."

"Ok love, hold tight."

Debbie and Pollard waited in the car.

The receptionist came back on the line. "Yes, the doctor will see you."

Pollard turned to Debbie. "Thank you for your kindness. I'll call you to pick me up. Should be just a few hours. Just go home and keep a low profile."

Pollard opened the car door and cautiously looked around. No people were in sight, just parked cars. He quickly hurried to the door of the medical office and pulled it open.

The air inside was frigid and antiseptic. To the left was a waiting room with a small TV on the wall. He glanced up at it and saw his own face on the screen. *ESCAPED CONVICT*, read the caption. *ARMED AND DANGEROUS*.

Pulling the visor of his cap low, he approached the receptionist who was behind a plexiglass barrier. "Charles Kaplan here to see Dr. Winston."

The receptionist looked up. She was accustomed to seeing the doctor's cosmetic surgery patients trying to hide their faces from view. "Hey sugar, I need that insurance?" she asked.

"My what?"

"Your insurance. Medicare? HMO? And please fill out this

form." She thrust a clipboard at him. "Answer the questions and sign the last page. You got this baby. Move along."

At that moment, the door behind the receptionist opened, and a man in a white coat leaned in. "Shirley, Mr. Kaplan is already in the system. He doesn't need to fill out any forms. Please show him to operating room three. I'll be along in just a few minutes."

Shirley stood up and came around to the door to the clinic rooms. With an annoyed smile, she said, "Please follow me."

Pollard followed her along a short hallway decorated with before-and-after photos of patients who had been given smaller noses, fuller lips, tighter necks, bigger breasts, smoother cheeks. She opened a door, and they entered a small operating room with one reclining chair and various cabinets and electronic instruments on wheels. A big circular light hovered overhead like a flying saucer.

"What do I have to do?" asked Pollard.

"Just sit back in the chair, relax, and the doctor will be in shortly." She left and closed the door.

Pollard did as he was told. His mind raced. What if it was a trap? He was a wanted man. They were actively hunting him. Could the cops have bribed Dr. Winston? They could be surrounding the office, waiting for the moment to swarm inside, guns drawn, dogs snarling. Pollard slipped off the chair and went to the window. Carefully, he parted the venetian blinds and peeked between the slats. His view was of the side yard and the neighboring liquor store. No cops. Just the highway off to the right.

He heard the door click open behind him and whirled

around. A middle-aged man in a white coat and with slicked-back hair entered. He eyed Pollard with a noncommittal expression. He closed the door behind him and said, "I'm Dr. Winston. Mr. Pollard, please sit down."

Pollard resumed his place in the chair. The doctor stood over him.

"I don't know if your uncle explained to you *why* I agreed to see you."

"No—we can't say much to each other because of the prison rules."

"Yes, of course." Dr. Winston gave a cheerless smile. "Here's the thing. You need me to provide a valuable service to you. Technically, it's not difficult. I'm going to re-shape your nose, lift your jowls, inject some filler into your cheeks, and give you a bit more chin. This will be sufficient to nullify facial recognition software. A photo of you, even full face, will not match what's in the law enforcement database. You will be able to move about freely in public, but this procedure will not change your DNA. You'll have the same fingerprints, the same retinas, and the same teeth, any of which could be used to identify you. You will always need to be vigilant.

"For this, I expect a service in return." Dr. Winston steeled himself. "A year ago, a drunk driver hit my wife's car. Stella was killed instantly. The police picked up the driver, who was miraculously unhurt. His name is Edwin Doolan. They arrested him and charged him. However, he was able to hire a very good, very slick lawyer who claimed to have found mistakes made by the cops and the prosecution. To make a long story short, Doolan was acquitted. After killing Stella, he just walked away a free man. He lives comfortably in Shelby Bottoms. Not a day goes by that I don't think about Stella and the degenerate who took her life and enjoys his freedom."

"You've got a deal," said Pollard.

Dr. Winston picked up his phone. "Nurse Kim? We're ready to prep the patient. Operating room three."

He then turned to Pollard. "We're going to give you an intravenous sedation, also referred to as 'twilight' sedation. The medication induces a calm, dreamy state, keeping you free from anxiety while still being able to respond to my questions and instructions. Some patients drift off into an unconscious state. That's normal. Throughout the surgery, your vital signs will be closely monitored by our medical team. After the procedure, the sedative's effects may linger, so you'll need a ride home—you won't be able to drive for at least six hours."

Pollard nodded. "Okay."

Nurse Kim, a stout woman with a no-nonsense attitude, prepped Pollard's right forearm by placing it in a rigid support held securely with Velcro straps. After swabbing it with alcohol, she brought the needle into place just above his cephalic vein.

Suddenly, Pollard saw himself on the death table at Riverbend, an instant before his life would be ended by lethal injection. As a wave of panic swept through him, he involuntarily jerked his arm away from the needle.

Startled, the nurse released his arm. "Sir," she said, "you need to hold steady for me. This isn't going to hurt. You'll feel

EVEN STEVEN

only a slight pinch."

Dr. Winston smiled. "Nurse Kim is extremely skilled at placing an IV. Just relax, will you?"

Pollard clenched his teeth and told himself to ignore his feelings of terror and think about being able to walk among normal people without fear of being captured.

Three hours later, as the sun was casting its late afternoon rays, Pollard groggily opened his eyes. He gingerly lifted a hand to his face and felt only gauze bandages. He tried to sit up but, feeling dizzy, slumped back into the chair.

The door opened. Nurse Kim entered and approached Pollard. "How are you feeling?"

"Like I just went five rounds with Mike Tyson."

"That's normal. Your vitals are good." She unclipped the fingertip pulse oximeter and set it on the stainless-steel tray. "Can you sit up?"

He tried again and managed to stay upright. He took a deep breath, and his head began to clear. He remembered why he was there.

"What's next?" he asked.

"You'll go home and take it easy. You'll feel some soreness during the first week, which can be managed with prescription pain medication, if you want it. The bruising and swelling should subside within two weeks. Avoid strenuous exercise for at least three weeks. Numbness around the incisions is normal and can take several months to go away. Stay out of the sun, apply sunscreen, and wear a hat with a brim. Is someone picking you up?"

"Yes—I'll text her now."

Debbie arrived and, without much conversation, they headed back to her house. The car radio blared the news of his escape. The cops had located Jimbo, the driver of the Estes & Sons Produce truck, and hauled him downtown for questioning. Jimbo told them everything—how he thought he was giving a ride to a prison employee whose name he never got, and how he had dropped him off at the White Bridge Car Wash. That was a little more than four hours ago.

Debbie was so nervous that Pollard had to remind her to drive carefully. On Charlotte Pike, just after the intersection with I-40, they came to a police roadblock.

"Oh shit, now we're screwed," whined Debbie as the car crept ahead toward the line of police cars with their blue lights flashing.

"Be cool," said Pollard. "Just remember: My name is Charlie. I'm your boyfriend. You drove me to the doctor at ten o'clock this morning. Charlie. Boyfriend. Ten o'clock."

"Charlie. Boyfriend. Ten o'clock," she repeated. "Charlie. Boyfriend. Ten o'clock."

They rolled to stop next to a state trooper. Debbie rolled down her window.

"What's going on?" she asked.

EVEN STEVEN

The trooper peered inside the car. "We're searching for an escaped prisoner," he drawled. "Please open your trunk."

Debbie popped the trunk. Another trooper behind the car closed it. "All clear."

The first trooper nodded at Pollard. "What's your name?"

"Charles Kaplan," replied Pollard.

"You look pretty beat up."

"Had some facial surgery done. Bad car accident a while back."

"You got identification?"

"Sure." Pollard handed over his Charles Kaplan driver's license. The trooper studied it.

"I took Charlie to the clinic this morning," volunteered Debbie. "At ten o'clock."

There was a deep gulf of silence. Then the trooper handed Debbie the Charles Kaplan driver's license. "Okay. You may proceed."

Once safely inside the house, Pollard went to the bathroom to change his bandages, as Nurse Kim had instructed. He stood before the mirror and, under the harsh glare of the lights, peeled off the gauze. He was both astonished and horrified by the face looking back at him. His nose was swollen but somehow flatter. His cheekbones were more pronounced, making him appear vaguely Native American. His chin, blue and tender, seemed to project forward with dramatic authority. And despite the swelling, the overall

EVEN STEVEN

shape of his face seemed more slender and less round.

He studied his altered image with increasing curiosity. He tried to smile, but pain shot through his cheeks. He opened his mouth, slowly and gently, to see if he could eat. Probably need to stick to a liquid diet for a few days. He made a note to ask Debbie to buy some hair dye—bleach blond would be good. And he could grow out his hair, which was now not much longer than a prison buzz cut.

Yes, he said to himself. *This is going to work out very nicely.*

10

Three weeks later, Earl Steven Pollard sat in his car—a ubiquitous used Chevy Malibu he had picked up from a local dealer—in the parking lot of the Village Tower Apartments on Electric Avenue in Shelby Bottoms. It was 7:30 on a frigid January morning. For a week, Pollard had visited this place every morning at this same time. Each morning, he watched the back door of the ten-story building and observed the residents going to their cars and leaving for work. The pattern was remarkably consistent. At around 7:15 a.m., a woman would come out, get into a Buick, and drive away. A few minutes a later two men would leave in a Jeep. Then an older woman would drive away in a Prius. Much to his satisfaction, Pollard had also noted there was no security camera covering this parking lot.

On this particular morning, he had snagged an empty spot next to a dark green Ford Explorer. This car was notable because of its owner.

At exactly 7:35 a.m., right on schedule, the back door of the Village Tower Apartments opened, and a man walked out.

EVEN STEVEN

Hunched against the cold, he wore a brown overcoat and a dark blue knit cap. His only distinguishing feature was an impressive handlebar moustache that clung to his upper lip like furry animal. Carrying a briefcase, the man hurried to the Ford Explorer, just as he did every morning at this same time.

Wearing gloves, a black ski jacket, and nondescript jeans, Pollard opened his car door and got out. He went around to the front and pretended to inspect something on his car.

The man in the brown coat arrived at his Explorer. With his key fob, he clicked open the locks, and the car beeped its friendly greeting. The man reached for the door, opened it, and slid onto the driver's seat.

At that same moment, Pollard reached into his jacket pocket and pulled out a .38 special snub-nosed revolver and held it down by his thigh. He sauntered around his car and deftly opened the passenger door of the Explorer. With one smooth motion he leaned in and pointed the gun at the man.

The man looked up. "What the—?" he muttered.

"Edwin Doolan?" said Pollard.

"Yeah—who the fuck are you?"

"Just a guy getting even. For Stella Winston." He pulled the trigger. The bullet drilled into Doolan's forehead and exploded out the back of his shattered cranium. The fragments clattered against the window glass. Bits of brain and bone splattered across the interior of the car. Doolan's eyes remained open as his mouth went slack and he slumped in his seat, supported by his shoulder belt. A peculiar gurgling sound came from his ravaged head. The blood

EVEN STEVEN

flowed from what was left of the back of his skull and began to pool on the floor.

Quickly, Pollard pocketed the gun and pulled out a box cutter. With his gloved hands he rudely pried open the mouth of the dead man and grasped his tongue, pulling it out with one hand while holding the razor with the other. He held the tip of the blade on the bloody tongue, ready to go to work.

He paused.

He asked himself if he were ready for the white-hot response that would come with the discovery of an eighth Even Steven victim, just weeks after he had made his daring escape from Riverbend. Perhaps he should give himself space to breathe and become more accustomed to his new identity. By eliminating Edwin Doolan, he was paying off a debt to Dr. Winston—no more, no less. No one else needed to know the motive.

Deciding this one should be incognito, he retracted the razor and put it in his pocket. He then removed the victim's gold watch, unbuckled his seat belt, reached into his rear pants pocket, and extracted his wallet. After opening the glove compartment door and flinging its contents on the floor, he backed out of the car and stood on the pavement. He looked around. A person was walking to their car with their back to him. He closed the door of the Explorer and hurried to his own car.

Let the cops worry about Edwin Doolan, he thought. I have bigger fish to fry.

Moments later, he was heading west on Davidson Street

EVEN STEVEN

bound for I-24 and the morning rush hour traffic.

In Cumberland Heights, he pulled off the highway and drove to a Taco Bell. He went into the bathroom and threw away the bloody gloves. He took the wallet and removed the driver's license. *I'll keep this as evidence*, he told himself. He wrapped the wallet in toilet paper and dropped it in the trash. The watch? It was a Rolex. He hated to just throw it away. After examining it to ensure it had no inscription linking it to the victim, he went into one of the toilet stalls and, handling it with tissue, hung it from the toilet handle. Some guy—maybe the janitor—will find it and keep it. He then drove to the office of Dr. Winston.

Shirley was behind the desk and said he was not available.

"Tell him Charles Kaplan is here. This will take literally one minute," Pollard replied.

Grudgingly, Shirley picked up her phone. She spoke and listened. Then she hung up.

Dr. Winston appeared at the door. "This way, please, Mr. Kaplan."

Pollard followed Dr. Winston into a private examination room.

"Mission accomplished," said Pollard as he handed the doctor the driver's license of Edwin Doolan. "Watch the news tonight. You'll see. May you find peace."

EVEN STEVEN

Dr. Winston sat speechless as he stared into the license. He quickly looked to Pollard with gaping eyes and began to stutter with his words only to be silence by Pollard with a sly shushing gesture.

Pollard turned and walked out. With a nod to Shirley, he left the office and returned to his car. He took I-40 to White Bridge Pike—within a mile of the Riverbend prison—and across the river to Bordeaux. He turned off Clarksville Pike into the parking lot of the Dew Drop Inn, a cheap motel catering to transients, owned by a corporate proprietor that paid minimum wage to the desk clerk who's stayed just sober enough not to get fired. Pollard parked in front of room 26, climbed the steel stairs and put his key into the lock. He went inside and closed the door behind him.

Edwin Doolan worked in sales, and it was not unusual for him to be on the road, out of the office. It wasn't until 2:00 p.m. that his body was discovered by a woman who parked her car next to the Explorer and, to her horror, noticed the bloody window and body slumped in the driver's seat.

She promptly dialed 9-1-1.

At that same moment, Sara was in the heart of downtown Nashville at the Justice A.A. Birch Building, a few blocks from the State Capitol. She was seated in the audience of the courtroom, attending the trial of her brother, Ricky. The man in the witness chair was a forensic accountant who, at the behest of the State, had examined the finances of North Star Properties, the real estate company owned by Ricky and his murdered partner.

The assistant DA was a new guy named Michael Withers. Sara had dealt with him only a few times and had no opinion of him other than he was prosecuting the wrong person and was relying on an unreliable witness.

Withers asked, "Please tell the court what you found out about the partnership agreement between the defendant and the victim."

"The agreement between Rick Mansard and Brett Millar," the accountant stated in his monotone voice, "provided that, upon the death of one partner, his ownership of half of the company would revert not to his heirs, if there were any, but to the other partner."

"And as a consequence of Mr. Millar being brutally murdered," said Withers as he turned his beady black eyes toward the defense table, "How much money did the defendant gain?"

"The value of the partnership was about ten million dollars, so half that."

"Five million dollars!" said Withers. "Not a bad payday for murder, wouldn't you say?"

"Objection!" said Ricky's defense attorney, a smart and capable woman named Ruth Blade.

"Sustained," said the judge.

"No more questions for this witness," said Withers.

Sara's phone vibrated. She glanced at it. Headquarters. Police business. She hurriedly got up and ducked into the hallway.

EVEN STEVEN

Responding officers had found a man shot to death. Village Tower Apartments on Electric Avenue in Shelby Bottoms.

The City of Nashville experiences about one hundred murders per year. Usual motives are gang related, domestic, or robbery. This one—a middle-aged male shot in his car early in the morning—seemed unusual. It didn't fit into an easy pattern.

Sara and Jake arrived at the scene at 2:15 p.m.

"Do we have an identification on this guy?" she asked a uniformed cop as she peered at the bluish corpse. Rigor mortis was setting in among the small muscles of the face and hands and would soon spread to the larger muscles of the abdomen and legs.

"The car is registered to a man named Edwin Doolan," replied the cop.

Sara recognized the name. She recalled that Doolan had been charged with drunk driving and vehicular manslaughter but was acquitted on legal technicalities. Immediately, she pried open his mouth and examined his tongue.

Nothing. No marks.

"We need to get him out of the car and back to the office," said Dr. Yeager. "We cannot wait another minute. He'll be stiff as a statue."

"Okay," nodded Sara. "Take him downtown." Then to Jake, she reported, "No marks. Just the one gunshot to the head. No wallet, even though he was in his car and probably going to work. Glovebox ransacked. Looks like a robbery, but something isn't right."

EVEN STEVEN

After the medical examiner had taken the body, Sara pulled out the driver's seat belt. She examined the shoulder strap. "Look," she said to Jake. "Blood and brain matter here on the strap. He was shot while he was buckled in, and then the killer unbuckled him and presumably took his wallet."

"No sign of a struggle," nodded Jake. "If the victim were being robbed at gunpoint, he'd unbuckle his seat belt to get his wallet. His belt was still fastened. I can't see a dope addict shooting first and robbing second."

Sara had told the uniformed cops to canvass the building, and one officer returned, accompanied by an elderly woman.

"Hello, what's your name?" asked Sara.

"Pauline Sanders," replied the woman. With a withered hand she brushed a stray gray hair from her forehead.

"Where do you live?"

Pauline turned and pointed at the Village Tower building. "On the fifth floor. The top. The last two windows on the right are mine."

"Did you see anything today?" asked Jake.

Pauline nodded. "Yes, I think so. It was about seven-thirty this morning. I know because the weather forecast was on the TV news and it's always at that time. I was in my kitchen—that's the window nearest us—and I happened to glance out the window, because they were talking about the weather. I wanted to see for myself what it was like. I saw this car"—she pointed toward the Ford Explorer, now covered in a plastic tarp—"with the passenger door open. Then a man got out of the car, on the passenger side, and got into the car parked next to it, here." She pointed to the empty parking place. "He drove away."

"Can you describe the man and the car?" asked Sara.

"He was just an average man. I didn't see his face. Average size. He was wearing dark clothing. Maybe a jacket or jacket. He had dark gloves. The car was blue. Just a typical sedan. I don't know much about cars. It wasn't an SUV or anything like that. Just a normal car."

"You didn't happen to see the license plate?"

"Sorry, no."

"Had you ever seen the blue car before?"

"Oh, I don't know," said Pauline. She took off her wire-rimmed glasses and wiped the lenses using the hem of her cotton dress. Then she put them back on. "There are so many cars out there. They all look alike to me."

"Thanks, Ms. Sanders," said Sara. "If we have any more questions, we'll get back to you."

A half-mile down Davidson Street was a pawn shop. Ray's Collectibles was of interest to Sara because it had a security camera pointed at the front door that also covered the street. Sara and Jake asked Ray to play his footage from that morning. At the timestamp of 7:38 a.m., a blue car could be seen driving past the storefront, headed west. There appeared to be just one person in the car, the driver. Either a man or a woman with short hair. Too far away to see anything more. The plate was not visible in the profile view.

"What kind of car is that?" asked Sara.

Jake peered at the grainy video. "It's a Chevy Malibu. But you can't tell what year because they've kept the same body styling for the past eight years. There are thousands of them on the road."

"All right," nodded Sara.

They returned to the station. Captain Riggs was waiting for them in his office.

"Close the door," he said tersely. "Okay—is this an Even Steven murder? People are freaking out. The mayor is freaking out. The press is whipping the Earl Steven Pollard escape into a frenzy. He's been running free for three weeks! Not a sign of him. He was last seen when the truck driver dropped him off at White Bridge Car Wash. By now, he could be anywhere. He could be in Nashville or even Texas by now."

"We understand," nodded Sara. "At this point in the investigation, we do not believe the Doolan murder was done by Pollard. The victim has no mutilation of the tongue. It looks more like a robbery gone bad. We have yet to get forensics back from the vehicle—the Ford Explorer. We have a witness who saw a man get out of the Explorer at the time of the shooting and then drive away in a blue Chevy Malibu."

"What about the Edna Shriver murder?" asked Captain Riggs. "Anything there?"

"We've got the list of prisoners released from Riverbend in the last two months," said Jake. "We believe the Shriver killing was done by a copycat or even a protégé of Earl Steven Pollard. One of these released prisoners is a likely candidate for the role."

"Among them, who do you like?"

"Elliott Toliver is one," said Sara. "He was convicted on charges of wire fraud and embezzlement and incarcerated at Riverbend for two years. He was released two weeks before Edna Shriver was killed, and let's just say he's on our list for a myriad of reasons. The victim was killed with the chain from his own bicycle. The jury found insufficient evidence and acquitted him, but then new evidence emerged—a single hair found embedded in the bike chain. DNA testing showed it could have belonged to Toliver. The match was ninety-nine percent certain. But it was too late. Toliver had been acquitted based on trial testimony and evidence, and the State was precluded from charging him again. They had to let him go."

"Okay, find this guy Toliver and talk to him."

According to prison records, Toliver had only two visitors during his stay at Riverbend. One was his lawyer. The other was his sister, Jasmine Toliver, who lived in Town Park Estates, just south of Nashville International Airport.

Sara and Jake wasted no time pulling up in front of a tidy one-story wood frame home on Pumphouse Drive. A car—a plain Nissan sedan—was in the driveway. As snow flurries scattered in the air, a cozy plume of smoke curled from the brick chimney. Sara and Jake approached the door. It was answered by a woman in a beehive hairdo and a cowgirl outfit, complete with white boots and a fringed jacket.

"Howdy," she said brightly. "What can I do for you?"

Startled by her friendly demeanor, Sara and Jake identified themselves. "We'd like to talk to you about your brother, Elliott," said Jake.

"I hope he ain't done nothing wrong," said Jasmine as she waved them inside. "Or, I should say, nothing *more* wrong. He did his time for the mistake he made."

The detectives found themselves in a living room that, by all appearances, was a shrine to country music. The sounds of Dolly Parton filled the air from a record player built into a bookshelf laden with vinyl albums. Pictures of country artists, old and new, decorated every inch of the walls—Hank Williams, George Jones, Tammy Wynette, John Prine. Small figurines and souvenirs of more artists stood on the tabletops. There was a big poster of the Grand Ole Opry covered in autographs. And in the corner, holding court over the whole menagerie, was a nearly life-sized statue of Roy Rogers astride his horse, Trigger.

"Let's go into the kitchen," said Jasmine.

They followed her and sat down at a wooden table with a red checkered cloth. The crowning decoration was a bobblehead of Charley Pride, singing into a microphone.

"Can I get you something to drink?" she asked. "I make a mean screwdriver."

"No, thanks," replied Jake. "We're on duty."

"I see you're a big fan of country music," said Sara.

"You bet," replied Jasmine. "I listen to it all day long. Go to the Opry at least once a month. I got Reba's autograph just last week."

EVEN STEVEN

"Reba?" said Sara.

"Reba McEntire," said Jake dryly. "She's sold sixty million albums."

"Oh," nodded Sara. "Have you heard Beyoncé's country album?"

"Oh, sure," replied Jasmine. "Not too bad. Not bad at all."

"Okay, let's get down to business," said Sara. "Your brother, Elliott. He was released from Riverbend six weeks ago. Have you seen him? Do you know where he lives?"

"Yep, I saw him all right. I was the one who picked him up at the front gate. He had nothin' but the clothes on his back and a few personal items. I drove him to this very house."

"Did he stay here?"

"For about a week. I helped him open a little bank account at Nashville One Bank. He said he wanted to get a job and save his money. I told him that was a good idea. He went out every day looking for work. It's hard when you're a convicted felon. No one wants to hire you. Then one day, he came home driving a pickup truck! It was a Dodge, I think. And he said he had found a place to live. I was astonished. I asked him where on Earth he got the money. He said he was going into business with an uncle of a guy he knew from Riverbend. I asked him what kind of business. He said import-export.

"I said to him, 'You don't know the first thing about importing or exporting!' He replied he had learned in prison, in the library there. They had books on it."

"The uncle of a guy he knew at Riverbend?" repeated Sara. "Did he ever mention this guy's name or the name of the uncle?"

"No," Jasmine shook her head. "He didn't talk much about his experience in prison. I think he wanted to put it all behind him. He was very quiet about it."

"You said he moved out," noted Sara.

"Yes. He told me he found a little house way out in Jacob's Valley. He said he wanted to be away from people, so I asked him how he could operate an import-export business from a place in the boondocks. He said, 'Don't be silly—it's all done on the internet.' I said, okay. As you can see, I'm not real big on new technology. I like to live in the time of vinyl records and FM radio."

"So, he's out there around Joelton Pike?" asked Sara.

"Yes. Here—I'll get his address."

"When did you last speak with your brother?"

"This morning. On the phone."

EVEN STEVEN

11

The house on 24 Marrowbone Creek Road, just off Clarksville Pike, about ten miles northeast of downtown Nashville, was set well back into the woods. According to city records, the two-bedroom wood frame structure was originally built in the early twentieth century. The retired farm had once encompassed over a thousand acres; it had since been cut down to just ten, with the rest sold off to developers. It had been owned for decades by the Woodmont Trust, a private trust controlled by yet another private trust. Sara was convinced that the trail of ownership would eventually lead to none other than Leonard Givens, who had added to his significant fortune by selling off the old, vast soybean farmland.

The long weedy driveway snaked through the woods parallel to the creek. A startled deer jumped across the road and vanished into the undergrowth. After a quarter-mile, the driveway took a sharp turn to the right, and the house came into view. Next to it was an old barn, painted red. In front of the barn was parked a Dodge pickup truck.

The little caravan of three police cars—the detectives, two pairs of officers, and the SWAT team—slowly eased up to the front porch of the house with its four decrepit windows and warped floorboards. As two officers circled around to the back, Sara and Jake, backed up by the four black-clad members of the SWAT team, boldly stepped onto the porch. There was no sound from within. Jake rapped hard on the wooden door frame.

"Elliott Toliver! Police department! We need to talk to you!"

Silence. In the distance, a couple of crows angrily squawked at something.

Again, he knocked.

"Okay, let's go in," said Sara. With gun drawn, she reached for the doorknob. It turned. She pushed it open. "Elliott Toliver!"

Her voice echoed in the vestibule. Before her, the old grand staircase spilled down from upstairs. The walls, papered in a vaguely neoclassical floral design, showed rectangles where the paper hadn't faded, shadows of where pictures had once hung. To the left was the door to the front parlor, which seemed to have been stripped of its furniture. Its only contents were one ratty old armchair with a fractured leg that made it sit askew. The fireplace was black and empty.

To the right was the old library, identifiable by its bookshelves built into the walls on three sides, now largely empty except for a few scattered dusty volumes. This room had also been depleted of its furniture, with only a dark oak table remaining in the center.

"Elliott Toliver!" Sara called out.

No answer.

EVEN STEVEN

"First floor all clear," said one of the cops. "No sign of him."

"Let's go upstairs," said Sara. Her pistol led the way up the grand staircase, past more outlines on the walls where pictures once hung. At the top, she paused on the ratty red carpet. The hall led to the left and right.

"Elliott Toliver! Police!" Sara called out.

Nothing.

"Jake, you take the left, and I'll go right," said Sara. In her half of the hallway, there were four doors. She opened the first one. It was a bedroom, overlooking the front yard of the house. Like the other rooms, it was largely bare. A closet door stood open. The air was musty.

The second door, facing the rear of the house, opened into a bathroom. Here, she paused. Lying on the flat marble counter of the sink were various toiletries—a tube of toothpaste, toothbrush, razor, nail clippers, comb. On the floor was a new bathmat, the cheap shaggy kind, bright blue. The bathtub had a plastic shower curtain. A towel hung from a hook. The sink had beads of water clinging to the sides.

Okay, thought Sara. *Proof of life.*

The third door, also facing the back of the house, opened into another bedroom. Also abandoned. Nothing but a few old cardboard boxes and some stacks of magazines from the 1960s.

One door remained. Facing the front of the house. Probably a bedroom—that's how all these old houses were laid out. Gun in hand, she reached for the doorknob and opened the door.

EVEN STEVEN

Before her was a gruesome scene.

Lying on the big four-poster bed in a mass of bloody sheets was a body. Male, about thirty. Naked. The torso was bruised and lacerated, but these were not fatal injuries. They were designed to inflict pain. The feet were tied at the ankles. The hands were upraised and tied to the headboard.

Holstering her pistol, Sara approached the body. The eyes were open and glassy. She touched the forehead.

It was still warm.

"We got here just minutes too late," she said to Jake.

The cause of death was obvious. A bicycle chain had been wrapped tightly around the victim's neck, causing slow, agonizing suffocation.

Sara glanced around the room. An ordinary second-hand bureau and a chair. A plain desk with a laptop on it, as well as a cell phone, wallet, and vehicle keys. A closet, door open, with some clothes hanging. Shoes on the floor below.

There were no signs of a struggle. Jake opened the wallet. The Tennessee driver's license said *Elliott Toliver*.

With gloved hands, Sara performed the usual inspection. She opened the victim's mouth and examined his tongue. Sure enough, it had been inscribed with the sign of the eye.

Elliott Toliver, released from Riverbend two weeks before the murder of Edna Shriver, was victim number 8. He had gotten his fatal payback for the rape and murder of the young boy in the park, who had been killed with the chain from his own bicycle. Fresh from his daring escape from

EVEN STEVEN

prison, Earl Steven Pollard—Even Steven—was back to his evil ways.

"Look at this," Jake said to Sara. He showed her Toliver's phone. On the screen was the image of the crushed head of Edna Shriver.

"He took a photo as a trophy," said Jake.

"That proves he was the protégé of Pollard," nodded Sara.

"Funny thing, this photo is stored in his deleted files folder. After thirty days, it would have disappeared."

"It wasn't a trophy," nodded Sara. "It was proof that he had done the job. But he couldn't risk going to Riverbend and showing it to Pollard, even through the glass at the visitor center. I think I know whom he showed it to."

"So, our theory is that Pollard coached Toliver to take over as Even Steven," said Jake. "Then Toliver was legally released from Riverbend and without remorse or reservation killed Edna Shriver? I suppose we can assume that Leonard Givens is the uncle of the guy he knew at Riverbend and he underwrote Toliver's freedom with the phony import-export business. But then Pollard escaped!"

"Perhaps he didn't know he *could* escape," said Sara. "Perhaps the opportunity presented itself after Toliver had found his freedom. So, Pollard escapes, and the first thing he does is put his own protégé out of business."

"That would explain why there's no sign of a struggle here," said Jake. "Toliver let Pollard come here for a friendly meeting. Toliver suspected nothing until *bam!* Even Steven strikes again."

"I want to make sure we analyze that phone and get the record of every call made," said Sara.

By the time they were ready to leave the scene, the press had descended on the property. Sara and Jake walked outside to be greeted by a gaggle of reporters and cameras, while their news trucks and vans waited in a broad circle around the driveway, satellite dishes pointed to the sky.

"Is this a homicide?" inquired one.

"Is it Even Steven?" asked another as she thrust her microphone in Sara's face.

"How is the Nashville Police Department going to keep people safe?" demanded a third.

"No comment," said Sara as she made her way to her car. "This is an ongoing investigation. We'll issue a statement as soon as we're ready."

EVEN STEVEN

12

The next day at 10:00 a.m., Sara hurried to the Justice A.A. Birch Building. The jury had returned with their verdict in the murder trial of Richard Mansard.

The courtroom was nearly full. A hush fell over the crowd as the twelve jurors filed in and took their seats. From her seat in the middle of the crowd, Sara could see her brother at the defense table, flanked by his lawyers. She couldn't tell his mood. His Army service had instilled in him a sense of discipline, and she knew he wouldn't show much emotion. Suddenly, he turned and glanced at the audience. She gave him a little wave but wasn't sure if he saw her amidst all the other faces. Then he turned away and faced forward. She could see only the back of his head.

"The defendant will rise," said the judge.

Ricky and his lawyers stood. They looked straight ahead.

The judge continued, "Members of the jury, have you reached a verdict?"

The foreperson stood. "Yes, Your Honor." She handed the jury form to the bailiff, who passed it to the judge. He opened it and read it, showing no expression. Sara scanned the faces of the jurors. The five men and seven women were impassive. None seemed to be looking at Ricky. The courtroom was quiet.

The bailiff passed the jury form back to the foreperson.

"On the count of murder in the first degree, how do you find the defendant?" asked the judge.

"We find the defendant, Richard Mansard, not guilty."

A murmur swept through the courtroom.

"On the count of murder in the second degree, how do you find?"

"We find the defendant, Richard Mansard, not guilty."

The courtroom erupted in applause. Ricky turned, and with a big smile, embraced his lawyers.

Sara felt as though a huge cloud had been lifted from over her head, and the sun was shining down its glorious rays.

"Court will come to order," said the judge with a bang of his gavel. "Members of the jury, thank you for your service. You are free to go." He turned to Ricky. "The defendant is free to go."

DA Withers, grim-faced, stood up.

Losing your first big case was a stupid career move, thought Sara, *but the evidence had been weak. You should have known better. Tough luck, buddy.*

She made her way forward to the defense table. Ricky's girlfriend, Julia, was already there with him, locked in a tearful embrace. Sara put her hand on Ricky's shoulder. "Congratulations, kid!" she said.

"Hey, sis," he greeted her with a jubilant smile. "I had faith. I knew they'd acquit me. This ridiculous nightmare is over! I'm just pissed they haven't found the real killer."

"We're working on it," said Sara. "Doing our best."

Suddenly, Sara became aware of a commotion in the courtroom. Someone began shouting.

"You bastard! You killed my son! You're going to rot in hell!"

It was Brett Millar's mother. She had been in court every day, sitting in the audience, alternately seething and crying and dabbing her eyes with a tissue. Other members of the Millar family were there too, but Carol Millar was the most vocal and even disruptive. On more than one occasion during the trial, the judge had to admonish her to be silent.

"This trial was a farce!" she cried as her family tried to console her. "That man is walking while my son lies dead!"

Ricky looked ashen. He shook his head. "I feel sorry for her," he said teary-eyed. "I feel her pain, but it wasn't me. I never touched Brett. He was my friend."

The court began to clear, and Carol Millar was escorted out. Ricky, Sara, and the lawyers lingered behind to give the grieving mother time to leave the building. Sara glanced around the slowly dispersing audience. In the back row, a man rose from his seat. He seemed vaguely familiar. Not the face, nor his short-cropped blond hair, but his overall size and shape. As if deep in thought, the man slowly walked

EVEN STEVEN

along the aisle and then turned and went through the door.

Sara returned to her office to find a message from Captain Riggs waiting for her.

"Report to the Commissioner's office for a high-level meeting."

Here we go again, she thought. *The top brass are looking for scapegoats to cover their asses so they can run for mayor or governor or congressman or whatever.* "I'm the crime control candidate," *they'll all proclaim.* "I got convictions! I made the streets safe for little old ladies and children!" *Meanwhile, it's the grunts like me and Jake who do all the work while those guys sit around in their big offices barking orders.*

Commissioner Gaines sat behind his big desk with the afternoon sun streaming through the tall windows behind him, giving him the appearance of some higher being, like a prince or a saint. Seated to his right was Captain Riggs. Assistant district attorney Jill Simmons was there too, as well as some guy from internal affairs and the department's press spokesperson.

Sara and Jake took their seats, facing the inquisitors.

"Detective Durant," began the commissioner, "As I'm sure you're aware, this series of so-called Even Steven murders that's been sweeping through our city has the public terrified. People are afraid to go out at night. Our tourist business is down twenty percent over last year. Our fabled music industry—which has its roots in the hundreds of local bars and night clubs where tomorrow's superstars get their start—has been crippled. And now we have the new nightmare of the convicted killer, Earl Steven Pollard, on the loose in our community. I'm not blaming you or your partner, Detective Patterson, for his escape. The responsibility for that lies squarely with the people at Riverbend. Apparently one of the guards was vulnerable to being bribed. But all this shit becomes *my* problem. I'm the one the mayor calls on the carpet. I'm the one who has to answer to the press."

"Yes, sir," replied Sara.

"Now—where are we?" said Captain Riggs. "What evidence are you developing?"

"We're still aggressively canvassing the area around White Bridge Car Wash," she replied. "Someone must have seen him or helped him. And we've learned that Edwin Doolan, the man who was shot to death in his SUV at the Village Tower Apartments, was recently acquitted of manslaughter in the drunk driving death of a woman named Stella Winston."

"And?" interjected Commissioner Gaines.

"We've discovered that Stella Winston has, or rather had, a husband," continued Sara.

"Yes?" said Captain Riggs. He leaned back, his red face showing impatience.

Sara took a deep breath and exhaled slowly. Don't let them rattle you! "Her husband is Dr. Mahmet Winston," she said. "He's a plastic surgeon. Does facelifts and such. His office is in the Oak Hills Medical Office Park. In Royal Oaks Square, by the river. It's only a mile and a half from the White Bridge Car Wash where Pollard was dropped off."

EVEN STEVEN

"You'd better get over there and talk to this Dr. Winston character," said Captain Riggs.

Sara *wanted* to reply, "That's where I'd be right now if I weren't in this stupid meeting." But instead, she simply said, "Yes, sir."

13

Sara pulled open the door to the Oak Hills Medical Office Park and went inside, where she found Shirley behind the front desk. "Detective Durant to see Dr. Winston," she said. "I called a few minutes ago."

"He's between patients and is expecting you," replied Shirley with some trepidation. She nervously picked up the phone and said, "That detective is here to see you." She hung up. "He'll be right out."

Shirley fussed with some papers and then got busy typing something on her keyboard.

Sara leaned closer and said to her, "Is there anything you want to tell me?"

"No, no, of course not."

The door opened, and Dr. Winston appeared. "Please come in," he said to Sara.

In his office, Sara sat opposite of Dr. Winston.

"Does the name Edwin Doolan mean anything to you?" asked Sara.

"It seems vaguely familiar," replied Dr. Winston. He looked

away, out the window.

"You should know it," replied Sara. "He was acquitted of killing your wife in a drunk driving accident."

"Oh, that guy," nodded Dr. Winston. "Well, I hope he rots in hell. I know he did it. He got off on a technicality. A flaw in our system of justice."

"Yesterday morning, he was murdered," replied Sara. "Shot to death while he sat in his car at his apartment building."

"Really?" shrugged Dr. Winston. "You'll forgive me. I don't keep up with the news. I suppose I work too hard. Well, if he's dead, he got what was coming to him. I know that, as a physician I should not derive happiness from the death of any human being, but I have my human feelings. He was a terrible person who did a terrible thing."

"We think we know who killed him."

"Really? Are you going to arrest him?" Dr. Winston said with edge to his voice. He gave Sara a sideways look.

"In fact, the suspect—a man named Earl Steven Pollard, otherwise known as the Even Steven killer—was last seen about a mile and a half from here, after he escaped from Riverbend."

"That's rather shocking."

"Have you seen him?"

"Seen him? Of course not! Why would you ask such a thing?"

"Has he ever contacted you?"

"No." Dr. Winston emphatically shook his head. "In fact, I don't think I appreciate your line of questioning. To suggest that I would aid or assist a convicted murderer and prison escapee is ridiculous.'

"I never suggested that you had aided or assisted him," replied Sara. "Do you know a man named Leonard Givens?"

"No, I can't say that I do. I'm sorry, Detective Durant, but if you're quite finished with your questions, I have patients to attend to."

On the way back to the waiting room, Sara paused in the hallway to look at the before-and-after photos on the wall. Nose jobs. Shaved or enhanced jawlines. Neck and forehead lifts. Cheek implants. So many ways one could alter their appearance.

She stopped to speak with Shirley. She showed Shirley a photograph of Earl Steven Pollard. When Shirley saw it, she blanched. After glancing behind her to verify the door to the medical area of the office was closed, she took pad of paper. She wrote a date and time, and then the words, *Black Camry. Titans bumper sticker. Woman driver.* She handed the paper to Sara.

"Thanks," whispered Sara as she handed Shirley her business card. Then, in a normal tone of voice, "If you happen to remember anything, please give me a call."

"Like I said, I really can't help you," replied Shirley.

Back at her office, Sara did a search for black Camrys in Nashville. There were over 300. She narrowed it down to a radius of one mile from White Bridge Car Wash. Now she had thirty-seven.

One of these owners, she believed, had given shelter to Earl Steven Pollard and had driven him to the office of Dr. Winston.

It was like looking for a needle in a haystack—but the good news was that Sara was certain the needle was there. Somewhere. And it had a Tennessee Titans sticker on it.

The snail mail was delivered. Sara looked through the catalogues and other useless stuff, searching for another letter from Even Steven.

She was not disappointed. It was a plain white envelope addressed to the Homicide Department. No return address. The postmark was from the post office on Woodland Street. It could have been dropped into any one of a hundred boxes in the area. Wearing gloves, she carefully slit it open at the end and pulled out the single sheet of paper. The letter read:

Eight down! Toliver got his own chain yanked! He thought he could take over my mission, but he was a total fool. Your friend, Even Steven.

The drawing of the eye was at the bottom.

Jake came over and examined the letter and envelope. He shrugged. "Both look very clean. Nothing distinctive about either other than that they come from Woodland Street. Okay, we'll mark it on the map. Maybe someday we can use artificial intelligence to predict the location of the sender."

Sara slipped the envelope and paper in an evidence bag and had them sent to the lab for analysis. She knew it wouldn't do any good, but they might as well go through the motions.

EVEN STEVEN

She glanced at the clock. Grabbing her purse before stopping in the ladies' room to freshen her makeup, she headed for the door.

Fifteen minutes later she walked in the door of Park Cafe, where she told the host she was joining a party of two others. Ah! There they were, at a table in the back. She hurried to Ricky, his attorney Ruth Blade, and his girlfriend Julia.

"This is a night for celebration," said Sara as she raised her glass of champagne. "To Ricky!" They all clinked glasses as Sara continued, "Ruth, you did an amazing job of getting my little brother out of trouble! But of course, the charges were drummed up. I knew the case was bad but had to keep my mouth shut because of conflict of interest. Michael Withers is a hack. He never should have been allowed to bring it to court. So, now that this albatross has been lifted from your neck, what do you plan on doing?"

Ricky smiled and took Julia's hand. "We're going to get away for a few weeks. Let the dust settle and the press move on to the next sensation."

"I think St. Lucia would be wonderful," said Julia. "A friend of mine went there last year and said it was heavenly. The mountains, the beaches, the romantic sunsets. And then, when we get back, we're going to find an apartment together, right, darling? I am *not* moving into your place. We're getting a place of our own. Equal partners."

"Good idea," nodded Ruth. "No girl wants to feel like a visitor in her boyfriend's bachelor pad. Too much emotional baggage. You need a fresh start."

EVEN STEVEN

"And perhaps you, dear sister, and your colleagues can find out who killed Brett," said Ricky. "Whoever it is, they're out there, running loose."

"Now that the distraction of your pointless trial is behind us," said Sara as she took a bite of her wedge salad, "We can devote more resources to the case. And my guess is that assistant DA Withers will soon be moving on to another city. He really humiliated himself."

"I'm sorry that Carol Millar was so bitter," said Julia. "You'd think that she would want the real killer to be found."

"I know her," nodded Ricky. "Once she gets an idea in her head, she never let's go of it. She's been leading the crusade against me. Got the whole town whipped up." He gave Julia a little kiss. "Even more reason why we should skip town for a few weeks. Get off her radar screen while you guys"—he nodded at Sara—"get to work." He took out his phone and quickly scrolled through it.

"Dear, can you please leave your phone alone for one night?" said Julia in a tone that was half-serious and half-playful. "We're here to celebrate."

"Sorry, love," he replied sheepishly as he put the phone into his pocket. "Force of habit. I don't want to miss any deals."

"Well, if you take it out while we're on the beach, I'm going to throw it into the ocean."

"Okay," he laughed.

At the end of dinner, they got up to leave, and Sara turned to her brother. "I'm so happy for you and Julia," she said. "Now you've got a chance to make a fresh start! When are

EVEN STEVEN

you leaving for St. Lucia?"

Ricky smiled. "Of course, this is all very last-minute. This morning, I didn't know where I'd be right now—a free man or locked up in prison. So now we're scrambling to get rooms and a flight. I would say a few days—by the end of the week. I'm willing to pay a premium to accelerate the timetable."

Sara nodded. "Promise me you'll be careful while you're still in town."

"Sure, sis, I promise," he laughed.

They parted ways, and Sara watched as her brother and Julia walked under the glow of the streetlights to his car.

14

At noon the next day, Sara called Ricky to ask him a question about his plans for the company. The call went to voicemail.

She tried again and hour later. Voicemail again.

How strange, she thought. Ricky was practically glued to his phone. He was constantly checking it for messages.

She called Julia. "Have you heard from Ricky?"

"No—I've called a few times this morning and he didn't answer. I hope he's all right."

"I'm going over there," said Sara. "You stay where you are."

Sara drove north through the center of town to Werthan Lofts in Germantown. The building, a nineteenth-century textile mill, had been renovated, and the interior carved up into big loft spaces with exposed brick and rustic beams. Ricky liked the vibe—it dripped youth and hipness.

She parked in the enclosed garage. On the way to the elevator, she passed Ricky's assigned parking place, and his BMW was there. With an increasing feeling of dread, she took the elevator to the third floor and hurried down the hallway to his door. She rang the bell. No answer. She

EVEN STEVEN

pounded on the door. Nothing.

She ran down the stairs to the super's office and brought him up. With his keys, he opened the door.

"Stay here," she commanded. Then she stepped into the big central area that served as a living room and kitchen. Sunlight poured in through the tall casement windows and scattered across the leather-clad furniture, the exercise bike, and a big wooden table piled with papers. His jumbo wide-screen TV was hung on the wall. Nothing was amiss—it looked the same as every other time she had visited.

She went to the bedroom—really just a generous space partitioned off from the loft with wallboard and a curtain. The bed was messy and unmade. Nothing unusual about that. The TV set was on. She clicked it off.

There was only one other space to investigate—the bathroom. It was a separate room, with tiled walls. The door was closed.

With a quivering hand and a knot in her stomach, she pulled open the door.

In the bathtub, fully clothed, with his head under water and legs splayed over the sides, lay the body of her brother, Ricky.

Shrieking and sobbing, Sara pulled him up by the shoulders and, with all her strength, hauled him out and onto the floor. She knew instantly from his cold, clammy skin that he was dead, but desperation triggers action, and she began CPR, pushing down on his unresponsive chest over and over again. His squishy shirt and pants formed a pool of water underneath him. Sara kept up her attempt at CPR but he was cold and inert. No sign of life. And then she noticed a trickle of blood at the corner of his mouth. Feeling sick to her stomach and with trembling hands she gently pried open his mouth to reveal his tongue. There it was, the horrible mark of the killer, the incised figure of an eye.

Even Steven had struck again. Her beloved brother had just become the ninth victim in the mad monster's personal campaign to rid the world of killers who had escaped justice. Only this time, Sara was certain Pollard had made a heinous mistake. Her brother, she believed, was an innocent man.

The room began to spin. Disoriented, she pulled out her phone and tapped the precinct. "Homicide. Werthan Lofts. Unit 311. Victim is Ricky Mansard. I need help." Her mind filled with images of death and violence, blood and tears. Then her legs grew weak, and she collapsed to the floor. She heard sirens and then footsteps, and suddenly people rushed into the room. Were they there to help or hurt her? She stood to defend herself and flailed at them as they tried to restrain her by holding her arms. But there were too many and they were too strong. Someone took her sidearm. She heard someone saying her name—"Detective Durant! Detective Durant!" She tried to kick them away, but the strong arms forced her to the floor, on her back. Someone sat on her to hold her down while more hands pinioned her arms and legs. She felt a sharp pinch in her neck. She suddenly felt relaxed, as if she were floating. Then all went dark.

She opened her eyes and saw a plain white ceiling. The light made her squint. She tried to sit up. In her arm was an IV.

A nurse leaned over her. "Stay calm, detective," said the nurse. She placed her hands on Sara's shoulders. "Just lean back and take it easy. You've had a rough time."

"Where am I?" asked Sara. Her voice sounded thick and distant.

"Vanderbilt Psychiatric Hospital," replied the nurse.

Sara groaned. "What the hell happened?"

"Do you remember anything?"

"I went to visit my brother. I was worried about him. He didn't answer his phone." She rubbed her head to get the blood to her brain. "I went to his loft. At the Werthan building. Then some people came in. I thought they were there to hurt me. There were so many of them. That's all."

Another face came into view.

"Jake!" said Sara. "What are you doing here?"

"I came to see you," he replied. "I wanted you to see a friendly face when you woke up."

"How long have I been here?"

"Since yesterday afternoon. About twenty-four hours. You've been quite a handful to the staff. A regular tiger. Are you okay now?"

"Yes, but what happened?"

"You don't remember?"

"Like I said, I went to visit Ricky. Is he all right?"

Jake sat on the edge of the bed and took her by the hand. "Sara, Ricky's gone. You found him in his bathroom.

Remember?"

As the images came flooding back, tears welled up in Sara's eyes. She struggled to breathe. She tried to sit up again, and this time, the nurse allowed it. Sara put her hands over her face and sobbed.

"I'm sorry," she said, wiping her eyes with the edge of the sheet. "I don't mean to make a scene."

"It's okay," replied Jake. "You've been through hell. Try take it easy."

"No!" she suddenly shouted. She twisted and fumbled for the IV in her arm. "I've got to get out of here! I need to find that motherfucker and kill him! Let me go!"

Jake stepped back as the nurses swooped in. "Sedative!" one of them shouted. As they restrained her on the mattress, a nurse jabbed her in the arm.

"Get off me, get off me!" shouted Sara as she tried to sit up. But her muscles quickly softened, and her breathing slowed. Her eyes lost their wild fire as she settled back onto the pillows. Her eyes closed, and she was asleep.

"How long will she be out?" asked Jake.

"I'd say two hours," replied the nurse who had administered the sedative. "Then we'll see what shape she's in. These things can take time. Some patients never recover. The shock stays with them for the rest of their lives."

The next morning, Sara was discharged, and Jake drove her

EVEN STEVEN

home to her house in Historic Edgefield on Woodland Street, facing East Park. It was a funky and untrendy neighborhood, which is why Sara liked it. They went into the kitchen—a showplace of retro-1960s styling with classic avocado-enamel appliances—and sat down on the sleek bar chairs huddled around the amoeba-shaped Formica counter that also housed the stove. Overhead, hanging lights shaped like UFOs glowed softly.

Her phone buzzed. It was Captain Riggs. She listened and nodded. Then she said, "Thank you," and hung up. She turned to Jake. "Captain says I'm on paid bereavement leave for one week. It's an order."

"Just one week?" Jake rolled his eyes. "The milk of human kindness flows like a river from the captain."

"I don't need it," she replied.

"Yes, you do! You've got to get back to being yourself. You know how it is when you're a cop. We experience more stress than anyone else yet are expected to remain cooler under pressure than anyone else. You were seriously traumatized only two days ago. You need time to recover and to grieve."

"Okay," shrugged Sara. "I get how the game works. Don't worry about me. I'll be all right. But I need to ask you one thing. Did Pollard send a letter to the station house?"

Jake hesitated. "I'm not sure if I should answer that."

"You just did. What did it say?"

"You can see for yourself, if you think you can handle it."

EVEN STEVEN

"I can handle it."

"Okay." He took out his phone and clicked open the photos. He chose one and showed it to her. It was the usual typewritten message on plain paper, plus the drawing of the eye:

Terminating number 9 felt dear to my heart! This scoundrel Ricky may have beaten the system, but your friend Even Steven fixed him!

Sara struggled to control herself. Seeing these gloating, hateful words brought the anger boiling to the surface—but she couldn't show Jake. Like a volcano with a tight lid, she kept it suppressed.

"Thank you," she said evenly. "Where was it mailed from?"

"Up in Oak Grove Beach. The usual pattern of no pattern."

"Are the paper and envelope being tested?"

"Yes. There's an interesting spot on the paper. Very tiny, but clearly not part of the paper. It's being examined now."

"Let me ask you a question," said Sara. "Do you think Pollard knows that Ricky was my brother?"

Jake shrugged. "I don't know. There was nothing in the court trial that would have provided that information. His last name was different from yours. I suppose someone like Pollard could find out if he dug back far enough to before you were married, when your last name was still Mansard. It's a fairly unusual name—not like Smith or Jones."

"Okay. One more question. How did he die?"

"Doctor Yeager is performing the, uh," Jake caught himself,

trying to be sensitive yet exact, "…examination. No results yet. But the preliminary indications are blunt force trauma to the back of the head. Ricky was hit from behind and was unconscious when he was put into the tub. If it's any consolation, my guess is that he never knew what hit him. The attack took place near the front door. There are smears of blood on the floor leading into the bathroom."

"Same manner of death as Brett Millar," said Sara. "He was hit and then pushed or rolled into Centennial Park Pond."

"Yes. No sign of forced entry. No weapon found—Pollard probably took it with him."

"So, Ricky opened the door, and for some reason, turned his back on Pollard, and that was it."

That evening, home alone and feeling like she was living as a strange, disembodied version of herself, Sara watched the local news. The lead story was Ricky. She saw Captain Riggs standing before the microphone with Jake and the rest of the squad behind him. It was the usual thing. Scant details about the cause of death. No reason for citizens to panic. Keep your doors locked and don't let strangers into your house. Report anyone suspicious. Photo of Earl Steven Pollard shown—but Sara knew that wouldn't do any good and might serve only to make life miserable for any poor guy who happened to resemble him.

Sara called Julia, who was beside herself with grief. Sara did her best to console her, and Julia said she was considering moving back to Baltimore to live with her parents for a while. Yes, that might be a good idea. Staying in Nashville might be too painful.

They hung up. It must be nice to be able to go live with your parents, thought Sara wistfully. Her own mother and father were gone. It had happened when Sara was at the police academy. Larry and Janet Mansard had taken a vacation to a lodge near Glenwood Springs, Colorado. They both enjoyed hiking, and the lodge featured spectacular mountain trails with varying degrees of difficulty. On the third day of their stay, they told the manager they were headed for the High Cliff Trail, the most challenging, which meandered for five miles through high, rugged terrain. They left at noon and were expected back before dinner. Witnesses reported they were both in good spirits.

They never returned. The next morning at dawn, a search party was sent out. Late in the day, Janet's body was discovered lying at the bottom of a 100-foot cliff, next to a swift-moving mountain stream. She had been killed by the impact of a fall. There were no traces of drugs or alcohol in her blood. The authorities concluded she had slipped and fallen to her death.

But the body of Larry Mansard was never found. He had vanished. No phone, no clothing, nothing.

Speculation ran rampant. Some say Larry had pushed Janet over the edge—murdered her—and then somehow disappeared to start a new life somewhere else. Others claimed he tried to save his wife but had slipped and fallen, his body swept away by the river. Or he may have struck his head, developed amnesia, and wandered in the forest until he either died or somehow survived. Indeed, a woman in Snowmass Village, about two miles from the lodge, reported seeing a man walking in the deep pine woods. He appeared disheveled, and at the time, she assumed he was one of the many hermit-type men who lived in tents and shanties in the mountains. But that was all. No further clues, no communication. Five years from the date of his disappearance, the State of Colorado declared that Larry Mansard was dead.

The uncertainty had long haunted both Sara and Ricky. Was their father a cold-blooded murderer still alive somewhere? Or was he a hero who had tried to save their mother only to succumb himself? Or the third possibility—he suffered from amnesia and genuinely didn't know his own past?

That night, Sara went to sleep beset by weird dreams and confusing thoughts. *Who am I?* she asked herself. *What am I doing here? What's the point of all this?* She imagined quitting the police force. Finding a new path in life. Maybe moving to a new city, a new state, a new country where she could start over again, free of the pain and constant mental conflict. *Julia was doing it—why can't I?* In bed, she tossed and turned, never feeling comfortable. Sleep finally came, but it stole up on her unannounced.

15

Suddenly, it seemed, the light broke through Sara's closed eyes. She awoke and glanced at her phone. It was 8:00 a.m. Rarely had she slept so late.

She sat up and looked around her bedroom. The past three days seemed like a bad dream, like she had been somewhere else, in some other time. So much had happened! Ricky was gone. He was not coming back. Sara was the last person in her family to be living and breathing. Earl Steven Pollard, her brother's killer, was walking free. Those were the immutable facts.

She rubbed the back of her head. The cobwebs that had plagued her since she came home from the hospital had dissipated. Throwing on her terrycloth robe, she went to the kitchen and made a coffee with her Keurig machine. Then she changed into exercise gear and worked out for an hour with her free weights. Barbell bench press, dumbbell incline press. Dead lifts, lateral raises, tricep extensions, pulldowns, bicep curls. Squats, leg press, standing calf raises. Then a cold shower. Feeling strong and invigorated, she ate breakfast standing up at the kitchen counter—two hardboiled eggs, whole wheat toast with butter, a banana, more black coffee.

While she ate, she turned on NBC's *Today*, which she

normally thought was nothing but foolishness. How many people really need to know where to buy the best pair of stretchy mom jeans for under thirty dollars? And why is Al Roker in drag again? But it was amusing and got her mind off her grief and her anger.

She had Ricky's funeral to plan. At 10:00a.m., she went online to research her options before calling Phillips-Robinson Mortuary. In her usual crisp and concise manner, she made arrangements for cremation and then a memorial service in their little non-denominational chapel. Burial would be next to their parents in Nashville City Cemetery. No flowers, please; donations would be gratefully accepted at the Nashville Rescue Mission.

With those tasks complete, it was time for action. No more lying around in a stupor!

She couldn't go to her office and had to be careful about contacting anyone on her team, including Jake. The investigation was supposed to proceed without her, but she knew the department was stretched thin with other investigations beyond the Even Steven cases. And of course, there was the manhunt for Pollard himself. But Sara had little confidence in how it was being conducted. Her colleagues were nice people, but sometimes they seemed clueless. Both literally and figuratively.

It was time for some old-fashioned gumshoe work. But first, she went to her desk drawer and rummaged around until she found what she was looking for—a palm-sized photo of Ricky. He was smiling as the sun shone on his face. She ran her fingertips over the gloss of the paper. "This is for you, my brother," she said before she slid the photo into her pocket.

EVEN STEVEN

Patrolling the neighborhood around the White Bridge Car Wash in her own unmarked car, Sara cruised up and down the streets, looking for a black Camry. North along Route 155 to Vine Ridge Road, then south down Neartop Lane, over Red Oak Drive, north up Hillwood Boulevard. Past houses and driveways and storefronts and gas stations. It was boring work, but strangely Zen-like and relaxing. Like washing dishes—she could do it with half her brain on autopilot, just going through the motions. East on Kendall Drive, then west on Stoneway Trail to Forestwood Drive. Before long, a black Camry pulled up next to her at a stoplight. She hung back and let it get ahead of her. No bumper sticker. She turned east on Knob Road and followed it all the way to White Bridge Pike, which she crossed, and kept going.

She happened to pass by the house of Debbie Chan. In the driveway was a Ford Escape. Taking no notice—why should she?—Sara drove on to where Knob Road met Kendall Drive, by the Richland Creek Greenway and the Army Reserve Center. She saw a black Camry in the parking lot. She swung around it, but it had no Tennessee Titans sticker.

Of course, this drive was bound to produce nothing, she told herself. It's just one of those boring, unproductive tasks that cops have to do yet sometimes enjoy precisely because they're dull and uneventful.

The dim Winter sun was slouching in the grey sky. Snow flurries scattered across her windshield, and the damp air promised more. She was on White Bridge Pike, headed south, ready to head home. "It won't kill me to check out Post Place," she said to herself as she turned east. To her left

EVEN STEVEN

she saw a sign: *Hadley Ford: New & Pre-Owned Cars and Trucks.* Absent-mindedly, she pulled into the driveway, surveying a dozen rows of vehicles in the lot, many with prices on their windshields or signs boasting, *Low Miles, Special!* and *Just In.* Chevys, Hondas, Toyotas, the odd BMW or Lexus here and there. A few trucks and campers.

Suddenly, she saw a black Toyota Camry. Its windshield sign exclaimed, *Hot Deal!* She stopped and got out. Expecting routine disappointment, she walked around to the back of the car.

A Tennessee Titans bumper sticker.

A jolt went through her body, and her mind, which had been in a comfortable state of cruise control, became electrified.

The ever-watchful salesman saw her and hurried from his office.

"Hello there, young lady," he said affably. At the sound of his voice, Sara glanced up to see a man about sixty, wearing a sports jacket and bow tie. An easy mark for her feminine charms.

"Why, bless my soul," gushed Sara in her most honeyed Tennessee accent. "I know the lady who had this car! You know—um—" and she waved her hand, indicating it was his turn to respond.

"Miss Chan," smiled the salesman.

"Of course! Her first name is—" Again with the hand waving and puzzled, damsel-in-distress expression.

"Debbie."

EVEN STEVEN

"That's right! Debbie. You know, the older I get, the more I keep forgetting things. Lovely lady." She admired the car. "Why, this creampuff is hardly three years old. Must have only, what, fifty thousand miles on it?"

"Good guess," he smiled. "Forty-five. Are you looking for a car?" He peered at Sara's ride. "You've got a nice Mustang there. Five hundred horsepower V8. Give a Porsche or Corvette a run for their money. Am I right?"

"Yes, sir, you are correct," oozed Sara, making sure to lower her head slightly so that she was looking up at him and her eyes appeared bigger. "It's got great performance. Never lets me down. Say, why on Earth would Debbie trade in her car? She always told me how much she loved it. And you can do worse than a Toyota Camry, am I right? Why, she could have put two hundred thousand miles on this car just by changing the oil now and then. These things last forever."

"Yes, they do last for many years and many thousands of miles! Well, Debbie didn't say much. She came in here just last week and said she needed to trade in her car for something else. She didn't go into detail, and I didn't pry. Her credit was good—that's all I cared about. The rest of it is none of my business."

"Of course not," agreed Sara. "What did she leave with?"

"A nice Ford Escape. Only twenty thousand miles on it. Good, clean little car."

Sara recalled seeing at least one Ford Escape on her drive around town. "Is it green?" she asked.

"In fact, yes, the color is called Clover Green. Pretty, isn't it?"

EVEN STEVEN

"Oh, that sure is nice," replied Sara.

"May I ask what you're looking for?" inquired the salesman.

"Me? Oh, I'm looking for a Jeep Wrangler, white, with a six-speed shift. You got one of those?" She knew he didn't because she had scanned the lot.

"Not at the moment," said the salesman. "Please take my card. Name's Rodney Bingham. I'm here just about every day. Leave me your name and number, and just as soon as I see one, I'll let you know."

She took his card and looked at her phone. "Dear Lord, I'm late! Listen—I have your card, Rodney. I'll keep it right here in my purse. I really must be off. Have a great evening!" With those words, she returned to her car and, with a cheery wave, drove off the lot.

She punched the name into her phone. Debbie Chan. 2765 Knob Road. Less than a mile away. A minute later, she was parked in front of the house. It was a brick one-story with blue shutters. In the driveway sat the green Ford Escape with *Hadley Ford—Nashville, TN* imprinted on the license plate frame.

Sara got out of her car and approached the front door. She knocked. After a moment, a woman answered. She was wearing white jeans and a ruffled, flowered top. Her blonde, rock-star hairdo gave her the look of someone who was getting older but didn't like the idea of it. Sara showed her badge. "Nashville Police Department. Detective Durant. Ms. Chan? I need to ask you a few questions."

"Yes, that's me."

EVEN STEVEN

After some hesitation, Debbie Chan opened the door, and Sara stepped inside. The living room was notable for being thoroughly unexceptional. The usual TV was hung on the wall with the usual 1980s faux-leather sofa facing it. The carpet was yellow shag. There was a fireplace, which could have been fake, with a real beagle-type dog sleeping in front of it. A bookcase stood against the wall, with a few books mixed in amongst the magazines, knick-knacks, and other junk filling the shelves.

"Um, what do you want?" asked Debbie.

Sara looked her directly in the eye and said, "I want Earl Steven Pollard."

"I don't know who that is," she stammered.

"Yes, you do. On the very day that he escaped from Riverbend Maximum Security, Pollard came here, to your door. You offered him shelter. Then you took him to the office of Dr. Winston, at Oak Hills Medical Office Park. You drove him there in your Toyota Camry, which you subsequently sold to Rodney Bingham at Hadley Ford. In exchange you bought that Ford Escape. At the office of Dr. Winston, Pollard underwent cosmetic surgery to alter his appearance and allow him to move about freely in public. When the surgery was complete, you picked him up from the office. You brought him here to recuperate, didn't you?"

"No, really, I don't know…" She sank into a recliner covered in plastic.

Sara stood over her. "Ms. Chan, you need to understand that there are only two sides to this story. The right side and the wrong side. The right side gives you freedom and the chance

EVEN STEVEN

to live a normal life. The wrong side gives you hard time in prison for conspiracy to commit murder. Which side do you want to be on?"

"I didn't kill anybody!" wailed Debbie.

"But Earl Steven Pollard did, and not long after he left this house where you protected him. That makes you an accomplice."

She covered her face with her hands. "I don't want any part of this." She began to cry. "Are you going to arrest me?"

Sara paused. Now that was an interesting question. Technically, she was on administrative leave. Not even supposed to be there. Even so, she could arrest Debbie right now. If she did, Debbie would be delivered into the very system that had failed to stop Pollard's vicious rampage.

Sara was beginning to doubt the very system she worked in. To arrest or not to arrest? That was the question.

Debbie dabbed her red-rimmed eyes. "I'm just a bookkeeper," she said. "An accountant."

Sara leaned down so they were face to face. "Let me guess… You work for Leonard Givens."

"How did you know?"

"And Givens put you up to this scheme. He paid you to take care of his nephew, Earl Steven Pollard. Right?"

She nodded weakly.

"Well, I hope it was worthwhile. You've been aiding and abetting a vicious serial killer. I'm frankly surprised he didn't kill *you* before he left here. People like Pollard don't like leaving witnesses around."

"What are you going to do?" asked Debbie.

Indeed, thought Sara, *what am I going to do?* Which would be better: to deliver her to the system and let the great and powerful machinery of justice squeeze what it can out of her, or keep her on the sidelines, out of sight, away from the hungry jaws of the Nashville Police Department and the Office of the District Attorney?

"Pollard got a new face, correct?"

Debbie nodded in agreement.

"Would you recognize him if you saw him?"

"I can't say for sure. His face was very swollen when I picked him up from the doctor's office. He was here for about a week, but he kept to himself. I hardly saw him. He did say to me, 'Debbie, the less you know, the better for both of us.' That made sense to me. I was doing it for Mr. Givens, not for any other reason."

"What name was Pollard using?"

"I don't know. Charlie something. That's all I remember—Charlie."

"When did he buy his car? And do you know the make and model? Was it a Chevy Malibu?"

"I never saw a car. He took an Uber when he left here."

"He had a phone?"

EVEN STEVEN

"Yes. A package was delivered here the day he arrived. It had some things in it, including a phone and a credit card."

"Do you have any way of contacting him?"

"No," she shook her head. "I think he wanted it that way."

Sara could feel that this particular vein of gold had been tapped out. Debbie was a useful informant and had shed light on Pollard's story, but Sara had gotten all she was going to get out of her.

"Okay, Debbie," said Sara. "Here's what I'm going to do. I'm not going to arrest you as an accomplice. There's no point in taking that step, but I need you to keep your mouth shut. If anyone else asks you these questions, you don't know anything. Nothing. Okay? And if anyone does come around, let me know." She gave Debbie her private cell number.

"You mean, if the police come around? But aren't you the police?"

"Yes, to both questions. Let's just say, this case is being handled differently. Okay?"

"Yes," nodded Debbie. "Sure."

"Okay. Keep this between you and me."

16

The next day dawned bright and clear, as the gloom of the previous was replaced by sharp sunlight. After completing her workout routine and eating breakfast, Sara sat herself down at her computer. Earl Steven Pollard was proving to be an exceptionally formidable foe who was highly skilled at covering his tracks. And now he was living somewhere in Nashville, right under the noses of authorities, with an assumed identity and a new face.

Sara had only two pieces of information about Pollard: his new name was Charlie, and he drove a blue Chevy Malibu.

In the job of policework, sometimes there are moments of excitement and even mortal danger, as violent criminals are apprehended and brought to justice. But there are more likely to be moments—or hours, or days—of grinding work, sifting through mountains of evidence (or more likely, non-evidence), chasing down fruitless tips, surveilling suspects doing nothing, and scouring databases for obscure matches that may lead to the development of a meaningful connection.

It was to this latter, supremely boring task to which Sara now set herself. Armed with coffee and refreshed by regular breaks on the treadmill, she began searching for people

EVEN STEVEN

named Charles or Charlie who had recently bought, rented, or leased a blue Chevy Malibu in the Nashville area.

Hertz, Avis, National, and the other rental companies all offered Chevy Malibus. There were roughly fifty auto dealers of all types in the Greater Nashville area. And of course, he could have picked up the car in a private sale. Or, better yet, how about from his indulgent sugar daddy, Uncle Leonard?

That would be a good place to start! She searched for records of car registrations by Leonard Givens or one of his companies. Many hours and cups of coffee later—Givens had a tangled network of companies and other business entities—she found a promising lead. Pennywell Real Estate, LLC, a company owned by Givens that was used for property management, owned several vehicles, including a blue Chevy Malibu. The license plate was BPN 1130. Sara did a search for that plate and found that, two weeks earlier, the car had been ticketed for speeding—going 45 in a 25 zone—along Manchester Avenue in the Bordeaux section of town. The driver of the car was a certain Charles Kaplan.

There were a dozen Charles Kaplans in Nashville. But this particular Charles Kaplan had to be newly invented—fake, in fact—and would not have any history of employment or home ownership, no LinkedIn page, no social media accounts older than a few weeks. One by one, with meticulous precision, Sara eliminated all the Charles Kaplans for being too well-established and too well connected to be a newborn.

All save one, that is. A person named Charles Kaplan was living at the Dew Drop Inn on Clarksville Pike in Bordeaux—not far from where the speeding ticket had been issued. The ticket had not yet been paid.

EVEN STEVEN

This was worth a drive.

At 2:00 p.m., Sara pulled into the parking lot at the Dew Drop Inn. The place was a classic American motel, with two stories of boxy rooms arranged in an L-shape around the central parking area, giving each occupant direct access to their room without passing through a central lobby. She scanned the cars. Near the furthest end of the building was a blue Malibu.

She parked her car and went into the office. Behind the counter was a man, about fifty, with a substantial gut hanging over the belt of his rumpled khaki pants. The buttons of his white shirt strained under the pressure of his bulk. A pair of reading glasses dangled from a thin chain around his neck.

"Nashville Police," said Sara as she flashed her badge.

"We got no hookers here!" the clerk said. "We run a clean establishment. No hookers, no dope dealers."

Sara smiled. "Glad to hear it. I'm looking for a man named Charles Kaplan. Is he a guest here?"

"Yeah," the clerk nodded. "Why? He wanted for something?"

"I just want to talk to him. What room is he in?"

"Two-sixteen," replied the clerk. "Down at the end." He pointed.

"What kind of car does he drive?"

"Uh, blue Malibu, I think."

EVEN STEVEN

"Stay here. Don't leave. Don't call anyone. Got that?"

"He's checking out in a few minutes."

"He's *what?*"

"He called a few minutes ago. From his room. Said he was checking out. Heck, you might bump into him. I'm waiting for him."

Sara leaned forward. "Keep your mouth shut! Don't say a word. Let him check out. Just like anybody else. Got that?"

"Sure," shrugged the clerk, who was thankfully more sober than not on that day.

Sara turned and scanned the steel walkway of the second-floor rooms. No one was in sight. She hurried to her car and got in. *Damn!* she said to herself. *I have a tracking device to attach to his car—but he might come out at any moment. There's no time. I'll have to do this the old-fashioned way, tailing him within visual contact.*

A moment later, the door to room 216 opened, and a man came out. He was wearing black jeans, a plain blue button-down shirt that service employees typically wear, and a tan windbreaker.

After cautiously looking around, he closed the door behind him and carried his suitcase down the stairs to his car. As she watched and snapped photos with her phone, Sara concluded that Charles Kaplan was the same height and build as Pollard, but facially, he looked more like he could have been Pollard's cousin. There was a familial resemblance, but too many of the features—the nose, the cheekbones, the chin, the jawline—were different, not to mention the unruly mop of blond hair. It was a brilliant transformation.

EVEN STEVEN

He started his car and eased along the parking lot to the door of the office. He stopped the car and went inside. Sara thought about the tracking device. Now? Should she risk being seen? It was tempting to try, but if he saw her, the entire case would blow up. No, it was better to wait. Suddenly, Pollard came out of the office. Sara thanked herself for staying in her car—he surely would have seen her.

Pollard got into his blue Malibu, rolled out of the driveway, and took a right on Clarksville Pike. He drifted into the left lane and then took a left at Courtney Avenue. Sara lingered behind him. A lumbering box truck cut her off, and it wasn't until Pollard had reached the big church on Ashland City Highway—Route 12—that she regained visual contact. Rush hour traffic was building, which was an advantage because it slowed him down but also a liability because drivers were jockeying for position.

They crawled their way up the highway, past the Get Glam'd Beauty Bar and the Hills of Calvary Cemetery, then across Route 155, the White Bridge Pike. The arc of the Cumberland River came into view on the left. The sky, which had started out clear and cold that day, began to darken with clouds from the west.

At the exit to Old Hickory Boulevard, Pollard was in the left lane and abruptly hit his brakes, veering into the right-hand lane and shooting off the exit ramp. Sara, behind a semi-trailer truck, glimpsed his exit and frantically forced her way in front of an angry Subaru, barely making it onto the ramp without getting impaled on a guard rail.

Was Pollard just a lousy driver? Did he simply change his mind about where he wanted to go? Did he suspect he was being followed? Sara didn't have the answer. She just had stay on his tail.

EVEN STEVEN

The blue Malibu headed northeast through the woods and pastureland, past Bells Bend Farm and the Baptist Church. Traffic was still heavy, and flurries had begun to swirl from the grey sky. Drivers were beginning to turn on their headlights. Suddenly, Pollard slowed and turned into the driveway of the Sulphur Creek Mini-Mart with its sign that boasted *Cold Beer, Cigarettes, Lottery*. Sara followed him but hung back near the entrance while he parked his car in one of the spaces next to the building. The driveway was a big "U" going around the back of the square structure, so she swung around the rear, past the dumpster. Close to the exit to the street, she deftly backed into a space next to a big camper, blocking the view of her car.

There she waited as the snow began to fall, driven by a hard west wind. She turned on her windshield wipers. Thump, thump, thump. She tapped her screen and checked the weather. *What the hell—six to ten inches of snow tonight? And the day had started out sunny!*

She peered at the cars leaving the Mini-Mart as they drove past her. Volkswagen. Ford pickup. Dodge pickup. Nissan pickup. Then the blue Malibu. As it passed, Sara saw the silhouette of the male driver. She eased out behind him, and he took a right onto Old Hickory Boulevard, resuming his former course. Traffic was still thick but going slower now because of the snow.

At Bull Run Road, Pollard turned left. The road wound northwest up through the wooded hills, and there were fewer cars among them, forcing Sara to hang back and follow his taillights in the whiteness. She passed a car that had slid off the road, the driver standing helplessly beside it. Sara shook her head. Every time it snowed, some people suddenly forgot how to drive their cars, as if they had never before experienced a slick road.

After about a mile the road curved west and followed the Bull Run Valley, which would eventually drain into the Cumberland River. But after only a thousand feet, the blue Malibu turned right onto Kirby Hill Road. As Sara followed, plunging into deep woods, the way became dark and winding, and there were no other vehicles. Sara slowed so that Pollard disappeared around each bend. Was this a trap? Would Pollard pull over, open his door, and spray her with an AR-15? She kept her eyes level and her breathing steady. There's no way he could know she was tailing him. *Right?*

The road was dirt now, and rutted. Sara saw the Malibu take another left. Instead of following, she stopped her car and shut off her lights. There was still enough light penetrating through the clouds and snow to see the road and trees. She pulled up her GPS. The map indicated Pollard had turned up a little road called Golden Lane. It meandered a mile into the woods before turning into a dirt path and then finally nothing. The satellite photo showed a structure—a cabin, perhaps, with possibly a small barn and some derelict junk cars around the perimeter. She input Golden Lane into the real estate directory. Yes, there was an old dwelling at 788 Golden Lane. Five wooded acres. Owned by Apex Trust.

She could easily guess who controlled Apex Trust. No doubt it was good ol' Uncle Leonard. For once, Sara felt a surge of confidence. She was now the predator; Pollard was the prey.

But with such a clever and vicious adversary, this was not going to be easy. One false step, and their roles would, again, be reversed.

EVEN STEVEN

To simply drive down Golden Lane would be madness. Even to walk down the road would be stupid because he would likely have warning devices hidden along the way. No, she was going to have to do it the hard way. The slow way.

Sara studied the satellite images. Then she started her car and crept along Kirby Hill Road for about a mile until she came to an abandoned barn with a space in front large enough to park. She was well beyond Golden Lane on a finger of Kirby Hill Road that dwindled into a rough trail another mile ahead. There was no reason why Pollard should ever drive down to that spot—at least, she hoped, not in the next several hours, during a blizzard.

She turned around, facing south, the direction she had come from, and shut off her engine. Now the only sound was the whipping of the snow that rapidly obscured the view through her windshield.

The daylight was waning. She had to hurry before night fell and, with it, more snow, making travel through the deep, dark woods treacherous.

According to her map, there was a creek about a half-mile to the north that passed within a hundred yards of the cabin. In fact, the cabin appeared to have been built on a piece of flat land with the creek at its back, running in a deep ravine between two hills—pretty typical for agrarian homesteads in the old days.

Taking only her Glock service pistol and her phone, Sara opened the car door and stepped outside into the falling snow.

EVEN STEVEN

She walked north, up the road, to where it turned sharply to the east. As she expected, the ground began to slant downhill, toward the creek. The prickly shrubs thinned out, and she found herself on a hillside, dense with soaring maple trees. Mostly bare now, their branches clicked and clacked high overhead as they caught the winter wind, but where she was, near the ground, the air was still, and the big heavy flakes fell straight down.

Half-sliding, half-walking, she reached the creek itself. Stepping over rocks, she could feel herself gradually descending with the flow of the creek.

How far should she go before heading back up the hill toward the cabin? She had estimated half a mile. Then to her left—the direction she wanted to go—she noticed an old trail meandering up the hill from the ground just above the creek bed. This was as good a place as any to begin her ascent, so she scrambled up the slippery clay banks of the creek and found secure footing on the damp leaves and exposed roots of the trail. The snow was now an inch deep, or two in some places, and the light was fading fast. Though the trail zigzagged its way up the hill through the swaying trunks, she managed to follow it, all the while keeping her eyes on the crest of the hill, where she expected to see the cabin. She suddenly slipped in the snowy mud and fell back down the hill until her foot made contact with a big fallen tree trunk. Scrambling to her feet, she used her hands to grab narrow saplings and hoisted herself back to the relative security of the path.

The ground began to level off. Sara knew she was near the upper edge of the ravine. But which way was the cabin? Through the snow-laced trees, she saw nothing. But suddenly she smelled smoke. A wood fire, drifting to her from the west. Carefully, she threaded her way through the trees and bushes until she saw a faint light. Working her way closer, she saw the silhouette of the cabin. Squat and square, it had two windows on the side facing her and a small brick chimney from which a thin plume of grey smoke snaked. A dish antenna was attached to the sloping roof, and a car was parked in front of the cabin—a blue Malibu.

Sara eased closer. One foot at a time. At any second, she expected an alarm to sound, floodlights to ignite, dogs to bark. *Surely Pollard had some type of defense system!* Or maybe not. Perhaps he didn't have time to put it together yet. Or maybe, just maybe, he felt so secure out here in the deep woods with his fake name and fake face that he didn't think it was necessary.

She stepped on a branch, and it gave a loud *snap*. She froze. The snowflakes stung her eyes and dripped down her cheeks as they melted. Then she saw the head and shoulders of a man pass behind one of the windows. The brief glimpse was enough to tell her the man was Earl Steven Pollard. But how to catch him off guard?

She saw an old door at the foundation of the cabin, leading to a cellar. Creeping to it, she grasped the battered metal handle and gently pulled up. It was not locked. Slowly, carefully, she raised the wood-slatted door, which resisted as if it hadn't been opened in years. But she got it open enough to slide her shoulder underneath it as she put one foot over the raised threshold and onto the rough concrete step. Keeping low, she moved down the steps until the bulkhead door was closed above her head—plunging her into complete darkness. The air was cold and dank, and she crouched on the steps, not knowing what lay before her. She took out her phone. Its sharp light revealed a second door a few feet in front of her. It was wood with peeling paint and a plate glass window. She grasped the dented brass doorknob and tried to turn it. It resisted. She applied more force, and it gave way; with a firm push, the door swung open.

Sara stepped into a rough cellar punctuated by timber beams supporting the cabin's ground level above. Under her feet was an unfinished dirt floor. The ceiling—the floorboards of the cabin above—was too low to allow her to stand upright. Around her she saw junk, scrap wood, moldering boxes, and cobwebs.

Suddenly, directly over her head, she heard, *thunk, thunk, thunk.* These were Pollard's footsteps. She froze. The footsteps went in one direction and then another before fading away.

Scanning the cellar, Sara found the rustic wooden stairs leading to the main floor of the cabin. Slowly, carefully, she ascended them. At the top was a door. There she waited, silently, gathering her thoughts.

Surprise was of the essence. *But then what? What was the end game?* Her choices were either arrest or kill. The former was obviously the legally appropriate choice, unless Pollard resisted and Sara's life were in danger, in which case lethal force would be justified. But this was a rogue mission. Sara wasn't supposed to be here. Pollard's defense team would try to throw out the entire case based on Sara's deviation from all law enforcement norms—the irony of such a twist was not lost on Sara, Pollard benefitting from the flawed justice system he's been fighting against all these years. But in the court of public opinion, she would be a hero.

EVEN STEVEN

She listened carefully but heard nothing except the rising wind. With her Glock in hand, she carefully turned the doorknob and gently pushed. The door cracked open with a *creak*. She paused and listened. Now she could faintly hear a television set. Good! It would mask the sound of her movements. She pushed open the door another few inches and braced for a response. But there was nothing but the drone of the television. She eased her way into the kitchen, a small area with a single light bulb burned overhead.

She turned in the direction of the television set sound. There was a doorway leading to the living room, and with her Glock leading the way, she edged forward. A big, high-backed armchair came into view. It faced the television, an old-fashioned box set on a table. Now Sara was in the door frame, just a few feet from the armchair. She raised her gun.

Suddenly something crashed into her arm. The shock sent the gun flying from her hand. It skidded across the floor. She pivoted to see Pollard wielding an axe handle, arm upraised, ready to strike again. His contorted face leered at her.

"How stupid do you think I am?" he sneered.

Sara leaned back and launched a swift kick to his body. It connected, and he stumbled backward, arms flailing. Recovering his balance, he swung at her again. The axe handle zinged by her head, brushing her hair before smacking against the door frame. Sara twisted to grab it, but Pollard wrested it free and raised it again. Sara countered by rushing at him headlong and driving her shoulder into his gut. He gasped and folded, and his blow with the axe handle landed weakly on her back. Sara hit him in the kidney with her fist, and he countered with a knee to her face. She fell back, dizzy and disoriented.

EVEN STEVEN

Pollard swung the axe handle at her again, but she rolled out of its path. She saw the gun lying on the floor under a low tattered sofa. Desperately, she lunged for it, but Pollard placed his boot on her arm—pain shot up to her shoulder. With a superhuman effort, she grabbed his leg and, using it for leverage, launched a kick at his lower back. It connected, and he howled in agony. He dropped the axe handle, lost his footing, and stumbled back, crashing into the television set and knocking it over. Still on the ground, Sara took the axe handle and swung at his head. He slipped to the side, and the weapon smacked into his collarbone. He wailed as his arm dropped uselessly to his side.

Barely conscious and lying on her stomach, Sara slid around to the sofa. She reached under it for the gun. She felt the cold handle in her hand. Swiftly, she seized it and rolled over to bring it up to shoot.

With his good arm Pollard took the axe handle and threw it at her. It glanced off her head and clattered across the floor. Through the searing pain Sara pointed the gun and fired. The explosion blasted through the room. Pollard gasped and grabbed his thigh as the blood began to seep through his jeans. Sara struggled to her knees, but the room was spinning. Pollard stumbled back and then turned and hobbled to the kitchen.

Sara's head cleared, and she stood up, but Pollard was gone. She lurched to the kitchen door, following the trail of blood spots. The door to the outside was open, and the snow poured in. Sara went to the door and peered outside. All she saw was white. She looked down: ragged footprints led to the left, around the cabin. She followed them. There, twenty yards ahead, Pollard hobbled away, limping and clutching his leg. She raised her gun and fired. Her aim was wild, and the bullet slammed into a tree. Suddenly Pollard was lost in the driving snow. She ran after him, though his tracks were quickly covered. *There he was, at the edge of the ravine!* She fired again but was barely conscious and didn't know if her shot had any effect. She saw him vanish into the trees, leading down to the creek. Exhausted and shivering, she trudged to the tree line and peered into the dark snow-filled woods.

Pollard had vanished. Sara fell into the snow. The cold against her face reminded her of the extreme danger she was in. With supreme effort, she stood up and stumbled her way back to the cabin. She closed the door and, feeling the soothing narcotic of warmth, went to the sofa, where she told herself she'd rest for a few minutes.

When she woke up, the room was silent. The windows showed light from outside, but it was nothing but white. She sat up. *What had happened?* It came back to her—the fight, the shots, and Pollard's escape into the blizzard. The deep, snowy forest had swallowed him up. *Surely, he was dead!* He had been bleeding from a gunshot wound to his thigh. If he did not receive prompt medical attention, he would soon fall unconscious in the snow. And if the bullet didn't kill him, he'd freeze to death.

Sara's head throbbed. She put her hand on the tender spot and felt a goose egg. At least her skull hadn't been fractured. Her entire body ached. She stood up slowly and took her phone from her pocket. The time was 7:15 a.m. She had been out for twelve hours.

She went to the front door of the cabin and opened it. The

morning sun cut through the trees, casting sharp shadows across the snow, lying smooth, fresh, and white. A couple of inches, at least. The sky showed scattered white clouds and patches of brilliant blue. It was going to be a beautiful day. She reached into her pocket and pulled out the photo of Ricky that she had been carrying with her. It was dog-eared now, and wrinkled, but she smoothed it with her fingertips. "We did it, my brother," she said before slipping the photo back into her pocket.

She went back inside the cabin and looked around. Then a thought occurred to her. Eventually, this dwelling was going to be found and searched. Wouldn't it be better if it looked normal, and not like a violent fight scene? She went into the kitchen and found a pair of dishwashing gloves under the sink. She put them on and went into the living room to straighten up the furniture. With a towel, she wiped the surfaces she had touched. When she was finished, she went into the bedroom and found the car keys on top of the bureau. She took them and, with one last look around, left the cabin and closed the door behind her.

The Malibu was poorly equipped to handle well in snow, but she managed to slalom it along the driveway onto Golden Lane and thence to Kirby Hill Road. The old barn was there along with her snow-covered Mustang. The door to the barn allowed itself to be opened, and she parked inside. Perhaps in fifty years someone would come along, open the barn door, and discover a perfectly preserved automobile. A "barn find," as they say in the classic car business.

She took off the gloves and stuffed them in her pocket. The Mustang roared to life, and within minutes Sara had left the scene of horror and retribution behind.

EVEN STEVEN

When she arrived at her house, it was quiet and welcoming. Not in a mood to work out today—she had enough exercise the day before. Maybe Jake and all the doctors were right; she should just relax, take it easy, and recover her strength.

But one dark thought irritated her mind and soul: she had not actually seen Pollard *die*.

She had merely seen him *disappear*, which was very different.

The man seemed to have superhuman survival skills. He had a way of evading the natural laws of life that governed normal people. Was it possible? Could he have made his way to some safe place? Becoming obsessed with this idea, Sara pulled up the satellite map of the area around Golden Lane. She found his cabin along with the creek in the ravine running behind it. There was the old barn where she had stashed the Malibu. The nearest house was about a mile from the cabin, to the north, across the ravine. To make it there, Pollard would have had to slip and slide his way down the steep hill to the creek and then haul himself up the other side. Was it possible?

With Even Steven, anything was possible.

17

On Monday morning, Sara arrived at headquarters and went to her desk. Jake looked up from his work.

"How are you doing?" he asked.

"Well enough," she replied. She looked through the pile of papers and messages. "This is what I love about getting time off," she sighed. "When you get back, you have to work overtime to catch up on all the shit you didn't do because you were away."

"You can ignore most of that," he replied and took a bite of a banana. "You had breakfast yet?"

"Black coffee," she laughed. "So, what's on the top of the pile?"

"Even Steven is still Public Enemy Number One. And I realize that now it's personal for you. I understand. We all want to get this guy. He's as bad as they get."

"Yeah," nodded Sara. She hated being disingenuous with her partner. That was the number one rule of the code of honor between partners: don't lie. Don't hold anything back. Your word is your bond. She looked at Jake. So guileless, so trusting. Perhaps she should tell him? But what she did was totally against any definition of appropriate police procedure. If brought to light, she could be charged with any number of crimes, up to and including first-degree murder if Pollard were found dead. No, she couldn't drag Jake into it. She couldn't ask him to participate in the lie.

"Sara—are you okay?" he asked.

"What? Oh—sorry. Just thinking."

"By the way, did you get anything from Dr. Winston? Didn't you interview him last week?"

"Yes, I did. His wife, Stella, had been killed by a drunk driver, and the late Edwin Doolan was accused and acquitted on a technicality. Even Steven did not claim credit for his murder, but I think Pollard could have done it. Anyway, Dr. Winston claimed to know nothing. He did not know Pollard. My interview produced nothing useful."

Sara paused. Should she tell Jake about Shirley and that she had tipped her off about a woman driving a black Camry? She decided it would be safe to let the investigation go as far as the Dew Drop Inn.

"However," she continued, "The doctor's receptionist, Shirley Barker, told me about a suspicious patient—a man—who had been driven to the office by a woman in a black Toyota Camry."

"You think this man could be Pollard?" asked Jake.

Sara shrugged. "Who knows? Lots of people act strangely when they visit a plastic surgeon. But this man stuck out to her."

"Did the guy have a name?"

"She thought maybe it was Kaplan."

"Okay," nodded Jake. "Guy named Kaplan, woman driving a black Camry. Is it possible Pollard could have had cosmetic surgery?"

"Anything's possible," said Sara. "I'll work on this lead. I'll get a list of black Camrys in that part of town. So—how about Ricky's case? Anything?"

Jake shook his head. "I'm sorry, but we've got nothing. The perp left behind no physical evidence. The only video we have is from a camera at the far corner of the building. It shows a man of average height and weight leaving just after your brother was killed. Even enhanced, you can't see his face very clearly."

"May I see the video?"

"Sure," replied Jake. He turned his monitor around and clicked his mouse. The screen showed the side door to the Werthan Lofts. The door opened and a man came out. The image was fleeting but, to Sara, it was unmistakable: the man was Charles Kaplan, or rather Earl Steven Pollard with his new face.

"Yeah, not much there," nodded Sara. "Why are these videos always so damned blurry? With my iPhone, I can film a mosquito at a hundred yards. But these surveillance cameras are crappy. Just cheap, I guess."

"Maybe Apple should get into the security business," smirked Jake.

EVEN STEVEN

Captain Riggs appeared at Sara's desk. "Good morning, Detective Durant," he said. "Glad to have you back. How are you feeling?"

"Ready for duty."

"Good to hear it. Nothing has changed since you left. Commissioner Gaines is demanding answers to the Even Steven serial killings. He's getting hammered by the mayor. We're heading into tourist season and need to make sure all of our citizens and visitors feel safe and protected. What's his last known location?"

"In the White Bridge neighborhood," said Jake. "But we have some leads."

"Well, you'd better turn those leads into an arrest!" barked Captain Riggs. "Or all of us will be back in uniform, working the midnight traffic shift. Got it?"

"Yes, sir," said Sara.

January melted into February. Sara slow-walked the Even Steven investigation. She allowed her team to uncover Pollard's movements to the Dew Drop Inn. But then he had vanished. He had checked out and was never seen again. The manager to whom Sara had talked—and who might have remembered her—had moved to California. The new manager knew nothing.

The people of Nashville gradually moved on to other concerns—fires, school shootings, political scandals, hospital closings. The Even Steven killings seemed to have stopped and began to fade into history as just another horrific

EVEN STEVEN

unsolved crime, like the Black Dahlia case in Los Angeles or the Zodiac killings in San Francisco.

One morning, a homicide landed on Sara's desk. A woman had been found shot to death in her kitchen. Sara and Jake hurried to the scene, a tidy suburban home in Cane Ridge, south of town. They went inside. The victim was lying on her back with a neat, single bullet hole in her forehead. Her eyes were open. It was about noon, and she was quite cold as rigor mortis had set in. Dr. Yeager, the medical examiner, put the time of death at twelve hours earlier, around midnight.

"Oh, my God," said Sara when she saw the body. "I know this woman. Her name is Lilly Clokey. We're friends from Sylvan's Gym. She also works at my bank as a manager. Nice girl. Always very sweet. When I needed a home improvement loan, she put it right through for me."

"Looks like a .38," said Jake as he peered at the entrance wound.

"Correct," said Dr. Yeager. "As it exited, it took off most of the back of her head."

Indeed, the pool of dried blood under her head was quite large, and the kitchen cabinets behind her were splattered with blood and bits of bone and brain.

"We have bullet fragments embedded in the wood," noted Jake.

Nothing else in the kitchen looked out of place, however. There were two wine glasses on the counter and an open bottle of pinot noir. The victim was dressed only in a sheer teddy nightgown. There was no sign of forced entry, no sign of a struggle, no robbery. Just a bullet in the head.

EVEN STEVEN

Out of an inexplicable sense of curiosity, Sara gently opened the victim's mouth and examined her tongue. It was unmarked. *Of course it was unmarked. Wasn't Earl Pollard dead?*

"Even Steven?" asked Jake.

Sara shook her head. "No."

"She was expecting company."

"Yeah. We need to find out who that was."

Before any of that, Sara had one dismal duty: informing the parents of Lilly Clokey that their daughter was dead. Murdered.

John and Mims Clokey lived in a tidy colonial-style house on a cul-de-sac in the neighborhood of Cumberland University in Lebanon. He was the assistant director of admissions there, and she worked for an insurance company. It was early in the evening when Sara pulled her marked cruiser into their short driveway and stepped up to the front door. She paused to collect her nerves, then pushed the softly glowing doorbell. After a moment, a woman opened the door. She peered at Sara.

"I'm Detective Sara Durant, Nashville Police Department. Are you Mrs. Clokey?"

"Yes," nodded the woman. "Oh—I know you. You're Lilly's friend. From the gym."

"That's right," replied Sara. "May I come in?"

"Why certainly, Sara—if I may call you that. Please do." She turned. "John! We have company! Lilly's friend Sara!"

EVEN STEVEN

Sara stepped into a typical family room with early American furniture and, on the walls, a pastiche of decorative paintings and family photos, many of them featuring Lilly at various ages and locations. In the fireplace a late-season log burned cheerily.

John Clokey emerged from the kitchen. With his kindly eyes, he peered at Sara over his silver-framed reading glasses.

"Hi, I'm Detective Durant," she said as he approached.

"Can we get you anything?" said Mims. "Coffee? Some cider?"

"Oh, no, thank you," replied Sara.

"Nothing serious, I hope," said John.

Now they were all sitting—Sara in her chair and the parents on the sofa.

"I'm afraid it is rather serious," said Sara, struggling to keep the tears from welling up in her eyes.

"It's not Lilly, is it?" asked Mims. She cast a worried glance at her husband.

"Yes, it's about Lilly," nodded Sara. "I'm sorry, but I have bad news. She's deceased."

"What do you mean, deceased?" said John. He gripped his wife's hand.

"She passed away last night. In her house."

"That's impossible!" cried her mother. "I spoke with her just yesterday! She was perfectly fine. Healthy and happy."

EVEN STEVEN

"We don't understand," said John. "Our only child is gone?"

"Yes," said Sara. She could feel her throat tighten. "I'm very sorry for your loss."

"What happened?"

"Her life was taken. She was shot. Around midnight in her home."

"Who would do such a horrible thing?"

"We don't know yet. We're beginning a full and aggressive investigation."

"I want to see her," said Mims through her tears. "I must see my baby. She's all I have. Where is she?"

"At the offices of Forensic Medical Management Services, on Louisiana Lane, in The Nations."

"What is that, some private company?" asked John.

Sara nodded. "They handle forensics for the city. Here—I have their card. The medical examiner is Doctor Pieter Yeager. You'll have to contact his office."

John took the card and, scowling, examined it.

"I'm so sorry," said Sara. "Lilly was a very special girl. I have such fond memories. She was always very kind and generous."

"I cannot believe my baby is gone," sobbed Mims as she sank into John's arms.

Sara stood up. "I know this is a terrible shock. If there's

anything I can do, please let me know."

"You can catch the bastard who did it," said John.

"Did Lilly have any problems with anyone? Anybody ever threaten her?"

"Not that we know," said Mims. "Everybody loved her."

"I'll be going now," said Sara. "I'll let myself out. I'm so very sorry. We'll be in touch."

She left the house and closed the door behind her. She stood for a moment on the front steps and looked around at the houses and trees and sky. Somewhere out there, a killer was walking free, the bastard was going to pay.

18

The investigation proceeded quickly. Sara uncovered the name of a lover. Actually, *three* of them. Logan Silva, Jimmy Kent, and Benny Shook—each with extensive message trails on Lilly's phone.

"Lilly Clokey was a busy lady," mused Jake. "Juggling three friends with benefits. I wonder which one got jealous enough to kill her?"

Kent and Shook were quickly ruled out because both were out of town on the day of the murder and had solid alibis. That left Silva as the number one suspect. And sure enough, there was a call from his phone to hers at 2:00 p.m. on the day of the murder. It lasted five minutes. But after that, nothing.

Jake interviewed a friend of Lilly's, who revealed she had seen Lilly and a man arguing in the parking lot of a restaurant a few nights before the murder. Surveillance video revealed the man to be Logan Silva.

Based on the accumulating evidence, Sara and Jake decided to pay him a visit at his apartment in Hillsboro Village, a few miles from the murder scene. When they knocked on the door, a man answered. He was six feet tall, had a man bun on his head, and wore big tortoise-shell eyeglasses.

EVEN STEVEN

He definitely wasn't Logan Silva.

The detectives identified themselves.

"Who are you?" asked Sara as she stood outside in the hall.

"I'm Chuck Forester," the man replied as he peered at them nervously. "Logan isn't here. He's at work."

"Are you his roommate?" asked Sara.

"I've been staying here for the past year," replied Forester. "I work in town. I'm a sound engineer. In recording studios."

"Yeah, we understand," nodded Jake. "Listen, do you mind if we come in and look around?"

"Um, I don't know," stammered Forester. He pushed his glasses higher up on his nose.

"It will only take a minute," said Sara.

Not wanting to seem like he was hiding anything, Forester agreed, "Well, sure, okay." He stepped back to let them enter.

The apartment was modern and ordinary. Jake and Sara found themselves in a living room furnished with a couch in faux black leather, the usual television screen hung on the wall, an exercise machine bolted to another wall, a table and chairs, and a bicycle in the corner. The walls were decorated with sports posters and a big panoramic photo of the Nashville skyline at night.

Sara moseyed into the kitchen. Nothing special there. Returning to the living room, she motioned to the two bedrooms. "Which one is yours?" she asked Forester.

EVEN STEVEN

"This one," he said, nodding to one with the closed door.

"Mind if we take a look in them?" asked Jake.

"Um, do you need a warrant?" Forester stammered.

"Not if you allow us. But if you want, we can go to a judge and get one, then come back with an army of cops."

"Okay, no problem," said Forester. "Go ahead and take a look. I've got nothing to hide."

Jake took Forester's room while Sara entered Silva's. She found the drapes closed. Shag carpet on the floor. An unmade bed with a plaid quilt tossed across it. Clothing on the floor. On the dresser were the usual personal effects—sunglasses, a toy football, cologne, a few framed photos of what appeared to be family members. There was also a framed photo of Silva and Lilly standing on a dock on a lake. They were arm in arm, smiling in the sun.

She opened the closet doors. Suit jackets, pants, shirts hung askew. It smelled musty. *The guy needs to clean his clothes more often*, she thought. She glanced down. A gym bag was on the floor. It was open. She could see inside of it.

And she saw a gun.

"What have we here?" she said as she picked it up with her gloved fingers. "A Taurus .38 special double-action revolver." She sniffed it. It smelled like gunpowder. "Jake!" she called. "We've got something!"

That afternoon, Sara arrested Logan Silva, and assistant district attorney Jill Simmons charged him with first-degree murder. At his arraignment, he was given fifty thousand dollars bail and ordered to stay at home with an ankle monitor.

The mood in the office was upbeat, nearly jubilant. Forensic tests proved the gun found in Silva's closet was the weapon used to kill Lilly Clokey. The case was a slam dunk, but Silva refused to confess. He resisted hours of grilling by the interrogation team, insisting that he was on a hiking trip in Warner Parks until 10:00 p.m. on the night of the murder, and then had come home and gone to sleep. No one had seen him. His roommate Forester had been working a late-night recording session and hadn't returned to the apartment until 3:00 a.m. Silva's door had been closed, and Forester had gone straight to bed, where he watched television for a while before falling asleep.

Silva's prints were found in Clokey's apartment, but of course, he said, he had been there many times. True. The prints of Kent and Shook were also found in the apartment.

Then Silva's lawyer filed a motion to dismiss. The motion charged that the seizure of the gun was the result of an illegal search, and therefore, the gun could not be admitted as evidence.

"Your Honor," argued Simmons before Judge Ito in his chambers, "the detectives asked the occupant of the apartment, Mr. Charles Forester, for permission to enter the premises. He gave his permission. The detectives asked Mr. Forester for permission to search the apartment, including the bedrooms. Again, Mr. Forester gave his consent. The gun was found inside an open gym bag on the floor of the closet. It was in plain sight. Therefore, the search and subsequent discovery of the murder weapon were entirely legal."

EVEN STEVEN

Judge Ito nodded and asked, "What does the defense say?"

"It's our position," said attorney Roberta Smith, "that while Charles Forester was an occupant of the apartment, he was, in fact, a guest and did not pay the rent. He may have had control over certain parts of the apartment, including common areas and his own bedroom, but he did not have the right to consent to the searching of Mr. Silva's bedroom, his private space. And the door was closed."

"Your Honor, this is absurd," said Simmons. "Mr. Forester had a key to the apartment. He had been living there for a year. He could go anywhere in the apartment he pleased. The fact that he had never *happened* to enter the defendant's bedroom is just a matter of chance."

"I'll decide what's absurd, Ms. Simmons," said the judge. "As a matter of fact, I find the argument to be quite reasonable. I'm getting concerned with what I see as recurrent police overreach. Your detectives went into that apartment knowing that Mr. Forester was merely a guest and had no control over the entire premises and, in particular, the closet in Mr. Silva's personal bedroom, which he had testified he had never entered. He may have felt intimidated by your detectives. Whatever the reason for his acquiescence, I'm ruling that Mr. Forester had authority to grant a search of the premises only for those specific rooms or areas over which he had control. He had no authority to allow a search of the closet and the gym bag. The gun is inadmissible."

"Judge Ito, that's crazy!" protested Simmons. "Forensics has proven it's the murder weapon!"

"Watch your language, Ms. Simmons. Your detectives failed to get a search warrant, which would have solved your problem. The gun is out. Return it to Mr. Silva. Good day."

When Sara heard the news of the ruling, she was astounded. Judge Ito was known to be tough on the police, but this was shocking. He could have easily ruled the other way. The idea of how much of Silva's apartment this year-long "guest" controlled was highly subjective. Any rational person could have concluded that Forester controlled the entire apartment.

"Without the gun, where's the case now?" Sara asked Simmons in her office.

"Down the toilet," she replied. "We've got nothing. No proof Silva was there. No other physical evidence. We all know his story about hiking in Warner Parks is bullshit. He couldn't even provide an accurate description of the stone steps and The Allee. Christ, he could have at least bothered to Google it to give some veracity to his story. I'm sorry, but unless we get more evidence, I've got no choice but to drop the charges."

Stunned, Sara went back to her desk. She felt both guilty and enraged. She knew that, technically, she and Jake could have gotten a search warrant. But it wasn't necessary—the damned guy living there had opened the door and given his consent for a search. And she had seen the murder weapon in plain sight!

Her phone rang. It was a call from outside.

"Detective Durant. How may I help you?"

"Hi, detective. John Clokey here. Any news? We heard you had arrested a man named Logan Silva. You found the gun?"

EVEN STEVEN

"Mr. Clokey, are you at home? I'll come out there to see you."

The news she had to deliver to the grieving parents was too awful to relay over the phone. With a heavy heart, she went to her car and made the drive out to Lebanon.

She arrived at the house and rang the bell. John Clokey answered the door.

"Please, come in," he said with a wave of his big hand. "Honey!" he called, "Detective Durant is here!"

They went into the living room. Mims came downstairs; she looked worn and haggard, as if she had aged a decade since her daughter's death. John and Mims sat on the sofa. Sara remained standing.

"What's so important that you had to drive out here to tell us in person?" asked John.

"I hope that bastard fries in the chair," said Mims. "What's his name? Something Silva? I recall Lilly mentioning dating a man by that name."

"Yes, the man we arrested is named Logan Silva," said Sara. "But I have some distressing news. The judge has made a ruling against us, and we have no choice but to drop the charges."

"What? Why?" asked John.

"We seized a gun from Silva, and forensics proved it was the murder weapon. No doubt about it. Silva did it. But the judge ruled that we found the gun improperly. To make a long story short, we cannot admit the gun into evidence. And without it, we cannot win. I'm sorry, but that's what happened."

"So, you guys botched the investigation?" said John with anger in his voice.

"We believe we handled it properly. But the defense made a motion, and the judge ruled in their favor. Unfortunately, this sometimes happens."

"You're fucking kidding me," spat Mims.

"No, I'm sorry. That's what happened."

"So, the bastard Silva is going to walk free? Without spending so much as a day in jail?" shouted Mims as she stood up.

"Dear, please calm down," said John, reaching for her.

"I will not calm down!" she said, shrugging him off. "This is outrageous! How could you let this happen?"

"I'm so sorry," said Sara.

"Detective Durant, I think you should leave," said Mr. Clokey.

"Yes, all right," she said. "If I can do anything—" and then she stopped. She knew that was the wrong thing to say. She went to the door and walked out of the house.

19

On the drive back to headquarters, Sara's mind was reeling. What could she do? Yes, the investigation had been botched. They could say it was her fault. Lilly was a sweet girl, a friend, and Sara had let her down.

When she walked into the office, Jake waved her down. "You're just in time to catch that blowhard Roberta Smith and her client Logan Silva gloating on the steps of the courthouse."

They stood in front of the TV monitor. Sure enough, Smith and Silva stood in front of a gaggle of reporters.

"My client has been unfairly persecuted by the Nashville Police and the district attorney," said Smith to the microphones. "He is totally innocent, and we are delighted that the judge put an end to this ridiculous charade. Now, perhaps, the detectives can turn their attention to solving real crimes instead of harassing law-abiding citizens."

"What a piece of shit," muttered Jake. "She ought to get down on her hands and knees and thank the good Lord for the spectacular stroke of luck that set her murdering client free."

Sara, seething, nodded. "What goes around, comes around."

EVEN STEVEN

"I wonder," said Jake, "if Even Steven is watching."

"What?"

"I said, I wonder if Earl Steven Pollard is tuned into this stunt. If I were Logan Silva, I'd watch my back. He fits the profile of an Even Steven victim, right? And Pollard hasn't been active in a few months. Maybe Pollard got smart and went to Alaska or someplace. Or maybe he's still in town, keeping a low profile with his new face."

"Yeah—Silva definitely fits the victim profile," mused Sara.

"Maybe we should warn him?"

"Why the fuck would we want to do that?"

Jake laughed. "Good point. You know, karma's a bitch. Let Silva worry about his own ass. If he were smart, *he'd* go to Alaska, where pissed-off friends and relatives of Lilly Clokey couldn't find him."

"He's not that smart. He's cocky."

That night, at home, Sara sat at her desk. Her computer screen was open to Facebook, and the profile she was looking belonged to Logan Silva. There he was, smiling and free, showing himself at night clubs with his friends, driving his new Corvette, watching a game at Nissan Stadium, eating a pizza.

What a pompous buffoon!

But Logan Silva was not just a clown. He was a dangerous predator who—having killed once—was capable of doing it

EVEN STEVEN

again.

She poured herself another shot of Jack Daniels from the bottle on the desk. Her mind raced. *Yes or no?* The whiskey burned its way down her throat. Should she walk through that door from which there was no return? Hunting down Earl Steven Pollard was one thing. He was a dangerous escaped serial killer. But Logan Silva? Maybe the universe would take care of him. Like Jake had said, karma's a bitch. But not always. Too often, karma seems to be on vacation. Absent. Not operative. Really bad people keep on being bad, with no consequences.

The door was open.

Within minutes, Sara had created a fake Facebook page. Her name was Sophie Hawkins. Thirty-two. Fitness instructor at Planet Fitness. Graduate of Hillsboro High School and Belmont University. Lived in Ashland Park, conveniently about two miles from Silva's apartment. She dug up some photos of herself when she had big hair and was into 1980s fashion—tight spandex leggings, high boots, and floppy sweatshirts that looked like they were about to fall off her shoulders. Plenty of skin and cleavage. She still had some of that stuff in her closet. The overall effect was of a girl looking for fun.

With her page populated, she sent a friend request to Silva.

Hey, didn't we meet at Brown's Diner one night?

(Their surveillance of him had provided this nugget).

Been thinking about you. DM me.

She closed her page and went to do the dishes and cleaned

the kitchen.

She came back half an hour later, and to her amazement, he had already answered:

Hey hottie!

Sara felt the puke rise in her throat. But now was no time for distractions. The dumb fish was nibbling at the bait.

What'cha doing tonite? she replied.

Hangin' out with you, I'd say.

Meet you at Brown's in 15?

You got it.

Sara quickly dressed in her 1980s outfit. This was too easy. An essential accessory was a brown floppy brimmed cowboy hat that she could pull down over her face when she entered and exited the pub, because that's where the cameras were. She also put on a pair of enormous hoop earrings, because when police interviewed witnesses the next day, all the witnesses would remember was the woman wore huge hoops and a big hat. Her face would go unnoticed.

She put a few accessories into her oversized purse. One was .38 snub-nosed revolver she had liberated from the evidence room. Connected to a gang slaying years earlier, it was not part of any active cases. Conveniently, it came with a suppressor. The second was a small bottle of TriGene disinfectant, capable of destroying DNA on the surface of an object or body, with gloves to go with it. The third was two

EVEN STEVEN

lengths of clothesline rope.

At 10:00 p.m., she pulled open the door to Brown's. The place was half full. Keeping her head down, she scanned the tables. Silva was sitting alone. Good—she didn't want to sit at the bar where the bartender could stare at her.

"Hey there, Ronnie, how's it going?" she said sweetly as she sat down.

"Hey, sugar, it's going good—or at least it is now. What are you drinking?"

I need to keep a clear head, she thought. "Oh, just a white wine spritzer. Thanks."

For the next half an hour, Sara—or rather Sophie—forced herself to smile at his smarmy face, laugh at his lame and often sexist jokes, and even pat his beefy hand to establish physical contact. What on Earth did Lilly Clokey see in this guy? There was no accounting for taste. Silva made Sara's skin crawl, but she kept her eye on the prize.

Sure enough, the dumb fish took a big bite of the bait. Looking her in the eye, he said, "Say, why don't we go to my place? I can whip up some omelets. Havarti, prosciutto, onions. With champagne. You'll love it."

"Sounds yummy. Let's go." She paused for effect. Then she frowned. "You don't happen to have a roommate, do you?"

Silva sank back in his chair. "Uh, yes, I do. Why?"

She nodded toward his phone. "Call him and tell him to get out. Don't come back until after midnight."

EVEN STEVEN

"He has a totally separate room."

"I don't care. Get rid of him."

Silva smiled. "Yes, ma'am." He picked up his phone. "Hey, bro. Listen, I need you to leave the apartment for a few hours. Until after midnight. Make it one o'clock. Yep, got a special visitor. Okay? Listen—I owe you one. Thanks, bro." He hung up and smiled. "Done deal."

Sara agreed that he should drive her to his place in his car, a Corvette. Nothing good could come from her distinctive Mustang being caught in his neighborhood that night. She hurried into the building with her head low and hat on. Within minutes they were inside his apartment—which she knew all too well.

"My, what a lovely place you have here," she cooed. "Pour us some drinks, will you, dear? I'm going to freshen up if you don't mind."

"How about that omelet?" he asked.

"Oh, maybe later," she smiled as she sashayed toward the bathroom, giving him a little hip waggle to affirm her intent.

Inside the bathroom, she touched nothing; she only pulled her pistol from her purse and checked to make sure a round was chambered. She knew she would get only one pull of the trigger. With her pistol concealed in her purse, she emerged to find Silva already in the bedroom with the lights dimmed.

"Hey, sweet thing," he said as he opened his arms to embrace her. He planted a wet kiss on her lips as his hands crawled south. She reciprocated, running her hands over his manly chest before sliding down to below his belt and

EVEN STEVEN

massaging his pants from the outside.

"Impressive," she purred.

"So I've been told," he thoughtlessly answered.

"I'll tell you what we're going to do," she whispered in his ear as she gently pushed him away. "I want you to put some music on. Something soft and sensual. Then I'm going to dance for you."

Nodding eagerly, Silva took his phone and brought up a "Slow & Sexy" playlist.

"Oooh, nice," she sighed. "Now take off your clothes, except for your boxer shorts. We'll leave those for last."

Silva hurried out of his shirt and pants.

"Lie down on the bed," she commanded.

He did as he was told.

"Give me your right hand."

He obeyed. Deftly, Sara took a length of clothesline from her purse and tied his wrist to the bedpost. He gave an expression of alarm. At this cue, Sara leaned over and gave him a deep kiss on the mouth. "I'm going to be kissing a lot of other places very soon," she smiled.

He relaxed. She took his left hand and tied it to the other bedpost. Now he was quite helpless; but he was happy, dreaming of the pleasures to come.

"Do you want me?" she said as she gyrated on him.

EVEN STEVEN

"Oh, yeah," he replied.

"Ok, just one more little thing, my love," she said. "Close your eyes."

"Close my eyes?"

"Trust me, you'll be amazed."

"Okay," he said happily, with visions of volcanic sex dancing in his brain.

Quickly, Sara reached into her purse grabbing her pistol as she rolled off the bed. It was loaded, and the bullet chambered. Safety off. Holding it in both hands. She pointed the gun at his forehead.

"Ready?" she said. "Okay, open your eyes."

He opened them.

"What the fuck are you doing?" he gasped. "Put that thing down!"

Sara smiled. "This is for Lilly Clokey," she said. She waited a brief moment while his expression changed from bewilderment to rage.

"Why you fucking bitch!" he spat.

She pulled the trigger. With a soft "*phhhht*" sound the bullet drilled a neat hole in his forehead and exited out the back, slamming through the pillow and shattering into the bedframe. Sara didn't look, but she knew that the back of his head was nothing but a mush of brains and blood and bone.

His eyes remained open and glassy.

EVEN STEVEN

Her hands shaking, Sara dismounted. No time to be nervous—she had work to do. She quickly stashed the gun in her purse. After getting dressed, she took from her purse a pair of standard police latex gloves. She went to the kitchen and found a sharp utility knife. Returning to the bedroom, she pried open his mouth and carved the signature eye design on his tongue. She untied his hands and put the ropes in her purse, along with the knife. Taking the bottle of TriGene and a paper towel, she wiped his face, hands, and body to remove her DNA. She opened his laptop and deleted their conversation from his Facebook page.

She went to the kitchen and washed her wine glass, dried it, and put it away. After one final survey of the scene, she opened the bedroom window to help dissipate the smell of gunpower. Then she closed the bedroom door, took his keys from where he had left them, turned out the lights, and locked the door behind her.

The time was 11:30p.m. The roommate, Chuck Forester, had agreed to stay away until 1:00a.m. Hopefully he would arrive home and, seeing Silva's door shut, not bother him and just go to his own room like he said he did the night of Lilly's murder. With luck, the body would not be discovered until the next day.

Sara drove Silva's Corvette back to Brown's and parked it a few blocks away. She locked it and took the keys. She went to her own car and drove away.

On the way home, she made several stops at restaurant and industrial dumpsters. Into each, she put one item. The car key. The door key. The knife. The gloves. She broke down the pistol into its component pieces and dropped them in various dumpsters. As a cop she had done plenty of dumpster diving, and she knew that, during a search, small random items devoid of context would not be noticed—assuming the investigators had any cause to search in the first place.

When she arrived home around 1:00 a.m., she had one more task to complete: the letter from Even Steven to the police.

To be sure, she had misgivings about continuing the legend of Even Steven. She could have simply shot Silva and walked away. His murder would have been chalked up as just another random homicide in a big city, probably committed by an angry lover. Sara knew that, if the police dug deep enough, behind Silva they'd find a parade of jilted women. Maybe a few men, too—one cannot jump to conclusions. Such murders don't receive the same white-hot intensity as the latest trophy claimed by a serial killer, though. Even Steven had become notorious, like Son of Sam or Ted Bundy. His near-miraculous ability to kill and escape undetected had earned him mythical status and instilled fear in an entire city, despite the fact that his victims were far from random. They were people whom the police were convinced were killers themselves and who had walked free because of the vagaries and failures of the criminal justice system.

Cops usually despise vigilantes, who by definition take the law into their own hands, and instead of reducing crime, compound it. They make tense situations worse and prevent the fair administration of justice. But Sara had heard enough idle chatter around the department to know that many of those who wore the blue had expressed secret admiration for Even Steven. Cops know they must operate within a strict set

EVEN STEVEN

of rules, and when a guy comes along who does the job with gleeful indifference to those rules for the sake of meting out justice, many cops nod their heads and say to themselves, *Mission accomplished.*

Yes, there would be a letter. The benefit of throwing a smokescreen over the case outweighed the possibility of inciting more public panic and pressure on the department's rank and file to apprehend Even Steven.

Sara donned a pair of latex gloves and an N95 mask leftover from the pandemic and went to her computer. She wrote the letter, printed it, added the pen sketch of the eye, and then printed the envelope with the address of the NMPD Homicide Section.

After sealing and stamping it, she put it into a plastic bag.

She was exhausted, but her job wasn't finished yet. After turning off her phone, she took the bag and went to her car. She drove north on I-24 to I-65 in Cumberland Heights and continued north. Traffic was sparse, and she could have easily hit eighty or ninety miles per hour, but she kept her speed within the limit. After half an hour, she came to the exit for Route 174 in Goodlettsville, where Janie Smalls, the victim of Edna Shriver, had lived. Sara took the exit and found the Holiday Inn, where she remembered there was a mailbox next to the street. Sure enough, it was there, and into it, she dropped her letter.

At 2:00 a.m., she put her key into the lock of her front door. She felt worn out, both mentally and physically, but her mind was racing, replaying the vivid scenes from the day. She took a sleeping pill and flopped onto her bed.

20

The next morning, bleary-eyed, Sara hoisted herself out of bed after hitting the "snooze" button more than a few times. No time for her usual workout. Feeling stiff and sluggish, she took a cold shower and had breakfast. While she stood at the counter and ate, she watched the local news. No mention of a murder. Her phone had been quiet all night. Good— Forester hadn't opened the door to Silva's bedroom. The odds were favorable he wouldn't until that evening.

She went to work. Jake was already at his desk, looking crisp and clean in his white shirt and black necktie. He peered at her.

"Are you okay?" he asked. "With those eyes, you look like a raccoon."

"Top of the morning to you, too, partner," she replied, stifling a yawn. "What's up?"

"Paperwork," he grumbled. "I've got a pile of MG forms to file. MG2, witness assessment for special measures. MG4, charges. MG5, police report for a new case, that guy who beat his male lover with a rolling pin. Fractured the victim's skull. MG9, witness list for the taxi cab rape case. MG19, application for compensation, same case. And there's more," he said with a wave of his hand toward a stack of papers.

EVEN STEVEN

She sat down. Like Jake, she faced a mountain of reports and filings. That's the way it was: the more you accomplished as a detective, or as any type of cop, the more paperwork you had to complete. It was like being punished for doing a good job.

"Do we have anything new on Pollard?" she asked as she flashed back to him hobbling away in the snow.

Jake shook his head. "I've got a pile of telephone tips to work through, but none of them are panning out. The clairvoyant woman is pestering me, as usual."

"The one who calls herself Madame Luna?"

"Yep. She's still around. She tells me that the person who killed your brother comes from the north."

"The north?"

"Yeah, because she sees a figure of a man in the snow. Like the abominable snowman. She can't see his face because of the blizzard. He's running through a whiteout. I told her to get back to me when the weather clears."

Sara gave a grim smile. Snow, huh? A shiver went down her spine. Better keep an eye on Madame Luna.

Her phone rang. It was Captain Riggs.

"Detective Durant here," she answered

"Sara, we got a bunch of 9-1-1 calls from Salemtown. Drive-by shooting at Delta and Garfield. Male victim dead at the scene. Many witnesses. Go there now. Take Jake with you."

"Yes, sir." She turned to Jake. "Let's roll. Drive-by in Salemtown. Victim deceased."

EVEN STEVEN

As they hurried to the cruiser, Sara could not help but think about the not-yet-reported death of Logan Silva. *When would the call come in?*

The scene in Salemtown was chaotic. The uniformed officers had closed off the block, but neighbors milled around, getting in the way. A man lay on the sidewalk, surrounded by a screen. Dr. Yeager had not yet arrived. Sara looked at the victim. Male, about twenty-five. Five-foot-eight, medium build. Had a ragged bullet hole in his chest. No visible gang tattoos. She searched his pockets. A wallet, set of keys, rolling papers, and a small bag of marijuana. Less than half an ounce—a misdemeanor, punishable by up to one year in jail and a fine. But this guy was not a dealer, at least not today. According to his driver's license, his name was Jerome K. Johnson. Lived just a few blocks away, on Cheatham Place.

There were witnesses. They saw a white Kia Optima with tinted windows. Tennessee plates, but no one saw the number. No security cameras covering the street. Blurry cell phone video of the car speeding away. A rapid-fire series of pops. Most likely an AR-style semi-automatic rifle. Spent cartridges littered the street.

Witness Harvey Gibson was in his house, directly in the line of fire.

"I rolled off the sofa and lay on the floor until the shooting stopped. Then I went to the door and saw all my glass blown out," Gibson said.

Indeed, bullet holes riddled the exterior aluminum siding of his home and picket fence. The glass of the front door was shattered, and holes punched through the walls of his living

EVEN STEVEN

room and bathroom.

"I'd like to know more about Harvey Gibson," said Sara to Jake as they compared notes. "It seems to me the shooter was aiming directly at his house."

It was time to notify next of kin. Sara and Jake drove to the victim's house and rang the bell. A woman answered. She was twenty-ish, slender, with bright eyes and a dancer's posture. Sara and Jake identified themselves as police detectives.

"Who are you?" they asked.

"Naomi Johnson," she replied, nervously clutching the fabric of her sweatshirt. "I live here."

"Do you know Jerome Johnson?"

"Yes, he's my husband. Is anything wrong? Is he in trouble?"

From inside, Sara heard the sound of a baby crying.

"May we come inside?"

They entered a tidy living room. A cross hung on the wall next to a framed picture of Jesus. Naomi went to a crib and soothed her baby.

Sara showed Naomi the driver's license of Jerome Johnson. "Is this your husband?"

"Yes. Why do you have that?"

"Please sit down," said Jake. "There's been a shooting. I'm afraid your husband was hit, and he has passed away."

EVEN STEVEN

Naomi collapsed into an armchair, sobbing. An older woman rushed in from another room.

"What's going on?" she demanded.

"Nashville Police," said Sara. "Do you live here?"

"I'm Naomi's mother. Helping take care of the baby. What happened?"

Sara told her. The mother-in-law insisted upon seeing the body. That was not possible now—perhaps later. Sara asked the two women if Jerome had any enemies. Would anyone want to kill him? No, he was a good man. Worked a steady job at the airport as a baggage handling supervisor. Smoked a little pot now and then but was never involved in gangs. The white Kia? No, never saw one at this house. Jerome was a quiet family man. Adored his daughter, Jasmine, who was just turning one year old.

Why had he gone out? His shift began at 3:00 p.m. Before work, he wanted to check on his elderly aunt, who lived on Ninth Avenue North, just a block from the scene of the shooting. He enjoyed taking the walk.

"Man, I hate this shit," said Jake as they left the dismal house. "It's one thing if gangbangers shoot at each other. But it really sucks when an innocent guy, a family man, gets caught in the crossfire."

Jake's phone buzzed. It was Captain Riggs. Probably wanted an update.

"Yes, Captain?" he answered.

EVEN STEVEN

"Got another job for you. Man named Logan Silva. Found shot to death in his bed. Avery Park Drive, Hillsboro Village. Medical examiner is on his way. Go there now and take control of the scene."

"How about Sara?"

"We need her to stick with the Jerome Johnson case. You're the lead detective on this. Got that?"

"Yes, sir." He ended the call.

Sara asked what was going on. Jake told her.

"I'm going with you," she said.

"Sorry—the captain explicitly said that you're in charge of this case. I'm taking the Silva case. Okay? I don't make the rules. If you have a problem with that, ask the captain. I'll see you later."

Jake walked away. Sara took her phone and called headquarters. She got Captain Riggs on the line.

"Sir," she said, "I really should be the one to handle Logan Silva. He's the guy who got off the hook for killing Lilly Clokey. He may have a connection to Earl Pollard and the Even Steven cases."

"Sorry, detective. We think it's better if you stepped away from the Even Steven cases for a while. Because of your brother. Detective Patterson will keep you informed. Now get started on your witnesses and that white Kia. I'm sure someone knows who shot our victim. All you've got to do is get them to talk. The code of silence is very strong."

EVEN STEVEN

"Yeah—snitches get stiches."

Dumbfounded, Sara ended the call. This was a headache she had not anticipated. Jake was old-school but he was sharp. Perhaps by careful coaching she could ensure he stayed off her trail.

She spent the afternoon doing the usual grunt work of interviewing witnesses who, despite being near the scene, all seemed to have been rendered temporarily deaf and blind. They saw nothing, heard nothing.

She shifted her attention to Harvey Gibson. He had a record of arrests, from drug dealing to sexual battery. His only conviction was for assault—he participated in the beatdown of another local guy—for which he had served six months. He collected Army veteran benefits and worked part-time at a local muffler shop. Why would a bunch of guys in a white Kia spray his house with bullets?

As for the car, it had been stolen the day before from a residence about two miles away, in Midtown. Surveillance video from a nearby liquor store showed two men approach the vehicle, jimmy open the door, and then enter the car. Within one minute, they drove it away.

Hyundai and Kia, nodded Sara to herself. *The easiest cars in the world to hotwire. The two most frequently stolen cars in America. Was it a drug deal gone bad? A turf battle? Or perhaps a war over a woman?*

While Sara worked the Jerome Johnson case, her mind was far away, thinking about the Logan Silva case and her partner, Jake Patterson.

21

When Jake returned to his desk that afternoon, he looked through the small pile of snail mail the mailroom guy had just delivered. Because of the eye crudely carved into the tongue of Logan Silva, and the victim's eligibility for targeting by Even Steven, he had been expecting a letter.

Sure enough, there it was. Just like all the others, it was addressed to Nashville Metropolitan Police Department Homicide Section. No return address. One ordinary postage stamp. Postmarked that morning in Goodlettsville. Wearing gloves, he carefully opened it. Inside was a neatly folded single sheet of printer paper. But this paper, he noted, was different from the previous Even Steven letters—recycled paper rather than the usual commercial stock, which had a slightly different texture and color. He thought, however, that might be consistent with Pollard having found a new place to live since his escape and assumption of a new identity.

The letter read:

Number 10 was a rotten guy! You botched the case and let him skate—but I got him on a deadly date! Your Friend, Even Steven.

Jake carefully analyzed the ink; it looked like it came from an ordinary home printer. When he bagged the letter and

EVEN STEVEN

envelope and sent them to the lab, he included a note to be sure to compare the paper and ink with previous Even Steven letters.

The murder had been reported online (*Hillsboro Village man found shot to death in bed*), but the department had not released the fact that the victim was marked with the sign of Even Steven. It was bound to leak out, and both Jake and Sara had advocated for full disclosure; but Captain Riggs and Commissioner Gaines had insisted on withholding that information. "No sense in getting the public riled up," Gaines had said. "It won't do any good."

"But what happens when the press gets wind of the facts?" Sara had asked.

"Let's make sure they don't—at least not until we find Earl Steven Pollard and lock his ass up again," said Riggs. "We have enough bad publicity from his escape as it is. We don't need to advertise the fact that we can't stop him from killing whomever he pleases. Find Pollard and put him out of business."

Jake forged ahead without his trusted partner. A review of Silva's credit card transactions revealed the last charge on his account was at Brown's Diner on the evening he was murdered, 10:35 a.m. Jake went to Brown's and asked the manager if they had video from that evening and a record of Silva's tab. Yes, he ordered a white wine spritzer, a Manhattan cocktail, and a hot chicken sandwich; and yes, they had a camera pointed at the front door entrance. In his office, he showed Jake the footage. At 9:50 p.m., the blurry image of Logan Silva could be seen entering the pub. Over the next few minutes, some other people, both men and women, came and went. At 10:00 p.m., a woman entered, alone. She was wearing a floppy brown hat, pulled low, obscuring her face, and big hoop earrings. She was medium height, fit and trim, about thirty years old. Then she walked into the pub itself, out of view of the camera. For the next half hour, people entered and left. At 10:40 p.m., a couple left—Logan Silva and the woman. Again, her hat obscured her face. She would be impossible to identify.

Jake asked the manager who had been serving Silva's table. Her name was LaShante, and she was on the premises. Jake had her brought to the manager's office and showed her the video. LaShante remembered the woman with the big hat. She thought it was frankly obnoxious, *but everyone has their own style, don't they?* She had no recollection of the woman's face, which she saw only briefly. About thirty years old. No particular distinguishing features, such as a tattoo. Just the oversized hoop earrings. Those really caught her eye.

Jake returned to police headquarters, and Sara arrived soon after.

"How's the Jerome Johnson case going?" Jake asked her.

"Difficult," she said as she pulled the lid off her to-go coffee. "No one is talking. Even the guy whose Kia Optima was stolen isn't cooperating. He just keeps saying, *I don't know, I don't know.* Our key is Harvey Gibson. I'm working on identifying his known associates, but it may take a while. It's tough when the man they tried to kill doesn't want your help! I'm trying to convince him that to flip is the rational choice, because then we could put him in witness protection. I think eventually he'll go for it, but I hope they don't pop him first. Tell me about Logan Silva. What have we got?"

"A very interesting development," replied Jake. "Silva was last seen at Brown's Diner. He was met there by a woman. She entered after he did, and then at ten-forty, they both left together. He was shot between eleven and one o'clock. So that's a pretty tight timeline."

"Okay," nodded Sara.

"Silva's phone showed a call to his roommate at ten-thirty, just before they left Brown's. I asked the roommate, Chuck Forester—you remember him—"

"The man bun."

"Bingo—I asked him about the call. He said that Silva asked him to vacate the apartment until one o'clock in the morning. He said he did. I checked out Forester's alibi. He was at the bar at the Metro Club from ten thirty until twelve forty-five, hanging out and playing pool. Lots of people saw him there. So, it's pretty obvious: Silva wanted to bring the woman back to his apartment. But she wasn't going to spend the night. She was going to be out of there before one."

"Could Forester have shot Silva?" asked Sara. "After all, we only have his word that he didn't discover the body until the next day. Could he have shot his roommate when he returned from the bar?"

"Theoretically, yes. But why? As far as we can see, Forester had nothing to gain. The apartment lease was in Silva's name, so now Forester has to move out. They have no business connection. And why carve the eye in his tongue?"

EVEN STEVEN

"But what if the woman Silva brought home was Forester's girlfriend, and he became enraged when he found out she was cheating on him right under his nose?"

Jake frowned. "That seems like a very unlikely scenario. I suppose it's possible, but I'm not going to spend a lot of time chasing it. I'm focused on the woman we *know* left Brown's with Silva."

"Do you really think he was killed by a woman?" asked Sara. "And a woman carved the design on his tongue?"

Jake shrugged. "If that's what the evidence suggests, we need to follow it. And there's one more odd thing. The letter from Even Steven arrived a short while ago. I sent it to the lab for analysis. But I was struck by a particular phrase." He brought up an image of the letter. "Read this: *You botched the case and let him skate—but I got him on a deadly date!* It seems like an odd choice of words, 'deadly date.' But suddenly it's not so strange if you consider the possibility that the killer is a woman. Specifically, the woman from Brown's."

Sara—caught off guard by the revelation of her inadvertent blunder when composing the Even Steven letter—shook her head. "I don't know about that. I think we may be jumping to conclusions. After all, the word 'date' rhymes with the word 'skate'."

"Perhaps. But we've got to admit the timeline points to the woman."

"Okay. But because your presumed killer—let's call her Madam X—did the tongue carving, which we have never publicized, then she must be another protégé of Earl Steven Pollard. We don't know for sure who sent the letter. It may have been the protégé or the master himself, Pollard. This guy is a brilliant opponent. I'll bet you anything that, if we find Pollard and arrest him, he'll have an alibi for last night."

Jake threw up his hands. "This is getting crazy! I think we're attributing to Pollard a set of superpowers that defy belief. He's in hiding. He may have a new face, but his DNA is the same as it's been since the day he was born. His fingerprints, too—you can obliterate them but you cannot change them. He needs to be extremely careful. He knows every cop in America is looking for him."

"Let's stipulate that Madam X is the killer," said Sara. "And this woman knows the secrets of the Even Steven murders. Therefore, she *must* be a protégé or maybe a lover whom he has trained. There's simply no other explanation."

Jake thought for a moment. "I guess you're right. It's the only way."

Sara nodded. "And let's further stipulate that it's extremely unlikely this Madam X is someone new to him, whom he recruited after his escape from prison. We know celebrity convicts often have groupies or female admirers on the outside, but we're talking about quickly recruiting and training a woman to perform a truly grotesque and horrifying act. Look at the Charles Manson family cult in the 1960s. He carefully groomed those women—brainwashed them, really—for many months before they willingly went on their gruesome killing spree. It takes a lot of conditioning to turn a human being into a killer. Madam X would have to be someone who has known Pollard for a long time and may even have conspired with him previously. Do you have a list of all the women known to have consorted with Pollard?"

EVEN STEVEN

"The first one who comes to mind is Debbie Chan, the bookkeeper who lives near the White Bridge Car Wash and gave shelter to Pollard after he escaped," said Jake.

Sara nodded. "I'd bring her in. Charge her with felony aiding and abetting a fugitive. She's no Snow White. She could be in this thing up to her neck. And get a search warrant for her house."

"Good idea," nodded Jake. "I'll set it up for tomorrow morning."

"And let me search the house while you apprehend Chan," said Sara.

That evening, Sara took the hoop earrings and big floppy hat she had worn to Brown's and cleaned them thoroughly. She had plans for them.

22

The next morning at 7:00, Detective Jake Patterson pounded on the door of the residence of Debbie Chan on Knob Road.

"Nashville Police Department! Open up! We have a search warrant!"

"I'm coming," called a woman's voice from inside. The door opened. Debbie stood there in her pink bathrobe. She looked terrified. "What's going on? Why is this happening?"

"Nashville Police," said Jake. "I'm Detective Patterson and this is Detective Durant. We're coming inside." He pushed his way past Debbie. "Is there anyone else in the house?"

"No—just me," she stammered.

"We have a warrant for your arrest." Jake turned to another female officer, "Go with her while she gets dressed."

Sara accompanied Debbie and the officer to the bedroom, where Debbie put on a pair of jeans and a shirt. Then she was cuffed, read her Miranda rights, and taken outside to Jake's cruiser. He then left the scene with Debbie.

Sara went outside to her cruiser. She opened the trunk and took out a large brown paper evidence bag. She quickly returned to the house and went to the bedroom. Two uniformed cops were in the living room as she opened the closet door, slipped the hat from the bag, and put it on the shelf with some other hats. Then she went to the bureau, where Debbie kept her jewelry and earrings in decorative ceramic dishes. She placed the hoop earrings on one of the dishes. Then she leaned the empty evidence bag up against the wall by the door.

"Officer Ridley," she called, "I need you to come here and video the search."

One of the uniformed cops stepped in with a video camera. Sara searched the bedroom, and from the closet she pulled the big floppy hat.

"Bag that," she told Ridley. Then she went to the dresser and, after rummaging through the drawers, poked around among the jewelry. She held up the hoop earrings. "Bag these too," she told Ridley.

There was a small home office with a laptop and a home printer. Sara saw that the printer was an Epson inkjet, the same brand as her own. *What luck!*

"Take them," she told the uniformed cop.

After a cursory search of the rest of the house, Sara returned to station with her evidence bag.

"Where's Jake?" she asked one of the other detectives.

"He's in the interrogation room with Debbie Chan," he replied.

Approached the room and knocked on the door. Inside, Jake was sitting at the small table across from Debbie. Sara asked him to step out and speak with her in the hallway.

"We've got solid evidence," she said. "In her bedroom, we found a pair of hoop earrings and a big brown hat that match what Madam X wore at Brown's. They're being processed now." She showed him photos of the items.

"They certainly seem similar," nodded Jake.

"What's her alibi?"

"She hasn't got one. Says she was home alone the entire night, watching television."

Jake and Sara returned to the interrogation room.

"Debbie, we have a problem," he said.

"What's that?" she said in a quavering voice.

"These earrings and this hat were found in your bedroom." He showed her the photos. "They match the hat and earrings worn by the woman who met Logan Silva at Brown's."

"That's impossible!" she retorted tearfully. "I've never seen those before in my life! I never wear hoop earrings. They pull at my ears. And I do not own that ugly-ass hat. Where did you say you found it?"

"We found the hat in your closet, on the shelf. The earrings were on the bureau with other pieces of jewelry. The search was captured on video."

"Who found them?"

EVEN STEVEN

"Detective Durant, as you can see."

"Then she planted them. Everyone knows how you cops work. You pick the person you want to frame and you plant the evidence. I'm surprised you just didn't go ahead and plant a gun, too."

"You have a gun?", said Jake.

"No! I don't have a gun. See, you're trying to trip me up. I do not own a gun. I do not own those earrings or that stupid hat. I was home all night watching television. I watched a movie—*Titanic*, with Leonardo DiCaprio and that woman—Mare of Easttown. Then the news was on at eleven. Then I went to bed."

"You never drove your car?"

"No."

"And you never wrote and printed a letter?"

"A letter? Are you crazy? Of course not."

"We have your home printer and computer."

"Fine. You're so smart, you'll see the printer is out of ink. I haven't used it in a month. It just sits there."

Suddenly, the door opened. A woman entered. She was dressed in a blue power suit and carried a briefcase. Behind horn-rimmed glasses, her eyes flashed wildly.

"This interrogation stops now," she said. "I'm Ms. Chan's attorney."

"Would you care to introduce yourself?" asked Jake.

"Regina Brooks of Thrasher & Rogers. I need to confer with my client alone, if you will excuse us."

Sara and Jake left the room.

"A Rolls-Royce lawyer for a Ford client," mused Jake.

"No doubt hired by dear Uncle Leonard," nodded Sara. "He must be protecting Pollard. That alone is evidence of her guilt—too bad we can't use it in court."

Debbie Chan was arraigned the next morning. Bail was set at one hundred thousand dollars, which Regina Brooks promptly paid in cash—Debbie didn't even have to borrow it from a bail bondsman. And perhaps even more surprising, the defense made no motions to delay the trial. "We want our client to have her day in court as soon as possible," said Brooks. "Full acquittal on all charges cannot come soon enough."

Sara picked up LaShante Valentine, the server from Brown's who had waited on Silva's table, and took her to an interrogation room, where she showed her a photo array that included the mug shot of Debbie Chan.

"Do you see the woman seated with Logan Silva here?" said Sara. "Take your time. Look carefully. You can be a big help to us. This person is very dangerous."

LaShante studied the photos. "I'm not really sure," she said.

"Imagine each of them with a big floppy hat and hoop

earrings," said Sara. "And you said the woman had no tattoos. You remember that? And you also used the word 'obnoxious' in reference to the woman. Does that ring a bell?"

"Yes, it does," nodded LaShante. Nervously, she scanned the photos. She pointed to a woman who was not Debbie Chan. "Maybe her."

"Really?" said Sara with a tone suggesting sarcasm. She leaned back in her chair and folded her arms. "Keep looking. Take your time."

LaShante sighed. "Okay—maybe this one." Again, she chose one who was not Debbie Chan.

Sara frowned. "Don't decide just yet. Keep an open mind." Still with her arms folded in front of her.

LaShante was visibly perspiring. "May I have something to drink?" she asked.

"Sure—just as soon as we're done, I'll get you a Coke," Sara said with an encouraging smile.

LaShante pointed to the photo of Debbie Chan. "It was her. This is the person I saw with the guy at the table."

"Okay!" smiled Sara. "Very good. You've been a tremendous help! Let's get you that Coke. So, you're sure—you'll testify that's the woman you saw that night?"

"If you put the hat on her, and the earrings—yes, it was her."

"Thank you, LaShante. Let the record show the witness chose the photograph of Debbie Chan."

EVEN STEVEN

And so, the trial began. Detective Sara Durant took the stand as a key witness for the prosecution.

"Because you were told that a supposed accomplice of the escaped prisoner, Earl Steven Pollard, was driving a black Toyota Camry," remarked Regina Brooks during her cross examination, "you concluded that my client, who at one time owned such a vehicle, had provided aid and shelter to the escapee?"

"Among other reasons, yes," replied Sara.

"Did you arrest her and charge her at that time?"

"No."

"Why not?"

"Because, when I interviewed Ms. Chan at her home, I was on bereavement leave from the police department."

"So, you were acting as a rogue cop?" exclaimed Brooks with a grand wave of her hand.

"I wouldn't call it that."

"A vigilante?" she said with a flourish.

"No."

Brooks paused to let the exchange sink in. "All right, Detective Durant, let's talk about the so-called evidence that the police assert links my client to the murder of Logan Silva. State's exhibit number five is a video surveillance tape of the front door of Brown's Diner, on the night of the murder.

You have testified the tape shows the victim leaving the restaurant with a woman whose face we do not see. She has never been positively identified. Correct?"

"Correct."

"But she is wearing a brown floppy brimmed hat and a pair of hoop earrings. Is that correct?"

"Yes."

"Detective Durant, I've introduced into evidence five pairs of gold-colored hoop earrings that I purchased from five different stores in the Nashville area." She presented a tray with pairs of earrings in plastic baggies. "Please tell me how these are different from the pair you see in the video."

Sara peered at the earrings. "They appear to be very similar."

"In fact, these hoop earrings are extremely common, aren't they?"

"Yes."

"All right. Moving on, I have five floppy hats, also purchased at five different stores in the Nashville area. Detective Durant, why do you believe the hat you found in my client's closet—which she denies owning—is the exact same hat worn by the woman in the video?"

"It appears to be a match."

Of course, Sara knew for a fact the earrings and the hat were the exact same ones the murderer had worn because she herself had worn them—but she could not reveal that inconvenient detail.

"You also seized a computer and a printer from my client's house."

"Yes."

"Why?"

Sara paused. The exact nature of the letters from Even Steven to the Nashville Police had never been made public. And the existence of the "eye" symbol carved into the tongues of the victims had been held in the highest secrecy.

"To determine if they had been used to write a letter to the Nashville Police Department."

"What letter exactly?" asked Brooks with a knowing smirk.

"A letter purporting to be written by Earl Steven Pollard, alias Even Steven, claiming credit for the murder of Logan Silva."

"Really?" said Brooks in a dramatic voice which almost dared Sara to respond. "And what exactly did this letter say?"

Assistant district attorney Jill Simmons rose. "Objection, Your Honor. No such letter has been introduced into evidence in this case."

"And yet the Nashville Police seized my client's printer," replied Brooks, "for the express purpose of determining whether it had been used to print a certain letter, received by the police, claiming credit for the murder," Brooks replied.

"The objection is overruled," said the judge. "The defense may proceed."

Brooks continued, "Detective Durant, is this a copy of the

EVEN STEVEN

letter?" Brooks handed Sara a sheet of paper.

Sara looked at it. "Yes."

"Please read it."

"Objection!" said Simmons.

"Overruled. Read the letter."

Sara read, "'Number 10 was a rotten guy! You botched the case and let him skate—but I got him on a deadly date! Your Friend, Even Steven'."

From her seat on the witness stand, Sara felt a commotion spread through the audience of the courtroom. Reporters were hurriedly writing their notes. This was the first time the text of any Even Steven letter had been made public.

"And is there anything else in the letter?" asked Brooks.

"What do you mean?" replied Sara, trying to delay the inevitable.

"Any other markings that make this letter interesting to the police?"

"Yes," nodded Sara. "A simple drawing, in pen, of an eye."

"And why is that significant?"

Simmons again rose from her chair. "We object, Your Honor! The defense is going far afield from the evidence introduced in this case. Any discussion of any such drawing is immaterial and irrelevant."

"Again, Your Honor," said Brooks, "my client is accused of

printing and sending this particular letter to the Nashville Police Department as a part of her alleged scheme to kill Logan Silva because he fit the pattern of previous victims of the convicted killer Earl Steven Pollard, who escaped from Riverbend Prison and is currently at large. The prosecution introduced the printer into evidence, not the defense."

This was true. While Sara had impulsively seized Debbie's computer and printer during the search of her home, in consultation with assistant district attorney Simmons, Sara had expressed doubts about its value as evidence. Despite that, Simmons had seized upon it and insisted on using it. And now, Sara realized, Simmons's strategy was coming back to bite them.

"But the drawing of the eye was made after the letter was printed," said Simmons. "It has no connection to the printer."

"Sorry, Ms. Simmons," said the judge. "The letter, in its entirety, is fair game."

"I repeat," said Brooks. "Why is the drawing of the eye significant?"

Sara swallowed hard. "Because it corresponds to the eye marking that we've found on every victim."

"Onto the body? Where?"

"On the tongue."

The room buzzed with this revelation.

"When you searched the residence of my client," said Brooks, "Did you find any razors or knives or any blood evidence suggesting the defendant had performed such an act?"

"No."

"Did you find a .38 pistol or, indeed, any firearm?"

"No."

Among the other witnesses was LaShante Valentine, who obligingly testified that Debbie Chan, the defendant, was with Logan Silva that night at Brown's, and they left together.

The trial was quickly wrapped up and the jury sent to deliberate. The mood in the detective division was sour.

"I think we jumped the gun on prosecuting Debbie Chan," said Jake as he picked through the box of leftover donuts in the break room. "Even with LaShante's identification, this case is very thin."

"But common sense tells us she's the one," said a cop getting coffee. "Everything fits."

"Yeah—that defense lawyer, Brooks, is a slick one," said another. "Most defendants don't have that kind of legal firepower. Brooks has got a small army of junior associates with her. They know how to exploit every angle."

"Look at this headline," said Sara as she showed the group her phone. "'Secrets of the Even Steven Killer Revealed! Maniac Mutilated Victims' Tongues With Bizarre Eye Design!' We don't need this kind of publicity. First, we had the killer himself, then we had the protégé, and now we're going to have copycats."

For Sara, the public revelations of the *modus operandi* of Earl Pollard were especially bitter. In her mind, she was the rightful heir to the legend of Even Steven. She alone had tracked down Pollard after his daring escape from maximum security prison. She alone had vanquished him. And she alone had masterminded the very first post-Pollard operation by the Dark Angel of Justice—as she had begun to think of herself—by eliminating Logan Silva. The job had been a stunning success. She was above any suspicion, and while the prosecution of Debbie Chan, who was of course completely innocent of murder, was unpleasant for Debbie, she stood little chance of being convicted. As Jake had rightfully pointed out, the case against her was thin, and (as only Sara knew) based on planted evidence. The prosecution of Debbie was a good smokescreen and an effective diversion; while her life was disrupted, in the long run, she'd recover, especially with the help of her generous benefactor, Leonard Givens.

But copycats were unacceptable. In approaching the job of vigilante, Sara was cool and professional. She told herself that she had moral justification for taking the life of Logan Silva and anticipated other targets emerging. She knew the flaws of the criminal justice system better than anyone and was confident it would, over time, churn out more miscarriages of justice and killers who escaped paying the price for their acts. With the sole and tragic exception of her brother, Ricky, the targets of Even Steven were bad people who had done terrible things and, by some defect in the criminal justice system, had walked away, free and unfettered.

EVEN STEVEN

No copycat would be as judicious and ethical as Sara—at least as she saw the question of ethics.

But on the flip side, one or two more copycat killings (all out of necessity and with righteous cause, of course) would muddy the waters and perhaps make her work easier and less likely to be discovered.

23

The detectives got the call—the jury had reached a verdict.

Sara and Jake hurried to the courthouse and took their seats in the audience. Prosecutor Simmons was at her desk with her team, and across the aisle, defense attorney Brooks and her team flanked Debbie Chan.

The judge took the bench, and the jury filed in. The prosecutors and defense stood.

"Have you reached a verdict?" the judge asked the foreperson.

"We have, Your Honor."

"On the charge of first-degree murder, how do you find the defendant?"

"We find the defendant not guilty."

Brooks smiled and patted her client on the back.

"On the charge of second-degree murder, how do you find?"

"We find the defendant, Debbie Chan, guilty."

A shock wave shuddered through the court. Debbie Chan

collapsed and had to be supported by one of her lawyers. Reporters frantically scribbled. Jake turned and clapped Sara on the shoulder. He was grinning. "Wow, we did it!" he said.

"Order in the court!" said the judge with a whack of his gavel. "Order in the court!"

The jury was polled. It was unanimous.

"Ladies and gentlemen of the jury," said the judge, "the court thanks you for your service. You are dismissed. The defendant is remanded pending sentencing."

As the court emptied out, Sara sat in stunned silence.

"Are you coming?" asked Jake.

Sara pulled out her phone. "Yes—I'll be along in a minute. Got to make a call. I'll see you at the station."

Guilty! This was not the verdict Sara had foreseen—or had even hoped for. Her diversion had worked too well. An innocent person was going to prison for a crime that Sara had committed, a crime for which Sara had framed her, deliberately and with careful planning.

It was true that Debbie had aided and abetted a dangerous criminal fugitive. Not because Debbie herself was a criminal—the poor unfortunate woman was just an ordinary citizen—but because she happened to work for a wealthy and corrupt man who recruited her to do his family a favor. When that type of pressure is put on a weak person, they usually succumb. Sometimes they do the favor and then fade away; other times the favor leads to more and bigger problems.

Sara had led the investigation into Debbie Chan. She had coerced—there was no other word for it—LaShante into identifying Debbie as Madam X. She had planted the hat and earrings in Debbie's apartment. The evidence to convict Debbie Chan had come from Sara, and she'd get the praise and the credit. So, too, would assistant district attorney Jill Simmons, who had notched an impressive win for her professional resume.

But how could the jury have unanimously convicted Debbie on such flimsy circumstantial evidence? The same way, Sara supposed, that juries could fail to convict when the evidence seemed overwhelming to police and prosecutors. It was just the way the system worked.

Enough introspection—there was work to do. The Jerome Johnson case was active. Real criminals weren't taking the day off.

Sara returned to headquarters, where she found the mood to be jubilant.

"Congratulations, Detective Durant," said Captain Riggs as he shook her hand. "Nice work with the Silva case. We got a dangerous criminal off the streets. Let's hope we have no more of these Even Steven protégés or imitators or whatever the hell they are. As for Earl Pollard, what's happening with him? Have we got anything?"

"He's dropped off the face of the earth," replied Sara. "We know he was at the Dew Drop Inn on Clarksville Pike in Bordeaux, under the name Charles Kaplan. He checked out and has not been seen since. We have no photos of Charles

EVEN STEVEN

Kaplan. His driver's license and other papers were faked. He could get new ones."

"Didn't the clerk at the Dew Drop Inn at least get his vehicle plate number?"

"He did. Charles Kaplan was driving a blue Chevy Malibu, Tennessee plates, number BPN 1130. No sightings. Every local police department has received the APB."

"All right," sighed Captain Riggs. "Keep digging."

Sara went to Jake and told him she'd be out of the office for a few hours.

She got into her Mustang and drove north to Bull Run Road, then Kirby Hill Road. She passed Golden Lane and carefully approached the old barn, where she had once parked and where she had stashed the blue Malibu. An unexpected late-season snow still covered the ground. She stepped out of her car. The only sound was the creaking and snapping of the winter trees swaying in the upper wind. She saw only animal tracks in the snow—deer, coyote, rabbit. No tire tracks, no human footprints. The barn door was closed. Grasping the rusted handle, she pulled it open and peered inside. Quickly her eyes adjusted to the silent gloom.

The car was gone.

She entered and looked around. It was just an old barn, dark, full of cobwebs. Light drifted weakly through two cracked and hazy windows. There was nothing on the wooden plank floor except bits of straw and old boxes and cans piled around the perimeter.

For a moment, she questioned her own memory. No, there

was absolutely no doubt. She had parked the Malibu in this barn. She had left the key fob under the front seat. Today, no car. What could have happened to it?

Two possibilities: Pollard could have survived and taken it. Or it could have been stolen and sold in some other state—shipped overseas, chopped up for parts.

When? Anytime. The snow was fresh and undisturbed. It could have happened the day after she parked it here or as recently as a few days ago, before the new layer of snow fell.

Sara turned, left the barn, and closed the door.

The weather was turning cold, and low clouds threatened more snow. But she had no choice—she had to investigate the cabin on Golden Lane.

The first time she had approached the cabin, she had gone north, down into the creek bed, and then had circled around and come up through the woods, flanking the ravine. This time, she chose a different, more direct route. She walked back to Golden Lane. The rutted, winding road led through the trees. There were no tracks in the pristine snow. Presently, the cabin came into view about one hundred yards ahead. Taking cover behind the trunk of a big oak tree, Sara watched the cabin. No smoke came from the chimney. No car was parked in front. No lights were visible inside the gloomy windows. She waited. Flurries began to fall, lightly settling on her shoulders. The chill wind whispered in the treetops. A crow squawked loudly, answered by others down in the ravine.

Slowly, Sara advanced on the cabin, making her way from tree to tree. In the waning light and steady snowfall, she came to within twenty yards. No sign of life. Sara took out her phone and selected the thermal imaging app. She pointed the phone at the cabin. On the screen, the cabin registered solid, even yellow. This meant the heat was on inside the cabin, but there were no hot spots of red indicating a human presence.

She knelt down and found a stout branch, which she snapped into a chunk the length of her forearm. Stepping out from behind the tree, she hurled the stick at the roof of the cabin. It struck with a solid *"thunk"* and bounced off into the snow. A flock of sparrows in the nearby trees startled and took flight. Then all was quiet. No response from the cabin.

With her gun drawn, Sara sprinted to the cabin and paused at the nearest wall. Hearing nothing, she eased to the front door.

The moment had come. With a gloved hand, she carefully tried the knob. She had left the house unlocked—was it still? The knob turned. The door swung open an inch. She backed away from it. The wind caught it and pushed it open. Flurries swirled inside. Sara peered around the door frame, into the simple living area. With her pistol leading the way, she stepped inside. It was as she remembered it. There was the ratty old sofa, the high-backed chair, the television set that she had put back on its stand after they had knocked it over in the fight. She went into the kitchen. As she entered, something scurried away. A mouse or a rat. The linoleum floor was stained with dark brown blood. Back to the living room and into the bedroom. A window had a broken pane through which snowflakes drifted. The bed was unmade, and clothes littered the floor, mixed with dead leaves. In the bathroom she found men's toiletries—toothbrush, a comb, deodorant, shampoo—as if the owner had just stepped out.

Could Pollard have just stepped out? The electric heat along the baseboards was still working. She turned on a light. Yes—the cabin still had power. But that meant nothing; you'd have to have months of outstanding payments before Nashville Electric Service would actually shut off your service.

As she searched the house, she recalled that Pollard had suddenly attacked her in the house, as if he had been lying in wait for her. How did he know she was inside? She stepped out through the front door into the softly falling snow. Looking up, she closely examined the soffit under the eaves. Sure enough, there was a tiny camera, no bigger than the tip of her thumb, mounted on a little metal bracket. She walked around the perimeter of the cabin. On each of the four walls, under the eaves, was the same type of camera. On his phone surveillance monitor, Pollard had seen her as she entered through the bulkhead door and had chosen to ambush her once she was inside.

She went back inside the cabin. The idea that Pollard could still be alive nagged at her. The Malibu was missing. He may have taken it. This cabin could still provide shelter to him. After pondering the question, Sara decided to eliminate the possibility.

Using an accelerant would not be a good idea—an investigation would reveal its presence. Sara gathered up all the loose papers and clothing she could find and heaped them on top of the electric baseboard in the kitchen. Then she lit a match.

The fire smoldered for a few minutes before curious flames began licking at the wall of the cabin. Smoke billowed and she retreated to the living room. The flames spread quickly

EVEN STEVEN

throughout the kitchen, and Sara felt the intense heat.

The fire was robust. It was time to get out. She went through the front door and walked into the falling snow, leaving the door open behind her. The more oxygen, the better for the blaze.

She walked down Golden Lane to Kirby Hill Road, and then to the old barn where her car was parked. As she quickly brushed off the snow, she watched the smoke curling above the treetops. The nearest fire station was well over five miles away. By the time someone noticed the smoke—if they ever did—and the fire department responded, the cabin would be fully consumed, and she would be long gone.

As she drove south on Kirby Hill Road, the wind and snow quickly covered her tracks.

24

She walked into the Homicide Section as the sun was setting. There was tension in the air.

"What's up?" she asked Jake as she passed his desk.

"The shit has hit the fan," he replied.

"What do you mean?"

"LaShante Valentine has recanted her testimony. She and her lawyer, Regina Brooks, are suing the department and you personally, accusing you of coercion. LaShante says you steered her toward fingering Debbie Chan for the murder of Logan Silva."

"What the fuck is she talking about? That's ridiculous."

Jake shrugged. "Somehow Brooks got ahold of LaShante, and now the whole thing is blowing up. And by the way, Captain Riggs wants to see you. He's in his office."

With a feeling of dread, Sara knocked on his door.

"Come in," said the deep voice with the southern drawl.

She went in. He was doing something on his computer, with his bushy eyebrows furrowed in thought. "Have a seat,

EVEN STEVEN

detective," he said without looking up. She took the chair opposite his desk and waited. After a minute, he clicked his computer shut and turned his steely eyes in her direction.

"You've been informed about LaShante Valentine and her allegations," he said.

"Generally, yes. She wants to recant her identification of Debbie Chan."

"She *already has* recanted," said Riggs. "Her statement is included in her ten-million-dollar lawsuit naming you, me, Commissioner Gaines, the Nashville Police Department, Mayor Noles, and the City of Nashville as defendants. She claims that, when you brought her in to identify the woman she saw at Brown's, you showed her an array of mug shots. Eight of them on the table. She chose one and you urged her to keep going."

"The first woman she selected was my fourth-grade teacher, Mrs. Hopple, who lives in Birmingham."

"Okay," nodded Riggs. "She pointed to a second person, and again you asked her to reconsider."

"The second person was Amy Goddard, who has been incarcerated for a year in the Arise Recovery Center. Not a possible suspect."

"And then she says she more or less randomly selected Debbie Chan."

"I cannot speak for her thought process or motivation," said Sara. "But she chose Debbie, she stuck by her decision, and she testified under oath."

"And do you want to know the kicker?" asked Riggs. "LaShante Valentine says that of all the people she's seen recently, this mystery woman at Brown's looks quite a bit like *you!*"

"Me?" replied Sara with an incredulous laugh. "That's crazy. Well, unfortunately, it makes our star witness seem highly untrustworthy."

"Yes, it does," nodded Riggs. "Brooks and her team are filing a brief with the Court of Criminal Appeals. The attorney from the Criminal Appeals Division of the Office of the Attorney General will respond. You will be called to testify. But I want you to know something."

Sara held her breath and then managed to say, "Yes?"

"The Police Department is standing behind you one hundred percent. We will not tolerate a wanton and baseless attack on one of our detectives. I'm sure your questioning of LaShante Valentine was professional and proper."

"Thank you, sir," said Sara. "What if the appeals court throws out the conviction?"

Riggs shrugged. "The decision to retry will be made by Jill Simmons and her office. It's out of our hands. We're cops. We investigate and arrest. We do our very best and then we move on. That will be all, detective."

With a huge sense of relief, Sara returned to her desk.

"I see you still have your head on your shoulders," said Jake. "I'm heading out for the night. Before I go, I have a number for you. A woman called, said she has information about the Jerome Johnson case." As he stood up, he handed her a slip

EVEN STEVEN

of paper. "See you tomorrow."

Sara took the paper. *Tiffany Oliver*. It was late, but Sara picked up her phone and dialed. A woman answered. Sara identified herself.

"Who is this?" the woman replied in an agitated voice.

Sara repeated herself.

"We don't want none," the woman said. "Why are you calling here?"

Sara heard a man's voice in the background. The woman shushed him and then said into the phone, "Like I said, we don't need no insurance. Okay?"

Sara made a calculated guess. "Listen, Tiffany. If you can leave your house and meet me somewhere, tell me to 'get lost'."

"Get lost, bitch."

"The McDonald's on Rosa Parks Boulevard. I'll be there in fifteen minutes. Black jacket, black slacks. Eating a Happy Meal. Sitting alone. I hope to see you."

Without waiting for an answer, she hung up.

The McDonald's was not busy. Sara went up to the counter and ordered a Happy Meal—a hamburger with kid-sized fries, apple slices, and a Dasani water, all packed in the distinctive red box. The toy was a miniature Squishmallow—specifically, an emerald-green pickle guy. Sara looked at the tiny figure with bewilderment.

Sitting alone at a table, with the red box in full view, she checked her watch. It had been seventeen minutes since the phone call. A few people had come into the store, but none who seemed to qualify as Tiffany.

Twenty minutes. Sara was losing hope. Suddenly, through the door came a young woman. She seemed nervous. Wearing sunglasses, she paused and looked around. She approached Sara's table.

"What's your name?" the woman asked.

"Sara Durant. We spoke on the phone."

The woman sat down.

"You must be Tiffany," said Sara. "You made up an excuse to leave the house."

Tiffany nodded. "Dwight thinks I'm at my sister's, helping with the baby."

"Is there anything you want to tell me?"

Tiffany removed her sunglasses. Her left eye was bruised and swollen.

"Dwight did this?" asked Sara.

She nodded. "He tried to kill Harvey. Something about missing drugs. Says he's going to try again, unless Harvey comes after him first. They hate each other."

"What about Jerome Johnson?"

Tiffany shook her head. "I feel sorry for his family. He didn't do nothing to nobody. He was just walking down the wrong street at the wrong time."

EVEN STEVEN

"Tell me more about Dwight. What's his last name? Does he work?"

"It's Dwight Downey. He works as an Uber driver. It's his cover. He's really just a mule for a gang."

"Which gang?"

Tiffany looked around and then leaned forward to whisper, "Silver Saviors."

"Okay," said Sara. "So, the gang wanted Harvey Gibson popped?"

Tiffany nodded. "They say he stole their dope. If Dwight helps, they might let him join."

"And how about you? Do you want to get away from Dwight?"

"Yes. You see, I'm pregnant. Dwight doesn't know it."

"Is the baby his?"

Tiffany bit her lip and shook her head, "No."

"Okay. I want you to call The Hope Center. They assist women just like you to escape abusive relationships and start a new life. Put this number in your phone. Give it some other name in case Dwight sees it. But call them. You deserve to be safe from abuse. And don't worry about being identified with us. The Metropolitan Nashville Police Department Gang Unit will be taking over this investigation. You will not be involved. Okay?"

Tiffany nodded. "Thank you," she said. She stood up and walked out the door.

EVEN STEVEN

I hope she makes it, Sara thought to herself.

Just then, her phone buzzed. She picked up.

"Yes, Captain Riggs?"

"Get over to Second Avenue South, near Dudley Park. Multiple victims of a possible drug overdose. Assist the Specialized Investigations Division. Commander Buckley is already there."

"Yes, sir. On my way now."

Sara arrived at modest two-story brick house with police and first responder vehicles crowding the street in front.

"Detective Durant," she said to a uniformed officer guarding the perimeter. "I'm looking for Commander Buckley."

"He's inside," nodded the cop.

She made her way through the small army of cops and paramedics to the front door.

"Coming out!" said a voice from within. Sara stepped back. Through the door came a gurney handled by two paramedics. Strapped on was a young woman who lay with her eyes closed. A paramedic held up a plasma bag. They rolled the patient to the open doors of an ambulance and quickly shoved her inside and slammed the doors. With siren wailing, the truck sped away.

Sara entered the house and found herself in a shabby living room. Through the crowd of people, she saw Commander Buckley. She approached him. He was talking to another detective—someone she knew from the narcotics squad.

EVEN STEVEN

Then Buckley turned to her.

"Detective Durant, I need you to interview a witness. She's upstairs in a bedroom. Her name is Karen something."

"Fatalities here, sir?"

"Yes—four. And at least a dozen overdoses. Now go."

Sara hurried up the stairs to the second floor, where there were three bedrooms and a small bathroom. Sitting on a bed in one of the bedrooms was a young woman. Standing next to her was a female uniformed cop.

"Are you Karen?" asked Sara.

"Yes," she nodded.

"What's your last name? How old are you?"

"Andrews. Karen Andrews. I'm eighteen."

"What happened here?"

Karen turned her red-rimmed eyes to Sara. With a sniffle she said, "Just partying. Having fun." She pushed a strand of hair away from her face.

"How did you get here?"

"Liam brought me here."

"Is he your boyfriend?"

Karen nodded.

"Where is Liam now?"

Karen fought back tears. "I don't know. The ambulance took him away."

"Liam Wright was one of the victims who did not survive," said the uniformed cop.

"Okay," said Sara softly. "Karen, were you taking drugs?"

She shook her head. "No. I hate that stuff. I just had a beer. But everyone else was doing it."

"How many kids?"

"Maybe a dozen. Or twenty. People were coming and going."

"What drugs?"

"Apache. Fent. TNT. Krok, mostly." She gripped her fingers nervously.

"Fentanyl and fentanyl derivatives," nodded Sara. "But many of the kids got sick?"

"Yes."

"Who provided the drugs?"

Karen looked down at the floor.

"Karen, whoever gave the drugs to Liam and everyone else here is guilty of murder. That person needs to be arrested and convicted. Don't you want to stop him from doing the same thing to other people?"

"His name is Tango."

"Where can we find Tango?"

EVEN STEVEN

"I don't know. Two of the guys went to see him."

"Which guys? Who made the arrangements?"

"It was Alex Monata. He collected everyone's money and made the call. Then he and another guy went to see Tango."

The uniformed cop interjected, "Alex Monata was taken to the hospital."

Fifteen minutes later, Sara walked purposefully into room 328 of Nashville General Hospital. She was followed by two cops. In the room were two beds. One contained an old man with a grey beard. His leg was in a cast. The other was for a young man with ragged brown hair and high cheekbones that gave him a rakish look. No wonder the girls liked him. He was on an IV drip.

"Alex Monata, my name is Detective Sara Durant. You're in very serious trouble. Do you know that?"

"Huh? What?" His heavy eyelids fluttered open.

"You killed three people. I'm placing you under arrest for second-degree murder for causing death by the sale or distribution of illegal drugs."

One of the cops took his wrist and handcuffed it to the bed rail.

"Hey, you can't do that!" he protested.

"Yes, we can and we just did,' said Sara. "That fentanyl you bought from Tango and handed out like candy at the party was cut with xylazine—you call it 'tranq'—and other deadly stuff. It was poison, Alex. And you were responsible for procuring it and distributing it. You're going away for a long time, my friend."

"But wait—I didn't know! I'm just as sick as the rest of them!"

"You're a lot healthier than George Wasatch, Susan Tuck, and Dell Lowery. They're dead, Alex. They're never coming back. You can think about them as you rot in prison."

Monata sank back onto his pillow. He stared at the ceiling. The corners of his mouth quivered.

Sara leaned closer. "But if you do the right thing, we may reduce the charges. You help us and we help you."

"What do you want me to do?"

Sara reached for his phone, which was in the bag of personal effects hanging by the side of the bed, and handed it to him.

"Open it."

He obligingly tapped his finger on the button to unlock it, and the phone lit up.

"Give it to me," said Sara. She scrolled to his recent calls. "Which number is it?"

He told her, and she put it into her own phone. Then she handed the phone back to him. "Call Tango. Tell him you need more stuff. Tell him you're sending a hot trick to pick it up. She'll be driving a Mustang Dark Horse. Name is Sara."

"I don't know if I can do this," said Monata. "He's a rough character."

EVEN STEVEN

"It's your only good option."

Tentatively, Monata tapped the phone.

"Hey, Tango. Wassup? That shit you dropped on me was drippin.' Yeah, peeps loved it. Listen, can you repeat the order? Same thing. Can you do it now? Cool. And get this—a smokin' hot trick is going to pick it up. Driving a Mustang Dark Horse. Her name is Sara. Where you at? Same place? Okay. Fifteen minutes. Thank you. Later."

She took his phone. "I'll keep this for security. Where do I go? What's the price?"

"696 Craighead Avenue. Black mailbox out front by the street, with a red bird on top, like a cardinal. Go to the side door by the carport. Five bucks a pill. I bought fifty of them."

Sara was amazed. Just 250 bucks to deliver death to a bunch of kids having a party. She left the room and called Special Operations and requested a fake Amazon truck to station itself on Craighead Ave as she went inside.

The house was in a row of unremarkable dwellings on the street: plain brick, one story, small brown lawn in front, a couple of bushes. She recalled to herself, *black mailbox with red cardinal on top. Car port on the side of the house.*

In the 1950s, the area was a suburban development, with nearly identical houses standing shoulder to shoulder. Since then, the interstate highway had virtually encircled it on the south and west sides, and Nashville International Airport, with its main runway ending just a thousand feet to the south, regularly sent big jets screaming over its rooftops.

EVEN STEVEN

Sara parked her Mustang in the short driveway. The Amazon truck was three doors down, facing her. The driver—a narcotics cop—pretended to fuss with a package.

The house seemed quiet. A nondescript Nissan sedan with Florida plates was parked in the carport. She approached the side door. It was an aluminum storm door, with the main door just inside. She pressed the bell. From inside came a musical chime. Footsteps. A man's face appeared in the window of the main door. The door opened. He was over six feet tall, built solid but flabby. Tattoos and piercings. Wearing a nylon track suit, blue with a silver stripe down each side.

"Tango," said Sara. She pulled open the storm door.

"Who are you?" he asked as his round eyes ran up and down her body.

"Sara. Looking for a refill."

Tango gave her a charming smile. "My man said you were hot. He wasn't kidding." He stepped back from the door, allowing her to step up into the kitchen. It was small and dirty, with dishes piled in the sink and the smell of vanilla air freshener mixed with rotting garbage.

"I could show you a good time," said Tango. He took a sip from the can of Colt 45 malt liquor in his hand and then wiped his mouth.

"I'm sure you could. Business first. Let's see what you've got."

Tango put the can on the stained Formica table. From the pocket of his track suit, he pulled out a plastic baggie full of

EVEN STEVEN

pills. "Got it right here, little lady."

Sara reached into her pocket and took out a wad of cash. She went to the table and counted out twelve twenties and one ten-dollar bill.

"Two-fifty," she said as she stepped away. She held out her hand. Tango took the cash with one hand and gave her the bag with the other.

"You ain't going to count them?" he said.

"You counted them, right?"

"Sure."

She looked him in the eye. "Then we're good. It was nice doing business with you."

"You ain't gonna stay? Like I said, I could show you a good time."

At that moment a young, emaciated woman entered the kitchen. To Sara, she looked strung out. She peered at Sara.

"Who is she?" the woman said to Tango in an accusatory tone.

"None of your damn business," he snapped. "What do you want in here?"

"Just some juice from the refrigerator."

"Well then get your damn juice and go back to the other room."

The woman, with an attitude of meek defiance, took the

carton of orange juice from the refrigerator and, with a dirty look at Sara, left the kitchen.

Tango watched her leave and then turned his attention to Sara.

"So, what do you say?"

Sara smiled. "Why do they call you Tango?"

"Stay a while and you can find out."

"I'm sure I would," she said as she pulled out her phone. "Maybe I should get to know you better. But first I need to make a quick call to my friends. They want to hear the good news."

Tango frowned but said nothing.

Sara tapped a number. Then she said, "Mission accomplished." She ended the call and put the phone in her pocket.

Tango sidled over to the kitchen window, which faced the street. The Amazon truck came into view.

He whirled around. "You're a damn cop!" he spat. With the agility of a wolf, he dashed to the door, knocking Sara off balance. He ran outside. Sara got to her feet. Tango got into the Nissan and gunned the engine. But Sara's Mustang was blocking the driveway. No matter—Tango floored the Nissan and spun the wheel, careening off the driveway and onto the lawn. The car slipped and slid its way in an arc around the Mustang, mud flying from behind spinning wheels.

EVEN STEVEN

Sara ran to her own car. From the Amazon truck, three undercover officers emerged, guns drawn. Sara slammed the Mustang into reverse. Too late—the Nissan had already skidded across the suburban sidewalk and landed with a *thunk* on the pavement. With wheels burning rubber, Tango rocketed the car down Craighead Ave to the sharp left onto Hampton Drive.

Sara careened onto the street, delivering a glancing blow to the black mailbox with the red cardinal and sending it, shattered, down along the sidewalk. She slammed on the brakes and her car jolted to a stop. Then into gear, and with engine screaming and tires smoking, she accelerated in pursuit of the Nissan.

Passing the Amazon truck and the three officers scrambling to get back inside, she saw Tango take a sharp left onto Elm Hill Pike, narrowly missing a kid crossing the street. With no time to use her phone and with no police radio in her personal vehicle, she depended on the Amazon officers to call in the details.

Tango accelerated east on Elm Hill Pike, narrowly skirting a city bus full of passengers. He sped under the Briley Parkway underpass only to suddenly pull a screeching U-turn and head back in a westerly direction. Sara jolted her Mustang over the median and, passing a cement truck within inches, sprinted up to the Nissan's bumper. But a reckless, desperate driver can make a mediocre car overperform, and once he had merged onto the northbound Briley Parkway traffic, Tango began weaving and slipping his way through traffic. Sara kept on his tail, not crowding him, but keeping him close.

At I-40 the chase was joined by a Nashville police cruiser.

EVEN STEVEN

Where the highway ran parallel to the Cumberland River, Tango pushed up his speed along the half-mile straightaway. Seventy miles per hour... eighty... ninety... one hundred. The Mustang and the police cruiser kept pace as they flew by slower traffic. At the old Wave Country water park, the highway arced to the left. Sara watched in horror as the Nissan rocketed up the exit ramp for the Two Rivers Parkway and hurtled straight through the red light. Instead of continuing down the entrance ramp to return to the Briley Parkway, Tango drifted onto the soft shoulder, weaved and wobbled, slowed, lurched to the left and right, and suddenly became airborne. It flew off the ramp and landed on the fairway of the Two Rivers Golf Course. Somehow, the car remained upright and plowed across the fresh turf, grinding to a muddy halt halfway submerged in a water hazard.

Sara pulled over and ran across the fairway to the battered Nissan. Followed by a uniformed cop, she reached the car and waded into the muck of the pond. She reached the driver's door and yanked it open.

"Okay, okay, I give up," muttered Tango with his hands raised.

25

The next day, having sustained only cuts and bruises, Tango was released from the hospital into the custody of the police. Bail had been denied. Sara visited him at the Downtown Detention Center.

"Let's see," she said as she read his rap sheet. "Your name is Jamal Franklin. Age twenty-six. Born in Gainesville, Florida. High school education. Played varsity football, in fact. Bunch of misdemeanor charges, with one conviction in Florida for assault. One month in jail and fined five hundred dollars. Lately, you've been commuting back and forth between Florida and Tennessee. I wonder why? No, don't tell me. Visiting your elderly grandmother, I suppose. Well, Jamal, you've graduated to the big leagues. Three counts of felony murder. Felony distribution of a Schedule 1 drug. You're looking at some hard time if you keep your mouth shut, so now it's your choice. Which will it be, Jamal?"

Franklin and his lawyer conferred.

The lawyer said, "Mr. Franklin is ready to cooperate."

"Good. Who is your supplier?"

After some hesitation and nervous glances, Franklin said, "His name is Henry Grey."

Sara typed the name into her laptop. In a moment, she had her results.

"Mr. Grey is well known to law enforcement!" she said.

Thirty-six. Born and raised in Nashville. A couple of minor offenses— petty crimes. Accused five years ago of drugging a runaway girl and having his way with her. He dumped her body at a construction site where his company was working. Destiny Troyce. He was arrested for the crime and tried. Despite compelling evidence, he was acquitted thanks to a scandal in the State Forensic Services Division in which a lab employee manipulated or omitted DNA test results of dozens of cases, including Grey's. Because of double jeopardy, the state couldn't try him again. Since then, he's been suspected of running a major drug operation, buying powdered fentanyl and fentanyl precursors from sources in China, Mexico, the southwestern United States, and India.

"In short, he's a massive drug dealer who cuts and otherwise adulterates product and sells it through a network of dealers." She looked at Franklin. "And you are one of those dealers."

Franklin nodded.

"Is it true that Mr. Grey lives on a houseboat on Norris Lake?" asked Sara.

"Yeah," said Franklin. "Near the town of Rocky Top."

"Where the hell is Rocky Top?"

"Used to be called Lake City," replied the lawyer. "A nice, quiet little town. About a mile west of the Norris Dam. Known for large striped bass angling. Then a big developer wanted to build a water park there for one hundred million dollars, but only on the condition that Lake City be renamed

EVEN STEVEN

Rocky Top. The city council voted to change the name, at considerable expense to the town, but the water park was never built. The name remains Rocky Top to this day."

"That's the stupidest story I've ever heard," said Sara. "Okay, what can you tell me about Henry Grey? Personal habits, his organization."

"Very lean organization," said Franklin. "He runs it like a nine-to-five business. Very disciplined. If you use drugs, you're out. Nobody swears. He doesn't even like tattoos. The operations are conducted out of an old shoemaking factory on Railroad Avenue. Just a few blocks from I-65—and as you know, once you're on I-65, in less than a day, you can be anywhere from New Orleans to Chicago. As for the houseboat, it's plenty big, with a couple of staterooms, a dining room, entertainment room, full kitchen. It's more luxurious than most regular houses. He moves it around once in a while, but he usually keeps it at Cove Creek Marina, right next to Norris Dam, about a ten-minute drive from the factory."

"Where do the sales take place?"

"In the back room of Super Health Supplements on North Main Street. They actually sell supplements—vitamins and protein bars—but it's just a front for the drug business. It's ninety percent mail order. Only a few of the biggest buyers ever see the factory or the houseboat."

"You say Henry Grey has no vices," said Sara. "Is he some kind of choir boy?"

"Oh no, not at all," said Franklin. "He collects expensive bottles of wine. The houseboat—which is named the

Diamond Cutter, by the way—has a walk-in wine cooler. One day, he showed me a bottle—I think it was a Chateau something—and told me it cost fifty thousand dollars. He has dinner parties for his friends, and they have all these different wines."

"Like a wine tasting," said Sara. "What else?"

"He likes women. Always has a few around. I don't know where he gets them. I've only been aboard the boat a few times and not for very long, but I've always seen women sitting around or lying on lounge chairs on the upper deck."

"Wine and women, huh. All right, Mr. Franklin, you've been very helpful," said Sara. "We'll be in touch."

Sara went to her office and wrote up her operation plan to travel undercover and meet Henry Grey, arrange a buy, and gather evidence for prosecution. There were various expenses—car rental, cash for drugs, food and lodging. And there needed to be a police escort for Franklin, if he were needed to personally make the introduction. All of this had to be reviewed and approved by Captain Riggs. Then the arrest would be executed, and eventually a trial.

As she was typing, she paused. Perhaps there could be a simpler, more direct way of dealing with Mr. Grey. Off the books, so to speak. After all, this scumbag had already skated on one set of serious charges, the rape and murder of Destiny Troyce. And now, even with three dead kids thanks to his poisoned fentanyl, a miscarriage of justice could very well happen again. This was just the kind of dirtball that Even Steven would eliminate, she thought.

She had claimed the mantle of Even Steven when she had

EVEN STEVEN

killed Logan Silva, and the ruse seemed to have worked, except that Debbie Chan had become collateral damage. Luckily, she had been released due to Sara's transgression in evidence collecting when she was the lead investigator, but the warning signs were there—Sara had to be more careful.

And how about her partner, Jake? He had been put in charge of the Silva murder investigation while Sara had been shunted over to the Jerome Johnson case. He was like a loyal hound, but he was a good investigator. With the Debbie Chan conviction heading toward a reversal, the Silva case would remain open. Sara had been very careful about not leaving evidence, but it would be a good idea to keep an eye on Jake.

Sara decided to handle Henry Grey herself. On her on her own time. To avoid conflict with her job as a cop, she had a week's worth of personal days she could take off. Normally, if you valued your upward career trajectory in the police department, you didn't use your personal days unless you really had to, like if there were death in the family. You had to always give the impression to your colleagues and superiors that your job with the department was your number one priority.

This was a choice she was prepared to make.

She tore up her operation plan.

But what about Tango? She didn't need him. She knew enough about Henry Grey to take him herself.

EVEN STEVEN

The next day, she drove to Black Creek Marina, on the main branch of Norris Lake, ten miles east of the dam and Rocky Top. Norris Lake itself was simply a flooded river valley, stretching over 200 miles in its twisting length up the Clinch River, but never more than a mile wide. The dam was at the far western end, adjacent to the city of Rocky Top.

At the marina she rented a small but luxurious Reina houseboat. Just twenty-six feet long, the *Margarita* was built for comfort and style and would mark her as a person of means. She piloted her little floating hotel along the winding curves of the long, narrow lake until the Cove Creek Marina came into view. Scanning the assembled vessels, mostly houseboats, outboard fishing boats, and waterskiing craft, she located the biggest of them; and easing closer, she saw the name *Diamond Cutter* emblazoned across the square stern. Just as Tango had said, it was an impressive boat for a relatively small lake—and not bad, she thought, as a permanent floating home. Low maintenance, easy security, and you could always move it around to any one of the other marinas dotting the hundreds of miles of Norris Lake shoreline.

The summer season was months away, so she easily found a space to tie up *Margarita* less than fifty yards from the *Diamond Cutter*. On a parallel dock projecting out into the lake, she gained a full view of Grey's boat separated only by one-hundred yards of cold, dark water. Measuring eighty feet in length, the *Diamond Cutter* had been built in the customary shape of a functional, spacious box. Sara went online and pulled up the typical floor plan of a big houseboat. There were three levels—the flat roof deck, which was partially covered by a hard-shell canopy, the main living level, and then a lower living level within the hull.

EVEN STEVEN

On the main living level, the "front porch"—what other boaters call the bow—was a flat, covered, open-air space with deck furniture. Entering the long cabin, you first came to the main living room area, which included the pilot's wheel and controls. Then you entered the kitchen/dining room space. Proceeding aft, you entered a hallway with a bedroom opposite a bathroom and then a ladder to the lower level, in the hull, with more bedrooms and a bath. At the stern would be the luxurious master bedroom and bath, with its private deck on the "back porch."

There were also two ladders, fore and aft, leading to the upper deck, which was just a big open space with a bar and chaise lounges, shielded by a metal roof. That was the basic layout—what Henry Grey had in his houseboat she couldn't be certain.

She pulled up a deck chair, got comfortable, and started her surveillance of the *Diamond Cutter*.

It was about noontime. She watched as two crewmembers, dressed in hatching blue jeans and white sweatshirts, went about their business maintaining the vessel. Washing the decks, polishing brightwork, touching up the paint. Occasionally another crewmember, whom Sara eventually surmised was the cook, would appear on deck. There was a housekeeper, too, wearing a grey knee-length tunic dress and white blouse.

The afternoon wore on as the languid pace continued. There was no sign of Henry Grey. Having seen enough, Sara got up and decided to take a walk. She put on a pair of big sunglasses and black puffy jacket and set out along the dock.

EVEN STEVEN

She casually strolled to the head of the dock and then walked the short distance to the next dock, on which the *Diamond Cutter* was tied up. Glancing up, she saw the usual security cameras used by every marina. One was pointing at her. The other was directed along the dock, at the boats. She made a mental note that this camera saw the sides of the boats facing the dock but was blind to the sides of the boats facing the water.

At the head of the *Diamond Cutter* dock, she encountered a young man sitting in a folding chair. A quick glance told her he was packing a handgun in his belt under his shirt. None of the other docks featured an armed guard.

She gave him a big sexy smile. "Nice day, isn't it? A tad chilly."

The man looked at her and grunted a vaguely positive response but made no effort to stop her. She strolled slowly down the clanky aluminum dock, casually glancing, like a tourist, at the houseboats tied up. On some of them were people, and she exchanged friendly greetings with them.

At length, she finally came to the *Diamond Cutter*, the last vessel on the dock and the largest. The two deckhands in their jeans and sweatshirts were cleaning the big main deck windows. Inside the cabin, at the wheel behind the front window, stood a man she hadn't seen before. He looked up and saw her and came out through the door onto the spacious front porch with its polished mahogany bar and sleek upholstered chairs and sofas. Like the man at the head of the dock, he wore a sidearm. He stood and stared at her.

She gave him a broad smile. "Lovely day today," she drawled in her best honey voice.

EVEN STEVEN

The man made no reply. She continued to walk at a slow pace alongside the gleaming cabin of the *Diamond Cutter*, occasionally casting a discreet look into the big rectangular windows, seeing only her own reflection against the dark glass. She came to the last set of windows that she assumed belonged to the master stateroom, and the curtains were drawn.

She went to the end of the dock and pretended to gaze out over the shimmering blue water. Hearing no footsteps behind her, she turned around. The man with the gun was standing on the top deck, looking down at her. Without acknowledging him, Sara retraced her path down the dock alongside the *Diamond Cutter*. The man with the gun moved discreetly along with her.

To her relief, she saw no cameras mounted on the boat. Clearly, Henry Grey preferred old-school human intelligence. She passed the man sitting at the end of the dock and strolled back to her temporary home on the water. The guards may have been watching her, but if they were, it didn't matter. The air was chill and damp with an errant flurry drifting every now and then through the sky. Perched on the dock next to her boat, she took out a submersible thermometer from her pocket and lowered it into the dark water. After a moment, she brought it up. Forty degrees. With a shrug, she stowed the thermometer and went into the kitchen to prepare an early dinner.

26

At 7:00 p.m., Sara noticed activity aboard the *Diamond Cutter*. She went to the railing. Lights were on now, and a man was walking purposefully on the top deck, a wine glass in his hand. Wearing a crisp white dress shirt and black slacks, he matched the photos of Henry Grey. There were other people there too—a half-dozen men and twice as many women. A heater glowed bright orange. Music started—*thump, thump, thump*. Disco and house. Dancing started. As the air became increasingly colder, the group descended to the main deck. Lights flickered warmly from within as people moved around like shadows in a dream. *Thump, thump, thump* continued the music. Occasionally, someone, or a couple, would come outside on the front porch, and Sara could see the red pinpoint of a cigarette or joint being lit. And all the while, a tough-looking man stood on the dock, arms folded, with his back to the boat.

The party continued until 11:00 p.m., when the guests began to drift away. *Of course*, thought Sara, *it's a work night for these people*. By 11:30 p.m., the boat was seemingly deserted save for a few lights in the windows. Under the streetlight at the head of the dock, the guard sat in his chair. *Good*, thought Sara. *You're creating the false sense of security I need.*

EVEN STEVEN

After changing into a black thermal legless wetsuit, she loaded a watertight backpack with a small tank of nitrous oxide and an inflatable life preserver, along with a combat knife and a Walther PDP compact 9mm pistol in case the operation went south. But Sara was ambitious: she didn't want to just *kill* Grey, which would have been child's play. She wanted him to know *why* he was being killed.

With her backpack slung on her shoulders, she went to the ladder on the back porch of her boat. Across the black water, the *Diamond Cutter* was dark except for the forward living area. Through the window, Sara could see a guard sitting with the blue light from a TV screen flickering across his face.

Now was the time to strike.

Inch by inch, she slowly lowered herself into the mirror-smooth, icy water. Her slightest movement sent ripples radiating outward. Releasing her hold on the cold aluminum ladder rail, she slowly and patiently began the swim to the *Diamond Cutter*. With her breath frosty in the cold air, she worked steadily and noiselessly.

She was not more than halfway across when she heard the sound of an outboard motor from out in the lake. Twisting around, she saw an inflatable dinghy, with its bow wake curling white. As she watched, it suddenly turned and began heading directly for her. *Damn!* There was no time to go back. The boat, with its small but deadly propellor, was no more than twenty yards away and closing in fast. She saw the dark silhouettes of two people on board. To save her life, timing was everything. She waited until the dingy was no more than five seconds from impact and then forced herself under water, using her arms and legs to backpaddle straight down. Deeper and deeper she went into the frigid darkness. The corkscrew sound of the propellor came closer, closer, until it was directly over her head. She felt the turbulence of its backwash as the dinghy passed over and continued toward the shore. Slowly, she ascended until her head broke the surface. Turning around, treading water, she saw the dinghy pull up to the dock, and the two people, illuminated by the streetlight, stand up in the swirling snow. One stepped onto the dock with a line to tie to the cleat.

Back to business. In her operational plan, she hadn't planned on getting her head wet by submersion because that's how she would lose the most body heat the most quickly. No matter—it was too late to turn back. She resumed her slow and stealthy swim to the *Diamond Cutter*. In another minute, she had reached the aluminum ladder to the back porch. She grasped the railing and paused to listen in the dark.

From overhead, she heard the *clunk, clunk* of footsteps. Someone was on the upper deck. A flashlight scanned the back porch. She sank back into the dark water, counted to ten, then cautiously came to the surface and listened. The footsteps receded. All was quiet except for the faint lapping of water against the metal hull and the barely perceptible patter of falling flakes.

She raised herself halfway up the ladder as the cold water streamed from her body. All was quiet. She carefully stepped onto the rough-textured deck. Her wetsuit made squishy sounds as she pressed water from it. Satisfied, she went to the door leading inside. She carefully tried the door handle. It moved, then clicked softly. She pushed it open and stood in the doorway. Her eyes adjusted to the gloom. She saw she had entered a carpeted lounge with plush chairs and a built-in bar. To the left, a narrow corridor led forward. Directly in front of her, a richly paneled bulkhead door. She crossed the lounge and tried the handle of the door. It clicked open, and she slowly, carefully pushed it.

She looked into the master stateroom. A king-sized bed dominated the space with a dresser, a small bedside table, a chair, and small sofa. A man lay on the bed, on his side. He was breathing slowly and loudly. An inch at a time, Sara crept her way to the side of the bed and peered at his face. Yes, this was Henry Grey, and he was alone.

Sara put her backpack on the floor. Carefully, she opened it and removed the small canister of nitrous oxide. Attached to it was a nose piece. She turned the valve of the canister and held the nosepiece against her cheek and felt the cool, slightly sweet-smelling gas escaping. She then leaned forward and held the nose piece an inch from Grey's nostrils.

She waited.

Grey groaned slightly and moved his head. Sara withdrew the nose piece until he had settled again. Then she held it up, hovering just above his nostrils. Twenty seconds passed. According to protocol, the gas should be affecting his brain. She held it in place for a full two minutes. If Henry Grey were in a dentist's chair, he'd be ready for the drill.

It was time to risk everything.

Sara gently put the nosepiece directly on his face and stretched the elastic strap around the back of his head. He groaned, and his eyes fluttered open.

"Wasss goin' on?" he mumbled.

EVEN STEVEN

"Just relax and enjoy the dream," she cooed.

"Dream?" he said. "Who are you?"

"An angel."

He moved his eyes in her direction. "From heaven?"

"Yes, from heaven. And you're going on a little adventure. Sit up."

She helped him sit up in bed. Hastily she strapped him into the inflatable life preserver. Then she put one of his beefy arms over her shoulder and maneuvered him to the edge of the bed.

Suddenly, from overhead she heard the sound of footsteps. The guard was making his rounds. She held Grey upright so he wouldn't topple over. His hand went to the elastic strap and fumbled with it. Gently, she pulled his hand away.

"Now sweetheart, just relax," she whispered. "Be a good boy."

The footsteps went to the very stern of the boat and then back over their heads toward the bow. In a moment, silence had returned.

She hoisted him to his feet. He was wearing nothing but a T-shirt and boxer shorts. Half-carrying him, she guided him to the stateroom door and through the lounge. Then she opened the door to the outside.

"It's going to feel cold, but you won't care," she reassured him. "Okay? You won't care."

They went out onto the back porch. Snow flicked at her face.

EVEN STEVEN

She maneuvered him to the ladder.

"You're going to take a cold bath," she said. "But you won't care."

She sat him down on the gunwale with his legs over the side. Grasping the life preserver CO_2 cartridge, she broke the seal and activated it, and the vest instantly inflated.

"Okay, here we go," she said as she lowered him by the scruff of his neck into the icy water.

Instantly, he stiffened and began to thrash his arms and legs. "Ahhhhh," he moaned.

She slid into the lake next to him. "It's all right," she said. "Feel the cold. It doesn't matter. Just ignore it."

She took Grey by the back of the neck and, with him lying on his back, began to swim to the *Margarita*. He began to thrash again and tore the nitrous oxide mask off his face. It dangled from the tank, bubbling in the water. She couldn't stop to fix it. She knew that she had a scant five minutes left before the effects of the gas wore off and Grey would be fully conscious.

Redoubling her efforts, unmindful of the sound of splashing, she quickly reached the ladder of the *Margarita*. Holding onto the preserver, she scrambled to the deck and then turned around to face the water. He was floating with his back to the boat. Taking him by the shoulders, with every ounce of her strength, she hauled him halfway out of the water. He twisted and fell back, but again, she mustered all her energy and, with one superhuman effort, hoisted him out of the water and onto the deck. She collapsed with exhaustion, but now was no time to relax. She roused herself, got him to his feet, and led him through the door into the warmth of the rear stateroom.

"Let's get you in a nice chair," she said.

Clumsily, he sat down in an armchair. "What's going on?" he muttered with irritation. "What are you doing?"

Deftly, she zip-tied his wrists and ankles to the chair and then tied a gag to his mouth. After removing the life vest and turning off the valve to the nitrous oxide tank, she stepped back, breathing hard.

Mission accomplished! But now he was fully awake and fully enraged, eyes blazing, struggling in the chair. Ignoring him, she shed her wetsuit and, without covering her naked body from his fierce gaze, toweled herself dry before dressing in jeans and a sweatshirt. Then she used the towel to dry his head.

"Shhh," she said. "Stop struggling. It will do you no good. This houseboat is soundproof. It's built so people can play loud music inside without pissing off all the people in the other houseboats parked nearby. Isn't that considerate? I'm going to remove your gag now. You can scream and yell all you want, but no one will hear you."

She took off the gag.

"You *stupidfuckingbitch*, what the hell do you think you're doing?" he sneered.

"Ah—the anger phase," she said as she pulled up a chair and sat facing him. "Just what I expected, Mr. Grey. Please allow me to introduce myself. I'm Even Steven. Does the name ring a bell?"

EVEN STEVEN

The blood drained from his face. "Yes," he said.

Sara smiled. "I'm glad that my reputation precedes me. It makes me feel like an important person."

"But you're a *woman*."

"Hear me roar," she said slowly, giving each word its proper weight. "With power too big to ignore."

"What do you want from me?" asked Grey. "Drugs? Money?"

"Ah—now we've entered the bargaining phase. You're making progress. No, I don't want drugs or money. I want to reach a level of understanding with you."

"What the fuck are you talking about?" He strained against the zip ties, which began to cut into his skin.

"Oh, so we're back to anger," she said in a disappointed tone. "I thought we were making progress. Oh, well. Let's get down to business. We'll begin with Destiny Troyce. Do you remember her? She was a runaway girl, young and vulnerable. You raped her and drugged her. She died of an overdose. You dumped her body at a construction site your company was working at."

"I was acquitted," he said through his teeth.

"Only because some idiot at the state crime lab mishandled evidence. But you know you did it and you walked away. Let's move on to the present day. Here are four more names: Liam Wright, George Wasatch, Susan Tuck, and Dell Lowery. You don't know who they are, but I do. They are four dead kids in Nashville. They're dead because you sold them adulterated fentanyl. Your product killed them."

"Listen, I don't know those people," said Grey. "I'm not responsible."

"Oh, so now we're back to bargaining," nodded Sara. "Mr. Grey, it's not going to work. You're selling death. It's as simple as that. These poor kids just wanted to party and get high. Maybe not the best idea in the world, but they shouldn't have to pay for it with their lives."

"Do you expect me to apologize?"

"No, Mr. Grey, I expect you to die." She glanced at the clock. "Your time has come."

With those words, she stood up. Taking the canister of nitrous oxide and the mask, she went around behind Grey. "I'm going to make it very easy for you," she said. Holding his head firmly with one arm, she snapped the mask over his nose. While he writhed in vain, she then took a roll of duct tape, tore off a piece, and sealed his lips. "We don't want you cheating by breathing through your mouth," she said.

As the gas took effect, his strenuous resistance faded. His muscles began to relax, and his eyes lost their fire. Sara sat in her chair and regarded him. He seemed smaller now, almost pathetic. She thought about the armed men who were paid to guard him, the people who worked in his drug lab and the distribution center at the supplements store, and the networks of petty dealers like Jamal Franklin who sold the stuff to unsuspecting kids. Henry Grey, who could be mistaken for an insurance executive, had built this drug machine and reaped the rich rewards—money, boats, cars, fine wines, hot girls.

EVEN STEVEN

And now, he sat in front of her, bound like a steer at auction, dazed and foggy from the gas, pliable and docile.

"Mr. Grey, can you hear me?" she asked.

His eyes met hers. He nodded.

She held up an ordinary plastic prescription bottle and gave it a little shake. The pills inside rattled. "Do you know what these are?"

From side to side went his head.

"No? I'll tell you. They're what's left of the product you sold to Jamal Franklin. The kids who died took only two or three of these. The ones who got very sick took just one. These pills contain fentanyl, heroin, xylazine, aminopyrine, talc, and other poisonous stuff we cannot even identify. They were made at your factory on Railroad Avenue and sold from Super Health Supplements on North Main Street. Do you know what I'm thinking?"

Again, he shook his head.

"There's an old saying in the dope trade: 'Never get high on your own supply'. Very apropos, I'd say. But I think you should break the rules. Just this once. You should have the opportunity to experience the high life too. It's only fair, isn't it? After all, they trusted what Jamal Franklin sold them. And Jamal Franklin trusted what *you* sold to him. You're at the end of the line, Mr. Grey. You're the one left holding the bag."

Without another word, she stood up and circled around behind Henry Grey and, with one swift motion, ripped off the duct tape, leaving one end stuck on his cheek. He greedily gasped for air. She unscrewed the top of the pill bottle and yanked back his head so that his jaw involuntarily slackened, and his mouth opened. She shoved the open end of the pill bottle into his mouth, which he tried to close but the bottle didn't break. Twenty pills tumbled into his mouth and back to his esophagus. He gagged, but Sara kept the pill bottle held tightly in place. After a moment, she deftly removed the bottle and slapped the duct tape across his mouth. Then she removed the gas mask.

The final sequence of events had been set into motion. She stepped around to watch as Grey, wild-eyed, struggled to open his mouth and spit out the rapidly dissolving pills.

He breathed hard through his nose. One minute ticked by.

"It won't be long, Mr. Grey," she said. "Two more minutes, tops."

But he couldn't reply. The fentanyl euphoria was setting in just as his breathing slowed.

"Fentanyl is a powerful respiratory suppressant," said Sara. "Just one of those pills would do the job on you. Do you feel like it's hard to get enough air? That you *want* to breathe but just *can't*? It must be terrifying, even for someone still high on nitrous oxide. Oh, I see the symptoms appearing. Your pupils are getting smaller."

She put her hand on his forehead.

"Your skin feels cold and clammy. I'd even say it's becoming rather blue. The fancy term for that is cyanosis. Are you feeling dizzy? Nauseous?"

His eyes became unfocused and glassy, his breathing slow

and shallow. He seemed to convulse, as if retching. Then his breathing stopped.

"Respiratory failure, Mr. Grey," said Sara. "Next stop is brain death. When it's deprived of oxygen for just four minutes, you suffer permanent brain damage. Then just four or five minutes after that, the brain completely shuts off. Like pulling the plug on a computer. Just like that, it goes dark. But here's the bad news—unlike a computer, which you reboot anytime, the instant the brain stops working, it's gone forever. No one can start it again. And from the moment of brain death, it begins to decay as the vital synapses between neurons are lost. All of your memories, your learning, your thoughts, your emotions—they vanish like snow melting in sunlight."

Henry Grey heard nothing. His eyes stared, unseeing. He was motionless.

"Just to be sure, let's give you a few more minutes to marinate," said Sara as she stood up and stretched like a cat. It had been a long day—but her work was not yet complete. She found her bottle of TriGene, paper towels, and a pair of latex gloves. "Got to get you cleaned up," she said as she wiped his face and arms.

Having done that, she left him in the chair and went forward to the wheel. She started the engine of the *Margarita* then went outside and cast off the lines that tied the boat to the dock. The air was still. Under the streetlight at the head of the dock, the guard was dozing in his chair. She looked over at the *Diamond Cutter*; the front window showed the flickering blue TV light. The rest of the boat was dark. Ignorance was bliss.

EVEN STEVEN

Sara backed the *Margarita* away from the dock and, once clear, turned it around and slowly cruised into the middle of the dark lake. Here and there, she saw the distant running lights of other vessels, large and small. She put the engine into neutral and let the boat drift.

She cut Grey free of the zip ties, and he slumped to the deck in a heap. She dragged his deadweight out onto the back porch and inflated his life vest, making it easier for him to be found, floating in the water. After all, that was the point. She wanted him to be found.

One more task. Taking a sharp knife, she pried open his stiff mouth and carved the distinctive shape of the eye into his cold tongue. Satisfied with her work, she tossed the knife overboard. Then she dragged him to the ladder and muscled him to the edge. With one final push, he splashed into the dark lake. The life preserver kept him upright, with his head and upper shoulders above water. She watched him float for a moment, bobbing like a cork.

"You're going to be one hell of a surprise to a lucky boater," she said. She went to the wheel and put the engine into gear. She steered to a municipal dock a mile to the east, where she could tie up for the night before returning the *Margarita* in the morning. Having secured the boat, she went to her stateroom, crawled into bed, and fell into a deep and dreamless sleep.

27

It wasn't long before the tattered body of Henry Grey had been found by a boater and taken to the medical examiner. Cause of death was a massive fentanyl overdose along with other toxic substances. A thin paste of partially dissolved pills was found in his mouth. Evidence of injury from ligatures on his wrists and ankles. And his tongue showed the horrible mark of Even Steven, inscribed posthumously. The medical examiner decided the cause of death was homicide.

The usual letter had arrived, addressed to the Nashville Metropolitan Police Department Homicide Section. It read:

Number 11 got a taste of his own medicine! He makes a good specimen, don't you think? But—no charge for me doing your job. Your Friend, Even Steven.

It was postmarked in Rocky Top, the same morning the body had been discovered.

After making a copy, Jake sent it to the Tennessee Bureau of Investigation, which would be handling this case. The word around police circles was that solving the murder of Henry Grey was not going to be a high priority because he was a known narcotics kingpin who deserved to die. What's more, his death gave the TBI a legal reason to search the *Diamond Cutter* and seize computers, phones, and other evidence of drug trafficking. All in all, in this particular case, law enforcement was quite pleased with the work of Even Steven.

But Jake was not happy.

"I'm puzzled by this murder," he said to Sara. "Why would the killer pretend to be Earl Steven Pollard if he were from a rival drug gang? It makes no sense. Gangs want the associates of the victim to know who was responsible. It's all about power. The message is, 'Don't cross us or you'll end up dead too'." This message sends a different signal. It's classic Pollard. It's about the criminal justice system."

"I don't know," shrugged Sara.

"And I find it interesting that Grey was killed just a few days after the drug overdose deaths of those four kids in Dudley Park. As if those deaths were what drew the attention of the killer—or killers. And they attacked from the water. It had to be a very sophisticated, commando-style raid. The guard at the dock saw nothing, heard nothing. The guard on the boat itself saw nothing. And they both swear Henry Grey was on board, asleep in his stateroom. In the morning, he was missing, and a few hours later his body was found in the lake."

"If it doesn't have the hallmarks of a gang conflict," said Sara, "how about a copycat?"

"An extraordinarily skilled copycat," mused Jake. "Or Pollard himself."

That evening, their conversation was far from Sara's mind.

EVEN STEVEN

Along with two dozen other honorees, she was seated on the dais in the Crystal Ballroom of the Nashville Sheraton Hotel. Before her, on the main floor of the ballroom at round tables of eight each, were over 200 members of the Nashville Police Department. The occasion was the Annual NMPD Awards of Excellence Banquet, during which outstanding members of the department, from support staff to detectives and commanders, were honored for service that surpassed even the high standards of the department and set an example for others to follow.

Sara had enjoyed the dinner (lemon chicken, broccoli, new potatoes, garden salad) but not so much the ridiculous small talk and fraternal banter. However, it was fun for her to wear her dress uniform and bask in the spotlight. Mayor Susan Noles was sitting on the dais too, along with Police Commissioner Joe Gaines, Vice Mayor and Metro Council President Lizzie Abood, and others—the cream of the crop of Nashville politics and law enforcement.

As dessert was served (flourless chocolate cake or strawberry sundae), the presentations began. Sara looked at the program for the evening. Commissioner Gaines would award posthumous Medals of Honor to two police officers who had been killed in the line of duty, followed by Medals of Merit for those who had been injured. Then Special Commendations for officers who, in a particular incident, had exhibited bravery and fortitude beyond the call of duty.

These awards were dutifully and properly distributed, applauded by appreciative fellow officers in the audience.

Then it was Detective Sara Durant's turn to be in the spotlight.

EVEN STEVEN

Commissioner Gaines regaled the audience with a set of stories and statistics that had set Detective Durant above her peers during the past year: a record number of arrests made, convictions obtained, cases closed, and families receiving justice for their loved ones who had been victims. *If they'd only known about her recent contributions!*

"Just last week," said Commissioner Gaines, "Detective Durant assumed authority over the investigation into the tragic deaths of four young people caused by the adulterated recreational drugs they had been sold. She quickly apprehended the dealer who had provided the illegal drugs to a group of twenty people, including the four who died, and the suspect quickly confessed and made a plea agreement. These are the outcomes we want. The Professional Standards Division, which ensures the department's integrity through impartial investigations and reviews, and the Community Review Board, which advises and reviews the Police Department, both agree that Detective Sara Durant exemplifies the highest expectations we have for police officers of all ranks. It's my pleasure to present Detective Sara Durant with the NMPD Annual Award for Investigative Excellence."

Everyone applauded. Sara smiled and humbly accepted the award—a handsome plaque. Commissioner Gaines beamed at her. She returned to her seat at the long table on the dais. Captain Riggs, seated next to her, leaned over and beamed, "Congratulations, kid! Nice job."

"But why me?" she whispered. "I don't get it. I do what every cop does."

"You're an outstanding detective," he replied. "Simple as that. And it doesn't hurt that the Department is trying to attract more female officers. It's their way of saying, 'See? You can succeed here. Look at Detective Durant. Look at the accolades she's receiving. It could happen to you'."

"So, I'm being held up as a role model."

"You might say that."

"But there are no women officers in command roles. None. It's a boys club. So have I hit the glass ceiling?"

Captain Riggs paused. He lowered his eyes. "It is what it is."

When the awards ceremony was over, the attendees mingled. One by one, officers and cops approached Sara to congratulate her. Others hung back, ignoring her or giving her the side eye. It was professional jealousy. Bitterness that a woman had received the award. Anger at a perceived threat to the system or unearned handout.

When the event finally broke up at 11:00 p.m., Sara didn't want to go home. She drove to Brewhouse and took a seat at the bar. There was a basketball game on the screen, but she didn't pay attention.

"Double bourbon," she told the bartender.

Her mood was sour. The awards ceremony had thrown into sharp relief the internal conflict brewing inside her. Just a week earlier, she had stepped outside the law and acted as a vigilante—the very type of person that cops intensely dislike. She had secretly and efficiently identified her target and eliminated him. This was a choice. She could have gone by the book. She could have investigated, acquired evidence, lined up witnesses, filed reports, and then, when all was ready, made the arrest of Henry Grey. Of course, he would have lawyered up. What kind of case could Sara give to the assistant district attorney? Eyewitness testimony? Who would turn on him? How about bank records? Or an inside informant? There was still no guarantee that the long arm of the law would ensnare him, as guilty as he was.

On the other hand, she had also planted false evidence against Debbie Chan and coerced LaShante Valentine into falsely identifying her as Madam X. That was very risky and unethical. Evil, even. But so many guilty people had been set free by the system Sara worked for, the same system which had just given her the NMPD Annual Award for Investigative Excellence. The tension was becoming intolerable.

A man approached her. "Excuse me," he said. "Do you mind if I take this seat?"

She glanced at him. Thirty-ish. Well-dressed in a button-down shirt and slacks. Clean shaven. No piercings. Fit but not musclebound like the guys at the gym. Horn-rimmed eyeglasses, giving him a Clark Kent look. Probably an office worker.

"You got a name?" she said.

"David Madden. And you?"

"Sara Durant. Sure, David Madden, take a seat."

"What brings you here tonight?" he asked. "Are you meeting someone? A boyfriend?"

She laughed. "Nah. Just sittin' and thinkin'. How about you?"

EVEN STEVEN

"Likewise, I guess." He nodded at the screen. "The Grizzlies are playing tonight against the Golden State Warriors. Big rivalry."

"I don't know much about that. My job doesn't leave much time for following sports."

"Oh? What's this job that keeps you so busy?"

She turned to him. This was the answer that sent most men packing: "I'm a cop. A detective with the Nashville Police."

David nodded and smiled. "Sure. I get it. My dad carried a badge. Twenty-five years on the force in Atlanta. My mom was a cop's wife, a special breed of person. They're both retired now. In Florida."

His drink came. He held up his glass. "Here's to the men and women in blue."

"Yeah," nodded Sara. "To the men and women in blue."

They took a sip and then sat for a minute. Sara found herself grappling with the weight of her predicament: chasing one man, mourning another, and having just killed a third. She wondered what she should do with this one.

She took a sip then slowly turned to him, "I'll bet you came here tonight looking for a hookup."

He laughed. "I wouldn't be so blunt about it."

"Well, did you or didn't you?"

Even in the dim light, he seemed to blush. "Sure, I suppose I did."

EVEN STEVEN

"David Madden, this is your lucky night. That is, if you want to."

"That fast?"

"You caught me in the right mood. I'm feeling restless. Let's get out of here. Your place or mine?"

28

At 9:00 a.m. the next morning, Sara slumped into her chair at her desk.

"You look like hell," remarked Jake. "Too much fun at the awards dinner last night?"

"No comment."

"Something interesting came in this morning," he said. "The detective at the TBI handing the Henry Grey case forwarded a video from the surveillance camera at the Cove Creek Marina. The time stamp is three-fifteen in the afternoon on the day of the murder. It's grainy, but it shows a woman. Here, take a look."

He showed his computer screen to Sara. Sure enough, she saw herself standing on the dock, talking to the guard in his folding chair.

"Who does that woman remind you of?" asked Jake. His eyes sparkled with excitement.

"Can't really say."

"Doesn't she look like Madam X from the video at Brown's?"

"I think you're getting carried away," said Sara. "There are a million women who look just like that. And didn't Franklin say that Grey liked to have women around him?"

"True," nodded Jake. "But this woman didn't stick around. She walked down the dock where the *Diamond Cutter* was tied up, but we don't know what she did down there because the security cameras show only a short section of the dock, and the *Diamond Cutter* was tied up at the far end. No surprise there; I'm sure the owners don't want their onboard activities captured on video! But we know that she went off-screen for five minutes and then returned. She walked past the guard and disappeared from view. That was at three-twenty, so we know she did not board the *Diamond Cutter*. Then at seven o'clock, we see a group of people, including Henry Grey, walk onto the dock from the land side and head toward the houseboat. Our mystery woman does not appear to be one of those people. The three women in the group are, shall we say, physically very different."

"Okay," said Sara. "File this information under 'Interesting Trivia'."

"Here's another piece of interesting trivia, as you call it," said Jake. "We've found Earl Pollard's Chevy Malibu."

Sara leaned forward. "Are you kidding? Are you certain?"

"Certain. The VIN matches. The vehicle was one of three found concealed in a shipping container on a dock in Savannah, GA. The container was bound for Nigeria. Customs officials cannot possibly inspect every one of the thousands of containers that pass through the port every day, but they use a risk-based targeting system, analyzing data from shipping manifests, country of destination, exporter history, and other intelligence to identify high-risk containers that are most likely to contain contraband. Then they select those containers for inspection using non-intrusive methods like X-ray scans or physical examinations when necessary. No one knows how much contraband gets through, but their batting average for inspected containers is pretty good. Anyway, Pollard's blue Malibu was destined to find a new home in Lagos."

"So, was it stolen?"

Jake shrugged and chewed the end of his pencil. "Maybe. Obviously, Pollard didn't report it stolen! But he certainly could have *allowed* someone to steal it, just to get rid of it. Better than selling it or trading it in—which would be impossible for a fugitive felon to do—and better than torching it or driving it into a river, both of which would be risky choices. If Pollard wanted the car to disappear, sending it to be sold in Lagos makes sense."

"Or if Pollard were dead, his car may have been stolen off the street by a car theft ring. Or by someone who killed him."

"Yes," nodded Jake. "There are many unknowns, aren't there?"

Sara went to her desk to work on a mountain of boring paperwork for the Jerome Johnson case. Her personal cellphone pinged. She glanced at it.

It was a text message that read, *Please visit me today. L.G.*

Leonard Givens?

She tapped back, *In half hour OK?*

EVEN STEVEN

The reply came, *Yes. Marcos will admit you. This is off the record.*

Off the record? Why would he say that? Was this a trap? Or an opportunity?

"I've got to do some canvassing for the Johnson case," she told Jake as she got up.

"Have fun," he replied dryly.

Sara drove the familiar route west along Old Charlotte Pike to the set of imposing stone gates, down the long, straight gravel driveway to the mansion with its six white columns framing the broad front porch. The day was warm, and the last traces of snow in the shady spots had melted away. Cheery little crocuses peeked out from under the protective shrubs. At long last, it seemed like spring was just around the corner.

She went to the big front door and pressed the softly glowing button.

"Hello, Marcos," she said as the door swung open.

"Detective Durant, Mr. Givens is expecting you," he replied. "Please follow me."

He led Sara through the ancient living room to the warm sunroom, with its big windows providing a vista of the pale violet hills in the distance. There, in his recliner chair, sat Leonard Givens. He looked the same as when she had last seen him—skeletal but somehow breathing and alert. Perhaps he had been this way and would always be this way, outliving everyone.

EVEN STEVEN

"Just in time for my morning grog," he said with a suggestion of levity that Sara found surprising. "Will you join me?"

"Just water, thanks," she said as she sat down in a wicker chair opposite him.

Marcos gave a little bow and disappeared through the French doors.

"Now then, Detective Durant, let's get down to business," said Givens. "May I call you Sara? I dislike formality."

"That depends on the subject of our conversation."

Givens gave a thin smile. "Very true. I assure you, it will be businesslike."

"Before we begin, I must ask you a few questions," said Sara. "Have you had any contact with your nephew, Earl Pollard, since his escape from Riverside Prison? Phone calls? Emails? Visits?"

Givens regarded Sara with his watery grey eyes. "I can't say that I have," he replied evenly. After swishing his glass, he took a swallow. "I assume he's smart enough to keep me out of his affairs."

"You own a house on 24 Marrowbone Creek Road, just off Clarksville Pike, about ten miles northeast of downtown Nashville? Under the auspices of the Oak Hills Trust?"

Givens shrugged. "I cannot keep track of every piece of property or crummy little house I may indirectly own through various family trusts. Why?"

"A man named Elliott Toliver was found murdered there.

EVEN STEVEN

We believe Earl did it, as Even Steven."

"If so, I'm sure he had his reasons."

"And do you own a cabin at 788 Golden Lane, under the name Apex Trust?"

"Again, I'd have to research that." He gave Sara an impatient look.

"Well, Earl was living there recently. It's his last known address. Do you know anything about that?"

Givens sat up in his recliner, as if his backbone had suddenly become stiff. "Detective Durant, enough of this. I didn't invite you here to interrogate me about my real estate holdings, which really do not interest me. Now it's my turn. I have a job for you."

"A job for me?" Sara stifled a laugh. "Mr. Givens, I can hardly imagine what that could be."

Without replying, Givens picked up a buzzer and pressed the button. A moment later, Marcos appeared.

"Please bring Holly to see me," said Givens.

With a nod, Marcos turned and left.

"Allow me to explain," said Givens. "As you may recall from our previous visit, my nephew is the product of the marriage between my sister, Judith, and her husband, Mark Pollard. Both were killed by a man named Tony Lafoy, who imagined Mark sold him a defective automobile that killed his wife."

"Yes, and Earl killed Lafoy in the very first Even Steven murder."

EVEN STEVEN

"Yes, yes, that's right," said Givens. "I also had a brother, now deceased. I seem to outlive them all! His name was Ernest. A lovely man, ran a flower wholesaling business. He and his wife had a daughter. My niece. Her name is Holly Givens. You will meet her shortly. As a teenager, she was quite ambitious, wanted to go into real estate and make her fortune. She was also quite beautiful and had many male admirers." Givens paused and reached for his wallet. He opened it and showed Sara a photograph of a teenage girl. "Here she is when she was eighteen."

"She's quite stunning," nodded Sara.

"There's a big shot real estate broker in town named Wally Hunter," continued Givens. "He made headlines when he sold the estate owned by country music star Ben Dupree. The mansion and horse farm fetched forty million dollars from an investment group. At the time, it was a record-setting price. He's also sold hotels and office buildings. These transactions don't make the headlines, but the money is bigger. Last year he brokered the sale of Jefferson Tower for a billion dollars. The commission was fifty million."

"Sure, I've heard of Hunter. I've heard the rumors, too. But nothing that ever got on the police radar screen."

"That's only because of the ironclad code of silence that Hunter enforces. He owns a big beach house on Dauphin Island, down in Alabama. He has his 'Nocturnals' there, as he calls them. He and a close circle of friends go there on weekends with girls who want to hang with country music stars and other rich men. But it's like Las Vegas—whatever happens on Dauphin Island, stays on Dauphin Island. No one talks. And everyone signs NDAs.

EVEN STEVEN

"Holly got mixed up with this group. Hunter has a personal assistant named Nicole Bouvier, and she tells the girls—young aspiring real estate agents (mostly college dropouts and high school girls)—that they can give their careers a boost and make money by attending one of Hunter's Nocturnals for a chance to show his guests their 'real estate', as she put it. Holly took the bait. She and some other girls were flown down to Dauphin Island on Hunter's private plane, so you can imagine that, even before they land, they're being groomed. Holly thought Hunter was very charming; she also met a Nashville record producer and some other rich men. At Nicole's urging, that afternoon, Holly gave the producer a massage. When he became aroused, Holly tried to leave the room. The producer complained to Nicole, who sat Holly down and threatened her; she told her, if she didn't 'do her part', as she said, her real estate career would be finished. Holly said she was terrified until Nicole began to console her with some warm tea and a blanket, but remembers nothing after that until she woke up nude on a bed in a desolate room surrounded by mirrors."

"Okay, go on."

"Over the course of the weekend, which she says she barely remembers, she kept finding herself in some new dark predicament every few hours. Then on Monday morning, Holly and the girls were flown back to Nashville and dumped at the airport, but not before Nicole showed her the videos of her other girls dancing naked and performing masturbatory acts on camera."

"Oh, my god. He blackmails them. Where is she?"

"You'll see," said Givens. He turned to the door. "Ah—here she is. Holly dear, please come in."

EVEN STEVEN

Holly hardly resembled the beautiful girl in the photo. Her hair fell in greasy strands across her plump, pimply face. Over her soft and flabby body, she wore a plain—dumpy, really—cotton housedress that would have seemed more appropriate on a granny of seventy years old. Her hands were folded in front of her, her fingers nervously intertwined. On her feet she wore a pair of canvas sneakers.

Holly drifted to her uncle's side. He gently put his hand on her forearm. "Holly, dear, this is a friend of mine. Her name is Sara. Say hello."

Holly gave a shy smile. "Hello, Sara. Nice to meet you."

"Nice to meet you too, Holly," she replied. "I recall that when I visited here a few weeks ago, I saw you in the living room, reading a book. Of course I didn't interrupt you. Do you enjoy reading?"

"Yes, very much," she nodded.

"Who's your favorite author?"

"Oh, I don't know. I read a lot of self-help books. Yoga and healing and spirituality. I suppose if I had to name one author of late, it would be Glennon Doyle."

"I've read *Untamed*," said Sara. "Very powerful and uplifting!"

Holly smiled. For a moment, she looked genuinely happy. Then she glanced at her uncle, as if for approval. She began to fidget.

"Well, it was a great pleasure to meet you," said Sara.

Picking up the cue, Givens said to Holly, "Thank you for

saying hello to my guest. I'm sure you have things to do."

Wordlessly, Holly turned and left the room.

"Your family has had more than its share of misfortune," said Sara.

"It's a tough world," shrugged Givens. "As you can see, my niece was severely traumatized by Wally Hunter and his friends. She's afflicted with serious post-traumatic stress disorder. The symptoms include feelings of intense helplessness and fear. She has trouble sleeping and difficulty concentrating, hyper-vigilant with an exaggerated startle response. And as you have seen, for Holly, making herself physically unattractive is perhaps her most powerful defense. Being invisible gives her a feeling of security. And the darkest part is she's attempted suicide twice and says that one of the other girls has succeeded at it. This is what one weekend with Wally Hunter did to her. He and his friends used her and then threw her away like a piece trash."

"Why didn't anyone file charges?" asked Sara.

"What are these girls—many more including Holly—supposed to say?" replied Givens. "No weapons were involved. No physical force. Alabama has loose laws, but a good lawyer could get the charges down to a misdemeanor. And it's rumored that the Mobile County District Attorney has been to Hunter's beach house. Wally Hunter has a lot of influence in high places.

"For the girls, fighting Hunter is just not worth it. They choose to close the door on that part of their life and move on. Some can put it behind them. But others are deeply traumatized like Holly. Even with professional therapy, which she receives, she's permanently damaged. She will never again be a happy, healthy woman."

"I'm very sorry for the evil that has been perpetrated against your beautiful niece," said Sara. "But you said you had a job for me to do. Let's get down to business."

Givens carefully set his empty glass on the small table next to his chair. He looked directly at Sara, his grey eyes hard and bright. "I've been looking for a person with your skill set to solve the problem of Wally Hunter."

"Solve the problem?"

Givens leaned forward, his chin quivering with emotion. "Kill the bastard!"

"You mean like Even Steven?" replied Sara. "What about your nephew, Earl? I thought he was the expert at revenge murder. And besides, I'm a cop! I could arrest you right now for attempting to recruit an assassin."

Givens leaned back and relaxed his arms. "You raise two issues. Number one, since his escape from prison, I have lost contact with Earl. I understand he may have been active—shall we say—immediately after his escape, and there's talk about the murder of the drug kingpin in Norris Lake. I'll have more to say about that incident shortly. But lately, it's been radio silence. For all I know, he could be in Lagos."

Lagos? wondered Sara. *Was that a random utterance—or was he hinting at something?*

"In addition," Givens continued, "in my opinion, his methods are somewhat crude. I'm not convinced he is not of a sufficiently high professional caliber to complete this task.

EVEN STEVEN

Number two, yes, you are a police detective. But I believe you feel as frustrated and angry as I do. Be honest with me—wouldn't you love to see a scumbag like Wally Hunter put out of business? He may not have murdered anyone, but he has condemned many innocent women to a life of living hell."

Sara stood up and walked to the window. She looked out over the serene rolling fields, drowsy in the early spring sunlight as thoughts swirled in her mind.

She turned around.

"Mr. Givens, I'm going to give you the benefit of the doubt and forget we had this conversation. Wally Hunter is an evil man. Many people, including myself, would be happy if a bolt of lightning turned him into charcoal. I'm tremendously empathetic about the crimes he and his friends committed against your niece. I hope she can recover and live a normal life. But I cannot see myself undertaking some sort of James Bond mission to assassinate him. This is real life."

"I was afraid you would be difficult to persuade," said Givens. He reached over to his table and opened his laptop. "Please give me a moment," he said. He fussed around with the computer until he smiled and said, "I've found what I wanted. Please, have a look."

He turned the device so that Sara could see the screen.

The video was dark, but she clearly saw the image of a big houseboat. The view captured the stern—the back porch. After a moment, a figure emerged from the glassy water. The person deftly climbed up the boarding ladder and stood on the deck. Then the person—now clearly a woman—opened the door and disappeared inside.

"Does this look familiar?" said Givens. "I'll fast-forward to the next scene."

The door opened and the woman emerged, half-carrying, half-leading a man. In the deep shadow of the covered deck, she maneuvered him to the boarding ladder and lowered him into the water. Then she followed. For a split second, her face caught reflected light.

Givens tapped the keyboard and the video froze.

"Does that woman look familiar?" he asked.

"Where did you get this?" demanded Sara.

"Let's just say I'm a meaningful investor in Cove Creek Marina! I'm very security conscious, as you may know, and I've installed a few extra cameras. The boat owners don't know—they would probably be very cross with me for invading their privacy. Especially a guy like Henry Grey, who's very touchy about such things. But I like to keep an eye on things. In any case, when I heard about his unfortunate demise, I reviewed my video footage from that night. You can imagine my surprise when I saw in the starring role, not my errant nephew Earl, whom I expected, but my new friend, detective Sara Durant!

"From the video, I concluded that you had to drag Grey to another boat, out of view, where you finished him off. So, I made a few calls to the other local marinas and learned from the nice lady at the Black Creek Marina that, earlier the same day, a young attractive woman fitting your description had rented a houseboat named *Margarita*. You returned it before noon the following day. She was annoyed because the carpet on the back porch was soggy and she didn't want it to freeze, so I paid her a handsome sum for the inconvenience and to forget it all. Now I'm, of course, sure that, if the state police had a reason to dust it for fingerprints, they would find yours."

Sara walked away from the computer, folded her arms, and stood silently.

"As I'm sure you ask your suspects in the interrogation room," said Givens, "where were *you* on the night of the murder of Henry Grey?"

She said nothing.

"Don't think about killing me," said Givens. "Other copies of this video exist, so that is not an option for you. I ask you again, will you do this thing for me? For Holly and all the other girls whose lives have been ruined by Wally Hunter?"

She turned to face him. "This is nothing like snatching a gangster off a houseboat at night. Wally Hunter is far more wealthy and powerful than Henry Grey. Getting close to him, and then escaping undetected, will be extremely difficult."

"I have resources to help you," replied Givens. "Let's begin with money. As a Nashville police detective, your base pay is seventy thousand dollars a year. With overtime and other benefits, it's one hundred thousand a year. Is that correct?"

"Sure," she replied despondently.

"If you left the force, with your exemplary record, you could get a job with any police department in the country. There's you have a safety net. Meanwhile, I'm offering to hire you to do what you really want to do: take down the worst and most

EVEN STEVEN

vicious criminals in America. Not just the guys who kill someone in anger and then get let off by the criminal justice system, but the really bad, evil guys who do it over and over again."

"You want to pay me to kill people?"

"I look at it a different way. I'm partnering with you to get justice for victims. To make right what is wrong. To bring hope to the hopeless. To tip the scales toward what is equitable. To make the guilty pay for their crimes."

"This is madness!" she belted.

Givens quickly interjected, "It would bring me great pain to see you go to prison—and perhaps face the death penalty—for eliminating a terrible person. I have the evidence proving your guilt. If you choose to bring no benefit to me, then why should I bring benefit to you? As for your squeamishness in carrying out this project—and possibly others—you've already done it once." Givens paused to regard Sara carefully with his keen eyes. "Or was Henry Grey not your first hit? Perhaps you've done this before?"

Sara stood muted.

Givens continued, "As for our project, people say that two wrongs don't make a right. But we could say that a wrong that goes unpunished, and is allowed to repeat itself, is worse. How many other innocent people did Henry Grey kill with his drugs before you caught him? And how many more would he have killed had he been allowed to continue? But you stopped him. That is a certainty."

"Why me? Why not Earl?" Sara quipped.

EVEN STEVEN

Givens shrugged. "Do you mean the mythical serial killer? We'll see about that. As of today, I don't think the authorities truly understand Earl's mission—and yours, should you decide to accept. There has never been cause for public fear or alarm. Even Steven, as Earl called himself, removed only those individuals who had flouted the law and brazenly got off scot-free after committing heinous crimes. Very few people fall into that category! The average citizen has absolutely nothing to fear from Even Steven. Am I right?"

"Yes, you're right," nodded Sara. "But Mr. Givens, this conversation is over."

Givens rubbed his chin with a skeletal hand. "Fair enough, then. A lot to consume I suppose. I guess I'd be happy to give you forty-eight hours. The choice is yours. Marcos will show you out. Have a good day."

Summoned by the buzzer, Marcos appeared and, expressionless as always, led Sara through the cavernous living room. She glanced over to the wingback chair and saw that Holly was curled up with a book. Sara stopped, thought for a moment, then turned to the impatient gaze of Marcos, and continued on her way to the door.

29

The next morning, Sara drove north on Granny White Pike toward downtown Nashville. But she was distracted and her mind unfocused. At the entrance to Radnor Park, she abruptly slowed and turned in. She parked in the little parking area under a stand of tall oaks and got out of the car. The day was warm, and the trees, while still leafless, showed delicate green buds of new growth. A path, with a map at the entrance, led into the woods. She started walking at a brisk pace as if she were late for an appointment. The tall canopy of sycamore, hemlock, and maple trees filtered and dappled the afternoon sun. Chipmunks scurried across the sawdust path, and squirrels chattered in the trees. She walked until she had crossed a low rocky hill and, turning around, could see nothing but the looming trees. As she continued at a slower, more measured pace, the winding trail descended until it reached the banks of a verdant pond. She paused to watch the ducks—paddling in groups, squawking and diving—go about their business in and off the water.

From the opposite direction, a couple approached. A man and a woman, looking to be in their seventies, walked slowly and carefully, as old people do. Arm in arm, they talked to each other in soft voices. As they came closer, the woman noticed Sara.

EVEN STEVEN

"Hello, dear," the woman said with a smile.

"Hello," nodded Sara as she forced a smile. She didn't want them to get the idea she was unhappy.

"Lovely day, isn't it?" said the kind-eyed old man.

"Yes, it is lovely."

"Stanley and I have been coming to this park for fifty-five years," said the woman. "Ever since we were first married. There's always something nice to see. Ah—the ducks are back. They were gone for a while. Some other pond, probably. But now it's brooding season, and they'll settle down."

"They build their nests in the reeds," nodded the man.

Sara felt as if she were going to burst into tears, but she kept a stoic face. Something about this sweet old couple hit her in the heart. Could she ever be like them? Could she ever live a normal, boring life where the most exciting thing was taking a walk in the woods with your life partner and seeing the ducks?

She had no answer. Every life is different, and at different times. The road you're on today may not be the one you're on tomorrow. And you can't do it all. You need to make choices. The elderly couple had made their choice—over fifty years ago, apparently. And there they were, arm in arm, looking at the ducks. They seemed very happy, but you never know what trials and tribulations they may have gone through to get here.

The couple said goodbye and continued on their way. Sara turned and, with firm resolve, pressed ahead along the path.

EVEN STEVEN

She drove home and went to her computer. She typed a letter, printed it, and, wearing latex gloves, put it into an envelope addressed to Captain Riggs at police headquarters. Then she got into her car and drove south to La Vergne, where she found a random post office drop box. After depositing the letter, she turned around and went home.

The next day at work passed without incident. Sara was assigned to a routine case of a guy who had shot his wife during an argument. Open and shut, but it still needed to be handled professionally and with the rights of the accused preserved.

On the following day, Captain Riggs called her into his office.

"Sit down," he said as he produced a clear plastic evidence bag.

Inside was a piece of paper and an envelope.

"I received this letter an hour ago," he said. "It was addressed to me. I will read it to you. It says: 'Sweet Sara Durant, I'm going to make her cry, for she will be the next rat to die. Your friend, Even Steven.' As you can see, it includes the distinctive drawing of the eye."

"This is ridiculous," said Sara. "It's just an empty threat. And besides, thanks to the LaShante Valentine trial, information about the letters and the drawings of the eye has been leaked to the public. Any whacko could have sent this letter."

EVEN STEVEN

Captain Riggs shook his head. "The drawing itself was never shown publicly. The one on this letter is an exact match to the previous drawings. We're convinced it came from Even Steven. He's still very much alive and in this area."

"Okay, then we've got to catch the bastard."

"*We* have to, yes," nodded Riggs. "But not you. I cannot take the chance that he'll pick you off in an unguarded moment. We need to get you off his radar. I'm placing you on indefinite protective leave. Go home. Keep a low profile. Watch out for anything suspicious. Better yet, go on vacation. Leave town. You're still on full salary—the union has seen to that. And this will not negatively impact your performance assessments. I need you to be healthy for a long time. Do you understand?"

"But sir—" Sara feigned protest.

"I'm sorry, the decision is final. Commissioner Gaines has signed off on it." He paused. "Of course, you have significant expertise that we would hate to lose completely, especially regarding the Even Steven case, so I will permit back-channel communications with your partner, Detective Patterson. But keep any such contact out of sight. Okay?"

"All right," she nodded. "I agree." She stood up and extended her hand, which Captain Riggs took. "Thanks, boss, for looking out for me. I'll see you around."

Sara returned to the office. Jake was at his desk, eating lunch.

"Looks like you'll be getting a new partner," said Sara as she began collecting her personal items and putting them in a box.

EVEN STEVEN

"What?" said Jake with disbelief. "You've been *canned?* But why? What for?"

"No, it's nothing like that. Captain Riggs received a letter from Even Steven specifically stating that I was on his hit list. I'm sure he's going to send it to you as evidence. You're now the senior detective on this case. Anyway, the Captain is taking the threat seriously, and he's put me on ice. Just temporary, for my own safety. Told me to lay low, even leave town on vacation. The union is okay with it."

"For how long?"

"Indefinite. Until Even Steven is either dead or in custody."

"Hey, can I get Even Steven to send a letter threatening *me?*" said Jake as he sipped his espresso.

"Very funny. But the Captain said that you and I could have off-the-record conversations. As long as I'm out of sight."

Jake acknowledged the decision, "Okay. I've got your cell number. You might hear from me."

Sara finished packing her desk—there wasn't much—and without further ceremony, turned and headed for the exit, passing Jake's desk on the way out.

As she passed by, Jake hurriedly shoved a piece of paper under a pile on his desk. Once she was gone, he pulled it back out. It was a grainy photo of a Ford Mustang Dark Horse, captured by a security camera on a liquor store a few blocks from Brown's Diner. The newly discovered video was taken on the night of the murder of Logan Silva—a case that, with the recanting of the testimony of LaShante Valentine, was certainly going to be re-opened. The distinctive Mustang, one of only twenty in the Nashville area, had been parked on the street at a few minutes before 10:00 p.m. by a woman in a floppy hat. The woman returned, without the hat, just before midnight and had driven away. Despite the best efforts of the department's tech people to improve the image, the woman's face remained a blur.

With a shrug, Jake slipped the photo into the 'Logan Silva' file.

Back home, Sara put the box on the kitchen table and took out her phone. She tapped the number of Leonard Givens. Marcos answered.

"Please tell Mr. Givens that Sara is on her way. Thank you."

Twenty minutes later, Marcos, with his customary funereal demeanor, ushered Sara into the grand dining room of the house, where Givens and Holly sat together at the end of a long table.

"Ah, Sara, will you join us for lunch?" inquired Givens with a sweep of his hand, indicating she should sit next to him. "I assume your presence here portends good news."

Holly glanced at Sara nervously.

"Good afternoon, Mr. Givens, Holly," she said as she took her seat. "No, thank you, I'll just have some water. I hope I'm not interrupting."

"No, we're happy to have some company," said Givens as he cut into his boneless breast of chicken.

EVEN STEVEN

"I just wanted to tell you that I'm declining your generous offer of employment."

Givens put down his fork and gave Sara a sharp look. "I wouldn't call that good news."

"There's more. Captain Riggs has put me on indefinite protective leave. For my own safety, he says. I'm still on the department payroll, but I'm not active duty. In fact, I'm supposed to be on vacation. In other words, your kind gesture is not necessary. I'm happy to work not as your employee, but as your partner, you might say, on the project you've proposed."

"But why?" asked Givens.

"Because I believe in the mission. It's righteous."

"By which you mean to say, acting in accord with divine or moral law, free from guilt or sin. Arising from an outraged sense of justice or morality. Which may not be the same as civil law."

"Correct."

Givens gave a tight smile. He took a sip of his water. He looked at Sara. "But you must admit, you are compelled by something more than righteousness alone. Many people *feel* righteous but lack the capacity and the will to *act* on their belief. Thoughts are nice, but taking action is a difficult, dirty business. You have both. The thought and the action. You are one of a select few."

"I suppose so. I haven't thought much about it."

"Still, you must forgive me for wondering why this is the

EVEN STEVEN

case. Do you, perhaps, share a tragedy similar to Earl's in your family history?"

Sara nodded and told Givens the story of how her parents had gone for a hike in the mountains. Her mother was found dead at the bottom of a high cliff, while her father disappeared and had not been seen since. Sara and her brother, Ricky, were caught in a maelstrom of speculation and intrigue.

"I'm sorry you had to go through such a traumatic experience," said Givens. "And never knowing the truth."

"And today, I solve murders," said Sara. "With cool and methodical precision."

Givens nodded. "One of my dear nephew's faults," he said with a glance at Holly, who seemed unconcerned, "is that he's compulsive and emotional. He gets careless, which, as you know better than anyone, led to his arrest and conviction."

"Yes. One simple mistake did it for him," Sara confirmed.

Givens continued, "My feeling is that you are more disciplined. More able to compartmentalize the various aspects of the job. The technical from the, as you say, righteous."

"I hope so."

"What do you need from me?"

Sara looked at Holly. "At the moment, I need to have a friendly conversation with your niece."

EVEN STEVEN

Givens stood up. "I see. Holly, why don't you and Sara retire to the library? I'm sure you'll be more comfortable there."

With a nervous glance at Sara, Holly carefully placed her napkin on the table, rose from her seat, and walked through a door at the end of the room. Sara followed her into the library, where the men would retire after dinner to smoke cigars, drink port wine, and play billiards in the old days. By the windows overlooking the terrace were two well-worn armchairs upholstered in leather. Sara settled into one. After a moment of hesitation, Holly took the other. She sat with her hands folded.

"I suppose you're wondering why I want to talk with you, just girl to girl," said Sara.

"Yes. I don't know why." She avoided eye contact.

"Because I need your help."

"How can I help you? I mean, look at you. You're like some sort of super-person."

Sara smiled. "No, I'm just like anybody else, trying to figure things out. Let me ask you something. How do you feel about Wally Hunter?"

Holly recoiled as if seeing a tarantula. "Are you kidding? He controls my thoughts," she spat with sudden ferocity. "He ought to rot in hell."

So much for the meek, mousy Holly that I assumed I knew, thought Sara. *This girl has some fire in her.*

"Yes," said Sara. "He ought to rot in hell. And my mission is to send him there."

"Great but he's surrounded by powerful men. He pays off the cops."

"Everyone has a weak spot. An Achilles heel. We just have to find Hunter's. How would you feel if I—or someone—sent him to the cemetery?"

"Wouldn't you have to arrest him?"

"In a perfect world, yes. But we live in the real world, where things are rarely black and white. Sometimes you just have to take action. Again, how would you feel if you knew he had suffered a painful death?"

"I try to be Christian," replied Holly. "But it's hard to forgive someone like that. To be honest, I would feel good. To know he had suffered would make me feel good. Is that a bad thing?"

"No, it isn't," replied Sara.

She wasn't sure if she really believed that or if it were merely part of her sales pitch to Holly. No matter—the course was set.

"What do you need from me?" asked Holly.

"I want you to tell me everything you remember about your trip to Dauphin Island. Everything about Nicole and Hunter, and how the system works."

"I don't know if I can," said Holly, twisting her fingers nervously. One of the long sleeves on her shirt inched up, and Sara glimpsed the tell-tale scars on her forearm.

"Holly," she said gently, "Are you a cutter?"

EVEN STEVEN

Holly pulled down the sleeve. "It's nothing."

Sara didn't want to push any further, so she changed the subject back to the task at hand, "You can help me take out Wally Hunter. Get payback for you. It may bring you some closure. Make you feel as though you're not powerless. I will act as your sword of justice. I will cut him the way he cut you."

"Are you sure you can do it? Make him pay, I mean."

"I can do it or die trying. Let's just take it slowly, one step at a time. Begin with Nicole. She recruited you, is that right? Tell me how she did that. Then we'll move on to Wally Hunter and what happened on Dauphin Island."

"All right," said Holly with quiet resolve. "I'll tell you everything I know."

30

When Sara returned home, her head was reeling with the information Holly had provided. Killing Wally Hunter was not going to be easy, but it was possible if every step and every move were executed perfectly. She set to work on her plan.

Her phone buzzed. Jake Patterson. *What could he want?* She picked it up.

"Sara, we need to talk," he said.

"Okay, sure," she replied without enthusiasm. "But what's the big problem?"

"Just meet me at Centennial Park in half an hour. At the James Robertson Founders Statue."

She found him sitting on a park bench overlooking the pond.

"What's so urgent, partner?" she said as she sat next to him.

"Evidence," he said.

"Evidence of what?"

EVEN STEVEN

"The fact that you killed Logan Silva."

"You're kidding. Why would I do that?"

"We talked about what a perfect target Silva would be for Even Steven. We even thought about warning him. But we figured, let's let nature take its course. And sure enough, he was killed. Not by Earl Steven Pollard, but by a woman, it appeared. A woman wearing a big floppy hat and hoop earrings. Very thin circumstantial evidence. The autopsy results showed that his skin had been cleaned with TriGene. No surprise there—Pollard had been known to be meticulous. But Sara, there was one problem."

"What was that?"

"You slipped up."

"What the fuck are you talking about?"

"There were a few female hairs retrieved from the crime scene, and one in particular, an eyelash, is a 100% match to your DNA."

Sara was silent. As a cop, she knew this was no joke. Science doesn't lie. It was just like she had said about Pollard—you can be highly meticulous in your work, but one mistake is all it takes to bring you down.

"So, you've played your cards," she said. "Well done. I guess I'll show you my hand. Does the name Judge Alonzo Rota mean anything to you?"

Jake scowled. "I've heard the name. He's a judge in criminal court. So what?"

"He's still a judge because of you, my friend. Last year, the distinguished jurist presided over the case of a Colombian kingpin accused of heading up a cocaine smuggling operation. It looked like a slam dunk prosecution, especially when the dead body of a rival was dug up in a construction site owned by the kingpin. But suddenly, to the shock of court watchers, Judge Rota dismissed the case on a technicality. You were assigned to quietly investigate. Is your memory improving?"

"Yes, so what?" Jake ran his fingers nervously through his perfectly trimmed hair.

"You came back and said the judge was clean. The world moved on. But I did my own digging. No offense—I was just curious, especially because, at that time, you were making frequent trips to Tunica, to the casinos. You were losing money, weren't you? And to keep yourself afloat, you accepted a hefty bribe from Judge Rota. It was probably laundered drug money from the mobster, but that's just a technicality. A bribe is a bribe. You had evidence that Judge Rota was crooked, didn't you? It was quite a tangled web of corruption. Lots of dirty people, including you."

"You know I don't go to Tunica anymore. I've quit gambling."

"And I applaud you for that! But let's get back to business. I'd say I just put down a royal flush. Beats your straight. My friend, you're my partner. You're a smart detective. But you have a lot to lose. The business about my DNA in Silva's belly button is a problem, but it could be contested for years. You know how that works! Delay, delay, delay. But the publicity that would erupt if some nosy reporter got wind of a highly placed Nashville police detective helping a controversial judge acquit a vicious drug dealer… well, it wouldn't matter if you denied it. You'd be disgraced. Finished."

"You're a bitch, you know that?"

"Yes, but a bitch with a heart of gold. I rather like you, Jake. I can't blame you for doing your job and following the evidence. That's what we all do. But I'm asking you to make the right choice. Bury the lab report. Move on to another case. It's not as if there's a shortage of murders in Nashville! Other, more deserving, victims need your help."

Jake said nothing but gazed out over the rippling water of the pond.

"You help me, and I'll help you," said Sara. "We'll each keep our little secrets. It's as simple as that."

Defeated, Jake turned to Sara.

"Okay—" he took a beat. "Well, shit! But tell me straight—do you know where Earl Pollard is?"

Sara stood up. "Partner, the answer is no. I do not know if he is alive or dead or where he is. He could be in this park, right now. He could be a thousand miles away or in some other country. But he has many admirers. Perhaps that's not quite the right word. Let's say there are many people who understand what he was doing and why."

"Including you," replied Jake.

"Cops see both sides. The good and the ugly. My friend, it has been a pleasure to see you. I'm happy we have come to a mutually beneficial agreement. Take care of yourself. And remember, I'm not off the force. I'm on protective leave. You can reach out to me anytime."

A she walked away, toward the parking lot adjacent to the Parthenon, she turned over in her mind the risks versus the rewards of killing Jake. *How did it come to this?* There was no doubt he was dangerous. He could send her to death row. But at that moment, he was loyal to her and could be a valuable resource within the police department.

For now, she would let him live.

From her home, Sara placed a call to Leonard Givens. As usual, Marcos answered, then Givens picked up the phone.

"I have a plan to eliminate our problem," she said. "It will take time and require precision. It will also require some resources. I need to appear to be a wealthy, successful person. To do this, I need you to set up an account that I can draw upon. Fifty thousand dollars to start. Okay? Good. You will not be disappointed."

Over the next few days, she hired a website developer and a business marketing firm. She bought some outfits that transformed her into a successful executive—Tom Ford, Stella McCartney, YSL. She leased a Mercedes S-Class sedan—her own Mustang would be too sporty, and her target could run her plates.

Finally, she got a new phone and commissioned false identity papers, including a driver's license.

EVEN STEVEN

When all the pieces were in place, she reached out to Nicole Bouvier.

First, a simple email:

Hello Ms. Bouvier,

My name is Daria Mellon, and I'm the managing editor at a new publishing house in New York, Athena Galaxy Press. We are planning a series of biographies of the most influential people in real estate and, naturally, we want to start at the top with Wally Hunter. After all, he is the undisputed master of the industry. The book will take the form of a "you-are-there" experience, with our author shadowing Mr. Hunter as he goes about his daily affairs. As you know, this approach has been used in the past for many New York Times best sellers of business leaders—including one who famously became President of the United States. Perhaps it can happen twice! We want the reader to see, firsthand, the scope and depth of Mr. Hunter's unparalleled genius as he makes record-breaking deals. Of course, we will arrange a generous profit-sharing deal with Mr. Hunter.

I look forward to hearing from you.

Sincerely,

Daria Mellon

Sara paused. *Am I laying on too much flattery?* she asked herself. *Is my tone too gushing? Too obsequious?*

Holly had been very clear: Wally Hunter's ego was beyond ordinary comprehension. His vanity was his most dominant trait. He lapped up compliments the way a pig slurps up its feed. She saw it often during her grotesque experience on

EVEN STEVEN

Dauphin Island. Wally Hunter didn't care who you were, as long as you were fawning and servile.

Sara hit "send" and went to make her dinner.

An hour later, as Sara was washing the dishes, her email pinged. She quickly dried her hands and checked her phone.

Dear Daria: Thank you for your kind inquiry. Please visit me at my office tomorrow at 10:00 a.m. We will speak then.

Sincerely,

Nicole

31

At 10:00 a.m. sharp, Sara entered the gleaming lobby of the Hunter Building, and after she cleared security, an elevator whisked her to the thirtieth-floor offices of The Hunter Group. Wearing a Michael Kors power suit, she strode purposefully through the glass and bronze doors and found herself in a reception area with silver silk wallpaper and plush gold carpeting. An attractive young woman looked up and smiled with crimson lips.

"How may I help you?"

"Daria Mellon for Nicole Bouvier."

"I'll tell her you're here."

Sara sat on the stiff little French-style couch and looked at the oversized framed photos of properties Hunter had brokered hanging on the walls. After a few minutes, a woman came through the door. She was about fifty years old, tall, square-shouldered, with slick dark hair and the same brilliant red lips as the receptionist. Sara made a mental note that, if she were so lucky as to return, she needed to sport the company lip color.

"Daria, I'm Nicole Bouvier, Mr. Hunter's personal assistant." Her hand, cordially extended, was cold. The flawless nails were the same red as the lips. "He's asked me to have a chat with you about your project. Please, let's go into my office."

Sara followed Nicole along a white-and-gold corridor and through a richly paneled door to a modern office with a picture window showing the Nashville skyline. There was a desk and several phones, a big video screen, shelves of books, and more photos of mansions and apartment buildings. Nicole took her place behind her desk while Sara took the single visitor chair. She put her purse, a Louis Vuitton, on the Persian carpet at her feet.

"I've been looking at your company website," said Nicole. She swiveled her computer so that Sara could see the screen. "Very impressive for a start-up." She indicated one of the photos. "Here you are with Oprah. Tell me about that."

"Oh, we were seated at the same table at the Met Gala," said Sara in an offhand tone. "Just by chance, really. She's truly an amazing woman. We chatted about her Charitable Foundation and its support for Nashville Nurtures, which served families in the Nashville area deeply impacted by COVID-19. Did you know she's a graduate of Tennessee State University?"

"No, I did not know that," smiled Nicole. "And here you are with our governor."

"Yes, at the Swan Ball at Cheekwood. Such a lovely event. In fact, that's where I picked up this Louis Vuitton bag. At the silent auction. Of course, I paid far too much for it, but isn't that the point?"

"Yes, of course one must be generous." Nicole lingered over the website for a moment, looking at the lavish photos, all of which, she did not know, had been fabricated using artificial intelligence. She turned to Sara.

"Tell me how books published by Athena Galaxy Press are distributed."

"We have a deal with Myers & Company, one of the Big Five publishers in New York. Our books will be sold in Hudson News, Books-A-Million, Barnes & Noble, as well as Amazon, course. We have access to *The New York Times Book Review* and all the other leading reviewers. For the proposed book on Mr. Hunter, we have a marketing budget of one million dollars."

"And of course, Mr. Hunter will share in the gross revenues," Nicole confirmed.

"Yes, of course. We sincerely hope to arrive at a deal that's a win-win for both parties."

They talked for a while longer. Then Nicole said, "Well, when do we meet our writer?"

"I'll be handling this assignment personally," replied Sara.

Nicole arched a hard eyebrow. "*You?*"

"Absolutely. I've written over a dozen biographies for our most demanding clients. We would not entrust such a high-profile assignment to anyone else."

"I see," nodded Nicole. She thought for a moment and picked up her old-fashioned office phone. "Mr. Hunter? Do you have a moment? It's about the woman with the book idea. Yes, she's here now. I'd like to bring her in to meet you. All right. Thank you."

EVEN STEVEN

She replaced the receiver on the cradle and looked at Sara. "Well, Daria, this could be your lucky day. Mr. Hunter will see you. Please follow me."

Sara followed Nicole down the same hall to a door at the end. Without knocking, Nicole cracked it open.

Stepping halfway through, she said, "Is now a good time, sir?"

A male voice drawled, "Yes," and Nicole pushed open the door.

The office of Wally Hunter occupied the entire north side of the floor, with windows all around, providing a breathtaking view of the city. Movable sheer curtains shielded the room from direct sunlight. Hunter's desk occupied the center of the space, and directly behind him, the section of wall was the only area to lack a window, as if the occupant of the desk didn't want anyone looking over his shoulder from outside. There was a small conference table to the left, and to the right, a quasi-living room setup with a sofa and chairs.

Behind the desk sat Wally Hunter in an enormous leather-backed chair. He was about fifty, with salt-and-pepper hair, a smooth complexion, and sharp, inquisitive eyes under hawk-like eyebrows. His blue business suit was padded in the shoulders, giving him a brawny profile. His mouth was wide and thin-lipped. He looked up, and his gaze fixed on Sara as if she were a deer in a gunsight at a thousand yards. Slowly, a wide grin spread across his face, indicating approval. His teeth were unnaturally perfect and white, leading Sara to conclude they were almost certainly veneers.

He stood up and leaned forward to shake her hand. "Nice to

EVEN STEVEN

meet you, Dawn," he said.

"It's Daria," corrected Nicole. "Daria Mellon. From Athena Galaxy Press."

His grip was firm but not crushing, and he showed no remorse for getting her name wrong. They all sat down. He pushed a button.

"Grapico for everyone, please," he said, just once, seemingly into the air. There was no audible response.

Sara scanned his desk. There was a computer and several phones, both of the landline variety and cell phones. Some papers piled up. No newspapers. Photos in little gold frames of Hunter with various famous people faced outward for visitors to admire. Behind the desk was a table, up against the wall. This had more framed photos and more papers and file folders. On the wall over the table hung more photos of Hunter with famous people, all smiling, some in restaurants, some at the ribbon-cutting of a new building.

"Nicole has told me about you," said Hunter. "You know I've been on the cover of *Nashville Lifestyles Magazine* more times than anyone else?"

"Yes, sir," smiled Sara. "Very impressive. That's one of the many reasons we want to make your book. We want a number one *New York Times* best seller."

"I want fifty percent of the gross sales," said Hunter. "Not profits, gross revenue. I don't give a shit if you make a profit. Publishing an authorized book about me, with my endorsement, will put your company on the global map. The value of that is beyond comprehension."

EVEN STEVEN

Sara perked up in her seat.

Hunter continued, "And I want fifty percent of the value of books given away for free to reviewers. In other words, if the book wholesales for forty dollars, I want twenty for every copy produced regardless of the format or what you do with it."

"You drive a very hard bargain," said Sara. Of course, she didn't give a shit about profits either. This project would be over long before a single book was printed.

A hidden side door eased open, and a man in black slacks and white coat entered, carrying a silver tray on which were three cans of Grapico and four glasses with ice. He set his tray on a small side table and, one by one, carried a can and a glass to each person, beginning with Hunter. As if serving vintage champagne, he opened Hunter's can, which made a faint hissing sound, and poured its contents into the glass at an angle so as to not create much foam.

Hunter picked it up and took a sip. He gave the server a nod of approval.

"When you order a Grapico, make sure they open the can in front of you," he said. "That way, you'll know it's fresh and has not been tampered with."

"Oh, yes, sir, very good advice," nodded Sara, as if receiving deep spiritual wisdom.

Hunter made a motion to the server indicating he was dismissed. The man wordlessly bowed and withdrew through the same hidden door.

The discussion continued—logistics, how many hours Daria

EVEN STEVEN

could shadow Mr. Hunter, who would pay for her meals. (Daria would, of course. Despite his wealth, Hunter was a notorious cheapskate).

"Daria, when do you want to start?" asked Nicole.

"Any time," she replied. "We'll just need to formalize a contract."

Hunter looked at her with his keen eyes. "You'll learn that, around here, we don't use contracts. We have a deal." He pointed his long, sharp finger at her. "If you screw me, then we have trouble."

"Yes, sir," nodded Sara. She got the feeling that, in the coming days, her vocabulary would largely consist of those two words. But soon enough, the trap would be sprung, and another unpunished criminal would get his bitter reward.

Nicole glanced at her phone. "Sir, you have an appointment in fifteen minutes at the Pinnacle Building. The prospective buyer wants to meet you personally before signing the final purchase & sale agreement. We need to get going."

"Okay," nodded Hunter. He looked at Sara. "She's a hard taskmaster, she is! Keeps my nose to the grindstone. You know I could be living on my yacht, cruising the Caribbean, but Nicole insists I stay at the helm here in Nashville."

Nicole made no reply, but her back stiffened.

She turned to Sara. "Thank you for your time, Daria. I'll be in touch about the schedule."

Hunter hauled himself to his feet. "Say, Darlene, why don't you tag along? If you want to write a biography of the greatest real estate broker in America, there's no time like now to get started."

"Um, okay, sure," said Sara. She glanced at Nicole, whose eyes were reptilian.

"Sir, we wouldn't want to inconvenience Ms. Mellon," said Nicole coolly.

"Oh, it's no problem," said Hunter with a wave of his hand. "As long as Darlene doesn't mind."

"It's Daria, sir, and it would be a great honor to accompany you."

"Well then, let's go," he said. "Daria. Got it. And by the way, I allow no recording devices in my office. You need to take notes by hand, the old-fashioned way."

32

They descended to the parking garage, and a man in a black chauffeur suit ushered Hunter and Nicole into the back seat of one of two identical white Cadillac Escalades. Another aide got in also, along with a bodyguard. Sara was standing on the concrete when Hunter waved her into the car.

"This is Daria from Athena Galaxy Press," said Hunter to the bodyguard and chauffeur. "A top publishing house in New York. She's writing a book about me. It's going to be a best seller. She's with the team now, okay? Full access."

Nicole interrupted, "Sir, we haven't fully vetted her yet. We need a few days—"

He waved his hand to shush her. "She's fine, Nicole. I mean, look at her! She's got style and class. No doubt about it."

"Thank you, sir," said Sara. She took a seat in the plush third row, behind Hunter and Nicole.

The two SUVs drove across town and arrived at the Pinnacle Building, a fifty-story gleaming tower of glass and steel. A fountain with a modestly naked sculpture bubbled in the grassy center of the driveway turnaround. They pulled up to the front atrium, piled out of the cars, and went inside.

Sara wisely hung back, out of view of Nicole. She didn't care what Hunter said to the potential buyer, a man named Abdullah. She watched as Hunter poured on the charm, clapping the guy on the shoulder, gesturing with his hand, the white plastic teeth gleaming. She caught a few snippets—phrases like "one hundred percent occupancy," and "a waiting list of dozens of A-list people," and "iconic address." She had to admit, the pitch was attractive if all you were concerned about was superficial status.

She followed the crowd into one of the two elevators and ascended to the top floor. There were two penthouse apartments here, and the group filed into one. It was unfurnished—just big empty rooms. (*So much for one hundred percent occupancy*, thought Sara.) The view over the city was terrific, and the spacious chef's kitchen with its sleek marble countertops impressive. Abdullah seemed happy.

Sara had lingered near the door of the penthouse suite, and as the group filed out, Hunter and Abdullah passed close to her. Hunter put his arm around Abdullah and leaned close and said, "Listen, my friend, after you make this deal with me, I'll bring you down to Dauphin Island for one of my weekend retreats. I'll show you a good time, if you know what I mean."

Abdullah nodded and said, "That sounds very nice, thank you," but his tone indicated he didn't place any particular significance on the island or the invitation.

Hunter must have sensed this, because he leaned closer and said, nearly in the man's ear, "You've heard of the Playboy Mansion?"

EVEN STEVEN

Abdullah smiled and said, "Yes, of course. It's very famous."

Hunter whispered, "My house on Dauphin Island is the fucking Playboy Mansion on steroids. It will blow your mind."

"Oh," nodded Abdullah as the light clicked on in his brain. "Okay, I see. Thank you very much. I'd be delighted to accept your invitation."

Sara eased back to let them pass. Nicole followed directly behind, holding her phone, dictating something into it. The group moved into the two elevators and descended to the atrium.

"So, we're good?" Hunter asked Abdullah. "We can let the lawyers take over?"

Abdullah nodded. "Yes, I'm satisfied. I will instruct my team to move ahead without delay. This is a very fine property and will be a profitable addition to my portfolio."

They shook hands with beaming smiles all around.

Hunter remarked, "I'll be seeing you again soon, I hope. My assistant Nicole will make the arrangements. We fly out of John C. Tune Airport. My private jet—a Gulfstream G550—is quite lovely. I can fly it nonstop as far as Paris, France! But you will be very pleased. Okay? Any problems, you call me directly."

The group was whisked back to the Hunter Building and up to the thirtieth-floor offices.

As they entered the outer reception area, Nicole turned to Sara and said, "Well, Daria, you've had quite an eventful day.

I'm sure you're ready to go home. I'll be in touch about your next appointment with Mr. Hunter."

Sara smiled and was ready to accept this power play when Hunter noticed her and said in a loud voice, "Say, Daria, why don't you stick around for dinner? We're eating in the executive dining room. It's where I take most of my meals. Our chef is pretty good."

Nicole turned to him and said something Sara couldn't hear. She edged closer to catch the conversation.

Hunter smiled at Nicole and said, "My dear, I'm grateful for your efforts to keep me from being distracted. But Daria is my official biographer! She needs to see me in action. Not just doing business but living my very enviable life. I want people to see what life at the top looks like." Hunter turned to Sara. "You're my official biographer, yes?"

Sara beamed. "Yes, sir, Mr. Hunter. It's my job to tell the world about your astonishing achievements and how everyone who meets you has such great respect and love for you."

As soon as the words left her mouth, Sara had a panicky feeling that she had ladled on the flattery a little too thick and Hunter would smell a rat. A split second passed as the words seemed to enter Hunter's brain and were processed. Then his face lit up like a Christmas tree.

"Yes! Exactly!" He turned back to Nicole. "Please ensure Daria has full access when I'm in any public or workplace setting. She will not be allowed in the private residence. Okay?"

Nicole nodded. "Yes, Mr. Hunter. Of course."

EVEN STEVEN

Progress will be slow, Sara thought to herself. *Inside the private residence is exactly where I want to be.*

The group—smaller now—headed into the executive dining room. This was Hunter's core business group. Sara learned their names and positions. Nicole Bouvier, of course, who sat on Hunter's right hand. Then, going around the table, were Ryan Goodwin and Victoria Adams, his top two producing agents. They seemed like typical high-powered real estate people—expensively dressed, perfectly groomed, and always "on." Pam Franklin was the office manager, and a bit more of the matronly type, wearing a nice diamond engagement ring along with her gold wedding band. Sara was next, then the firm's controller, Macks Wilson. He was about fifty, curly reddish hair, ruddy complexion, and pasty skin that rarely saw sunlight. From the moment they sat down, he was clearly smitten with Sara, peppering her with questions about her work and personal life. He wore no wedding ring. When he put his hand on Sara's shoulder, she shifted away from him and tried to strike up a conversation with Pam Franklin.

There were no choices for dinner. Everyone ate what Hunter ate—Caesar salad, filet mignon, mashed potatoes, and stuffed mushrooms. For dessert was Brandy Alexander.

Hunter presided over the group like a king holding court. Nicole, in particular, doted upon him and made sure he had whatever he asked for. At his insistence, his wine glass was kept topped up by the silent server.

At 8:00 p.m., Hunter rose from the table. A server in black pants and white shirt swept in to clear their dishes.

EVEN STEVEN

"Well, back to the salt mines," Hunter said.

Without further comment, he went to his office. Sara followed, all the while taking notes in her notebook. Nicole came as well. It was just the three of them.

Hunter was strictly business on the phone. Every call was the same. The other person—a buyer—would offer a price. Hunter would tell them their price was too low, insulting, ridiculous; and sometimes, would just tell them to go to hell. If the caller were a seller, the same thing would happen, only this time the price was too high, insulting, ridiculous—just go to hell. He closed deals this way. Sara found herself admiring his negotiating skill.

Eventually, he hung up the phone. It was after 9:00 p.m. Hunter turned to Nicole.

"How do things look for this weekend?"

It was Wednesday, so he was talking about two days hence. Nicole shot a glance at Sara, then back to Hunter.

"We can discuss this later, Mr. Hunter," she replied.

"Aren't we going to the island?" inquired Hunter.

"Yes, but let's excuse Ms. Mellon. I'm sure she's had a long day."

Hunter swiveled in his chair. "Are you tired, Daria?"

Sara smiled and said, "Not at all. I find all of this quite fascinating."

"So, she can stay," said Hunter.

EVEN STEVEN

Nicole looked ashen, as if she wanted to speak but was holding back.

"Don't worry, Nicole," soothed Hunter. "No secrets will be revealed!" He turned to Sara. "You see, I own a little getaway property on Dauphin Island in Alabama, on the Gulf coast. It's quite a charming place. The island was first discovered in 1519, when the Spanish explorer Alonso Álvarez de Pineda landed there. But things didn't really get going until 1699, when the Frenchman Pierre Le Moyne D'Iberville established a port and built a fort, a chapel, and a bunch of warehouses and houses.

"Today, maybe fifteen hundred people live there. Plus, loads of tourists visit in the winter. My place is ten acres just off the Bienville Boulevard on the very eastern tip. Nice old Spanish-style house. Lots of space, lots of privacy. Got my own airstrip." He grinned at Nicole. "Getting that baby permitted was quite a feat, wasn't it? The locals were up in arms. 'You can't fit a damned runway on that property,' they all said. I replied, 'I can if I tear down a row of these old worthless shacks!' I won. I tore down those crappy houses, filled in the wetlands, and built my airstrip. The Gulfstream can just slide right in there."

"Very impressive," said Sara. "I look forward to seeing it."

"Mr. Hunter, *please*," interjected Nicole.

But he was just warming to his subject. "I call my little estate the Palais de Plaisir."

"Pleasure Palace," nodded Sara.

"Yes, and on a regular basis I throw parties that I call 'Nocturnals'. These are weekend get-togethers with A-list

EVEN STEVEN

friends where we can kick back and relax."

Nicole rose to her feet. She glared at Sara. He'd said too much for her liking.

"Please excuse us for a few minutes, Ms. Mellon," she said icily.

Sara, who needed no tutorial on the Nocturnals at the Palais de Plaisir, agreed and got up to leave. Under the watchful eye of Nicole, she exited.

The door closed behind her. She took out her phone and held it up against the wooden door. With its sensitive microphone activated, she listened.

"Are you *insane?*" Nicole's voice was muffled but understandable. "The woman is a *writer*, for God's sake. Almost like a *reporter*. How can you dream of bringing her to the island?"

"Okay, okay, I get it," replied Hunter. "I just want her to see my success. I want her to see the high caliber of people who attend my parties. Senators. Governors. Artists. Celebrities. Movie stars. Sports heroes. No one has the guest list I do!"

"Yes, I know," replied Nicole. "You have the very best. The cream of the crop." Her voice lowered so it was barely distinguishable. "But the *girls*, Mr. Hunter. The *girls*. So many are underage. Minors. You know that."

Hunter ignored her.

"You don't want word getting out about what we do. It will be bad for business. There are a lot of conservative people in this market. Churchgoing people."

EVEN STEVEN

"Yeah, and half of them are at the Palais de Plaisir on weekends."

There was a pause.

Then Nicole said, "Do you want Daria Mellon? Are you attracted to her? Tell me."

"Are you kidding? She's over thirty years old."

"Just asking. She may not be your type, but you've got to keep her out of the loop. Okay?"

"Yes, my dear. Whatever you say. What time on Friday are we leaving?"

"Takeoff is at three o'clock sharp."

When Sara was admitted to the room again, Hunter invited her to fly with them down to Dauphin Island. She accepted.

Then she said to both of them, "Strictly off the record, I know all about the Nocturnals at Palais de Plaisir."

"What are you talking about?" said Nicole sharply.

"The girls. You recruit them for the OnlyFans webcam operation."

"So much for our little secret," smirked Hunter. "Hell, by now I suppose every young female aspiring real estate agent in Mobile knows, to make real money, you first must auction your real estate at my parties."

Nicole looked at Sara with suspicion. "How do *you* know this?"

"Like Mr. Hunter said, it's no secret, and besides, you're not committing crimes if you're paying them for the real estate training and work you've contracted them to do, right?"

Hunter, "Yes, exactly!"

"What the hell, are you really writing a book?" asked Nicole. "Or is this all just bullshit?"

"Yes, I'm writing the book. That's the only thing I know how to do. But don't worry, Mr. Hunter. You have full veto power over anything in the manuscript. You're going to look like a hero."

"I like the sound of that," he replied.

On Friday, at a few minutes before 3:00 p.m., Sara parked her leased Mercedes at John C. Tune Airport. It seemed strange—almost dreamlike—to simply walk out of the lounge, cross the open tarmac, and climb the steps into the sleek jet. No ticket, no TSA, no lines, no baggage search. She turned and found herself in a galley kitchen. Walking aft, she entered a lounge area with plush leather swivel seats.

Nicole greeted her. "Here, Daria, keep me company. The men are in the back." Sara put down her Dior travel bag and sat down.

Turning her chair to face Daria, Nicole said in a low voice, barely audible over the hiss of the cabin air system, "Congratulations, Daria. You've made it into the inner circle. Not many grown women do. Honestly, I think Mr. Hunter is crazy to trust you. I'm sorry, that's just how I feel. I'm very protective of him. He's much too—what's the word— garrulous. He's a sucker for flattery. And when he starts drinking, he loses his judgement. He's really a wonderful

EVEN STEVEN

man. He just has his hobbies. Girls are his hobby."

Sara remembered looking into the eyes of Holly Givens and seeing the abject misery and pain in them. Keep focused on the mission, she thought. The mission is to send Wally Hunter to hell.

"I understand," nodded Sara.

Nicole regarded her for a moment. "I must admit," she said, "It will be nice having a real woman to talk to. Sometimes I feel like it's just me, the horny men, and a bunch of teenage girls. It can get exhausting."

A life sentence in prison for sex trafficking would be even more tiresome, thought Sara. But she just smiled.

Another guest boarded the plane and walked past her. She recognized him—Josh Whitmire, United States senator from Kentucky.

Nicole leaned forward and whispered, "He's a regular." Then suddenly, she got up and went to the front of the plane.

Sara watched as Nicole stood at the door, talking to two girls. They each looked about fifteen. One of the girls seemed confident, while the other was plainly nervous. Nicole held the hands of the nervous one, like a summer camp counselor with a newbie. She brought the girls to where she and Daria were sitting.

"You guys take these seats until takeoff and, of course, sign the NDAs—we won't take off until you do," she told them.

They dutifully obeyed and signed the documents.

EVEN STEVEN

"I'm Daria," said Sara. "What are your names?"

"Krissy," said the confident one. "And this is Mia."

"You seem like you've done this before," said Sara to Krissy. "Made this flight, that is."

"Sure," she said with bravado. "Five or six times."

"And you like it?"

"Yeah. It's good money."

"So how does it work? I mean, does Nicole just call you and tell you to show up?"

Krissy nodded. "She's got a list of girls who sell property for Hunter. She calls and tells you you're wanted for work. Sometimes you get called, sometimes you don't. Some girls drop out. Those ones—well, they don't like it. Can't handle it." She brightened up. "You know, Mr. Hunter is a great man. He can make you successful. And not just in the real estate business. He knows Nashville music producers. He knows everybody. Do you know Colette Castle? Big country singer. Has a number one hit. Mr. Hunter introduced her to her producer. He got her started."

Sara was familiar with Colette Castle and her success story. Wally Hunter was not part of it. His claim was nothing more than more bullshit from a professional bullshit artist.

"Are you in school?" asked Sara.

Krissy frowned and pulled back. "Yeah. So what? This is better than school. School is boring. I just go to keep my parents at bay. Selling Mr. Hunter's real estate is all the money I need, and besides, it's too easy. I've maybe seen two of the twenty-five units I've sold."

She walks and talks, thought Sara, *but she's dead inside.*

"And how about you?" she asked Mia.

"Krissy told me I should try this," Mia said. "Hoping I can break into in real estate after the connections I make this weekend." Her eyes darted nervously around the luxurious cabin.

Nicole reappeared.

She went to Mia and said, "Here, the Captain says there's going to be a lot of turbulence with the coming storm, so take this pill to relax." She put the pill into Mia's hand. "Take it. You'll feel better."

Mia thought for a moment.

Krissy said, "Go ahead. It's okay. We all do it."

Mia swallowed the pill with some water Nicole offered her.

The stories were true. Part of the grooming process was keeping the girls comfortably numb with drugs, so they'd go along with whatever Hunter wanted to do with them.

The pilot announced takeoff, and they buckled their seat belts. The plane roared into the air and, within minutes, was cruising at forty thousand feet, and the girls were fast asleep after the champagne and pills overcame them.

Sara turned to Nicole, "You practically tranquilized them. What was that?"

EVEN STEVEN

Nicole snarked, "Oh, just an Oxy. It keeps them in line for the weekend. Hunter insists."

"So, you give him what he wants," said Sara.

"Yes. I'm not here to judge him. I'm here to keep him happy."

Sara effaced her disgust with an agreeing smile.

You may not be here to judge him, she thought, *but I am. And you, too, Nicole. You're a key part of the system. But I'm not going to get distracted. My mission is to eliminate the most important source of evil—Wally Hunter.*

33

The Gulfstream touched down on Hunter's private airstrip, rolled down the runway, and came to a halt adjacent to a nondescript service building.

They deboarded and got into two white Cadillac Escalades, which drove them a short distance to the main house—the Palais de Plaisir. In the car, Sara found herself sitting in the third row next to Mia.

"How are you doing?" asked Sara.

"Okay, I guess," mumbled Mia. Her eyes seemed unfocused, and her breathing was labored. She was like an exhausted antelope pursued by lions, who, on the verge of giving up, has made her way into the cool shade of a tree. It was the drugs, the psychological shock, and the loss of bodily autonomy that had beaten her down. In Mia, Sara saw another Holly—a bright and beautiful girl on the verge of physical and emotional ruin from abuse and blackmail.

If that weren't bad enough, the unfortunate girl faced two more days of this living hell.

The cars pulled up to the front entrance of the house. They all piled out and were greeted with champagne and more pills, which Mia took this time without hesitation.

EVEN STEVEN

Like a tour guide, Wally Hunter assembled them.

"This wonderful cottage—as they used to call it—was built by Mere Bradley, the granddaughter of the famous Confederate General Doke Bradley. It was completed in 1925, during the height of the Roaring Twenties. Crowned by a forty-foot, tile-roofed tower, the house includes bedrooms, baths, and an observation deck offering expansive views of Dauphin Island".

"Notable imported materials include limestone from Genoa used in exterior walls, interior features, and arches. This fossil-rich limestone was selected for its ability to age quickly and accommodate detailed carving. The house has fifteen bedrooms, a grand ballroom, library, game room, banquet kitchen—well, you'll see for yourselves soon enough! Please—enter!"

They filed into the grand foyer presided over by a medieval suit of armor and colorful tapestries featuring people on prancing horses. Nicole took Krissy and Mia aside.

"Follow me," she said. "You're staying with the other girls in the former servants' rooms in the east wing."

"Other girls?" asked Mia.

"There are always more girls than guests," said Krissy. "You'll see. It means you get a break once in a while."

A butler, wearing the usual black slacks and white shirt, led Sara up the grand sweeping staircase to the second-floor hallway.

He steered her into the first room.

EVEN STEVEN

"This will be yours," he said. "It's one of the original guest rooms. You share a bath with the room next door, where Nicole will be staying."

"Thanks," she said as she put down her bag. "I didn't catch your name."

"Philippe," he said. "Dinner is at seven o'clock." Then he turned and left.

The house seemed quiet. People were getting settled in. This might be a good time to innocently explore the house. After all, she had a mission to complete—and the Palais de Plaisir might be just the place to get it done.

In the grand foyer, her footsteps echoed as she walked into the cavernous grand ballroom with its gilded ceiling and mirrored walls. She went through an arched doorway and found herself in the paneled dining room, with its long table already laid out for dinner for seven people. *Not the girls*, Sara concluded. *They were probably fed in the kitchen, like servants. Which way would that be?* Sara pushed through a swinging door and found herself in a brightly lit area with counters and cooking gear and cabinets full of fine china and glassware. At the other end of the kitchen a man stood at a counter, chopping something with a knife. He wore white chef's pants, coat, and hat. She approached him. He did not hear her over the sound of a phone playing music over a set of speakers. He turned to take a bowl from the rack, and as he stepped to the side, Sara noticed his slight limp. He set the bowl down on the counter. Then he picked up his knife. Reaching for something in a bin, his face came into view.

The man was Charles Kaplan. Or rather, Earl Steven Pollard.

EVEN STEVEN

Sara froze with shock as his eyes zeroed in on her presence. He stared deeply at her with a tauntingly sad, clown-faced smirk. His expression became darker as he moved his hand towards a large knife on the table in front of him.

"Don't fucking move! Let me see your hands" Sara shouted as she quickly retrieved her gun and pointed it at him.

Pollard ducked out of sight behind the kitchen island.

"You fucking bitch." he snarled.

"Drop it, Pollard! Don't make me kill you. God knows I want to."

Pollard glared at the knife as he realized he was trapped.

"I'm not kidding. Hands up. Show me the knife!" she implored.

No reply.

"The knife, Pollard. Now!" Sara yelled as her mind raced with confusion on how the hell she was going to handle the shocking predicament.

She cocked the chamber, "Do it!"

Sara prepared to shoot him with any sudden movement, but then, to her surprise, Pollard slowly stood as he dropped the knife to the counter with his hands raised in surrender.

"So, what the hell now?" Pollard irked.

"I'm here for Hunter, not you."

Pollard processed her words with skepticism, but she had his attention.

"We're here for the same reason," she professed with the gun still raised. "Holly."

The adrenaline began to fade.

"I'm here to kill Hunter," she emphasized while lowering the gun. Pollard couldn't believe what he was hearing.

"How cute, Detective Durant has moved to the dark side," he chuckled.

A line cook suddenly burst into the kitchen with a hot plate paying them little attention. Sara moved her jacket to conceal the gun while keeping her aim at Pollard.

They waited impatiently as it took what seemed like a lifetime for the cook to move out of ears reach.

"If it wasn't for a deal I made with your Uncle Leonard, I'd kill you right now for what you did to my brother. Fuck maybe I should just get it over with!"

Ricky's lifeless body flashed before her eyes as she instinctually raised the gun and imagined unloading the chamber. BANG!

Time froze. She expected Pollard's body to collapse, but she quickly came to as a large pot ricocheted off the floor at her feet.

She regained her composure, "Lucky for Holly, or better yet you, today's simply not your day Pollard. Hunter is the prize."

She waited for her words to sink in. The cook exited and she

EVEN STEVEN

continued, "The alternative is I waste you now. What's it gonna be?"

"Are you fucking serious?" he barked in astonishment.

"Serious? Who the fuck do you think killed Logan Silva?"

Pollard couldn't believe it.

She didn't slow up, "It's either you or Hunter. What's it gonna be?"

Pollard unexpectedly erupted into a twisted laughter that alerted Sara to refocus her aim.

"Don't shoot," he pled. "I'll do it."

With that Pollard slowly extended his hand.

Sara stood firm, "I'm not shaking your filthy hand. My only promise is to let you live until Hunter is dealt with".

Realizing he was out of options; Pollard nodded his head in compliance.

The most unlikely of deals had been made. There was no going back.

Sara didn't skip a beat, "So what do you know about this hellhole?"

Pollard exhaled, "You don't know the half of it. I'm just glad Holly got away. Most of the American girls get out. They have a chance to go home and try to lead somewhat of a normal life. The undocumented girls are left to a hellish fate."

EVEN STEVEN

Sara was all ears.

"Some of Hunter's guests want real prostitutes, but it's risky with the American girls. The Americans are for other things. Anyways, these big shot guests come to get their rocks off however they choose at these Nocturnals and then go home to their ignorant wives. To them, it's all just harmless fun. Now, let me guess—" his face devolved into a sneer, "you don't know about the Special House."

"The Special House? Here on the estate?"

"Yes. Right next door to the main house." Pollard relaxed his arms, but his eyes still burned.

"What happens there?"

Pollard shook his head the way one would shake their head at someone who was appallingly stupid. "You think Hunter is rich, right?

"Yeah, he's rich."

"Do you think he makes all his money in real estate? Don't answer. He makes some, and it's a nice front. A good legitimate business front. But his *real* money—his Gulfstream money—comes from porn."

"Porn? Does he shoot it here at the estate?"

"In the Special House. Most of his weekend guests don't even know about it. Through shell companies, Hunter owns Black Cash Productions."

"I've heard of it from the guys who work vice. They put out some sick shit of these American real estate agents being forced to perform in front of live cameras."

"Yep. Porn is the big business for Hunter. Worth thirty billion dollars annually in the United States alone, with most of it on the internet, so Hunter is naturally all in. You'd think the prostitution makes more money, but no, it's his exclusive cams for international elites. And it's the live viewing of these cam sessions via the see-through mirrored walls that these high-profile guests truly are here to witness."

"Dang, so he's able to control them with blackmail and, of the course, the NDAs and a constant salary of hush money."

Pollard limped over to the single window in the kitchen. He paused and looked out at the long afternoon shadows.

"Sorry about your leg," said Sara. "But after all, you tried to kill me."

Their quick camaraderie caught her off guard at first but was an oddly welcome feeling in such a strange place.

"I usually finish the job," he said. "You were the exception. Most people are easy to dispatch. Some put up a fight, but few have the stomach to follow through and kill another person. When they need to act, they flinch or hesitate. They lose their nerve. That's their mistake. That's when you strike." He turned to face Sara. "You're different. You have the killer instinct. Either you have it or you don't. You can't learn it. You can't teach it. It's in you or it isn't. And I've learned you cannot tell by looking at someone if they have it. A person could be fat or thin, young or old, handsome or ugly, male or female—only their actions reveal their thoughts and capabilities."

"All right, Mr. Kaplan, if that's the name you're using here.

EVEN STEVEN

Let's talk business."

Pollard nodded but said, "Not now. The other cooks will be here in a few minutes to prep for dinner. We can talk after. Meet me at ten o'clock by the helipad. I'll show you the Special House."

What a coup! Working alongside Pollard was a shock to Sara, but she needed all the help she could get.

Until dinner time, Sara shadowed Hunter as he played tennis and then went for a swim. He said little of value to a biographer, but Sara didn't mind because her time was better spent keenly observing him and how he interacted with Nicole, his guests, and the staff.

Dinner was served at 7:00 p.m. in the main dining room. No girls, just the adult guests. Sara asked Nicole where they were.

"Eating in the kitchen," she replied.

The food wasn't bad—Sara wondered where Pollard had gotten his culinary training or whether, like some type of Frank Abagnale, Jr., he was just extraordinarily skillful at picking up knowledge and making it his own.

At 10:00 p.m., she went to the darkened helipad. Pollard joined her there.

"I didn't ask you what your angle was," he said. "You're obviously not here as a Nashville police detective."

"No, I'm on leave from the force," she replied. "I'm here as an author working on a biography of Wally Hunter. From Athena Galaxy Press. My name is Daria Mellon."

"Oh, I'll bet he's eating it up," smiled Pollard. "A book about the great Wally Hunter."

Sara thought it was the first time she had seen him smile. Ever.

"Vanity, Earl," she said. "Vanity is what drives him."

"Then vanity is what will kill him. But why are you really here?"

"I'm here to make sure justice is served, just like you."

They shared a surprising moment of agreement but quickly got back to business.

"Okay, let's go to the Special House," declared Pollard.

"How do we get in?"

"The food for the girls is delivered through a back door. I have the key."

They walked around the side of the main house. Sara could hear the *thump-thump* of dance music emanating from the Grotto, the disco that Hunter had built in the lower level. The dance floor area was ringed by private alcoves where the guests could have sex with the girls either in privacy or out in the open, whichever they preferred.

The Special House was a separate structure with a stand of honeysuckle and indigo bush forming a natural barrier from the main house. Like the main house, it was built in the Spanish Revival style, but from the outside at night, it was a looming, dark shape with heavy hurricane shutters covering the windows.

Pollard led Sara along a flagstone path around the back. *If he's going to try to kill me*, she thought, *this would be a good place*. But he went to a door, barely discernable in the weak moonlight, and took a key from his pocket, put it into the lock, and pushed open the door.

They entered a darkened kitchen. Pollard led the way through a set of doors to a dining room. Sara could hear voices from the next room. A man dressed in jeans and a T-shirt came through the door, carrying a piece of lighting equipment. Ignoring them, he went out through another door.

Sara and Pollard advanced to the threshold and looked into the living room, a cavernous space that had been converted into a movie set with several subsidiary sets—a fake bedroom, an exercise room, a kitchen, a dungeon.

A dozen girls, mostly naked, sat or loitered around the perimeter. They looked miserable, dejected, beaten down. In the fake dungeon set, two naked girls were chained and getting whipped by a man in a black leather gladiator costume. The girls screamed as he lashed them while a lone cameramen recorded it all.

"All these girls are undocumented. They'll endure just about anything to stay here because, if they go back home, they'll be killed," said Pollard.

Across the room, Sara noticed Wally Hunter standing in the shadows, arms folded, watching the filming. Occasionally, he'd say something to the man with the whip, who would nod and inflict a new dose of pain.

"We'd better get out of here," said Sara. "We don't want Hunter to see us together."

They retreated to the empty dining room and made their way outside.

"Listen, Earl, we're on the same team here," said Sara as they loitered under the overhanging honeysuckle. "We both want to eliminate Wally Hunter. But we're not going to just shoot him and leave. That would be too easy. Wouldn't you agree?"

"Yes. That's why I'm here. This isn't some hit-and-run job. I've spent weeks insinuating myself into this place. Hunter is as bad as they get and he needs to feel it."

"I have a plan," said Sara. "We're going to need something sharp. A tool from the kitchen."

Pollard bucked up, "Well, I've been daydreaming with the metal cheese wire… you know with the two opposing wooden handles? It cuts through a large wheel of parmesan cheese like butter."

They grinned in agreement and parted ways.

34

Later that night, Sara found Nicole in her room, working on her computer.

"Do you mind if I come in?" asked Sara. "I have a quirky idea inspired by some of Mr. Hunter's art I've noticed while walking around that I want to run by you."

"Sure," replied Nicole. "Here, let's sit on the sofa. Would you like something to drink? Glass of wine?"

Sara sensed a bit of loneliness in Nicole.

Nicole poured two glasses of chilled chardonnay, and they sat down.

"So, I couldn't help but notice Mr. Hunter's incredible taste in art. It's quite a collection, but in particular, I felt drawn to his Rodin sculptures," said Sara.

"Yes, remarkable pieces," said Nicole.

"Well, I have an idea that I'm hoping Mr. Hunter will love!"

Twenty minutes and another glass of wine later, Nicole clapped her hands and exclaimed, "It's brilliant! He'll be thrilled. Let me ring him now."

After a short conversation, Hunter agreed to meet them in his private suite.

"Welcome, Daria and Nicole!" he said as they walked in. The rooms were done in white and gold, with ornate French-looking chairs and sofa, and several mirrors in gilded frames. The ceiling was painted with a blue sky and fluffy white clouds, not unlike the Paris casino in Las Vegas. An ominous stuffed bear stood in a corner, frozen in time, baring its teeth.

It was like being in carnival funhouse designed by Louis XIV.

"Who is this?" Hunter motioned to Pollard, who entered after the two women.

"Oh, just one of your chefs," remarked Sara. "Steven, wait Charles I believe, but I just grabbed him from the kitchen to assist with thoughts on the project, knowing a chef is good with their hands."

"Okay," said Hunter with hesitation.

They sat on a silk-covered sofa that had lion's claws for feet. Hunter produced a bottle of twenty-year-old bourbon whiskey and told Nicole to serve drinks, which she dutifully did.

"Now what's this all about?" he inquired as he swished the single ice cube in his glass.

Nicole jumped in, "It's about your hands, or as Sara

described, your hands of magic which have built such and incredible empire."

"And?" replied Hunter.

"The idea is to immortalize them," Sara jumped to express. "If you'll allow me—I couldn't help but notice your Rodin hand sculptures in the gallery. I was captivated by them and how they embodied your firm character. I've only seen Rodin before in the Philadelphia Museum of Art."

Hunter interjected, "Yes, a couple of those on exhibit there are on loan from my collection."

Sara, "Oh, wow, even more incredible—so you'll hopefully appreciate this idea even more than I thought you would."

"Indulge me."

"I'd like to propose we make a Rodin hand sculpture replica of your own hands. You'd, of course, keep the sculpture, but we could use it for the press circuit and on the cover of your biography. All we'd need to do is get a casting of your hands."

Hunter perked up, "I actually love it. But why so urgent? Why now?"

"I ran it by my team, because we did something similar years back for a client's basketball shoes, and they said it takes a minimum of a year to complete. Best to get things in motion."

Sara paused, but Hunter was all ears.

"If you're up for it, I can facilitate it all. Considering all that you've built, it would truly be a magnificent symbol of the man you are, and we can include a chapter covering your introspective thoughts into your affinity for Rodin."

Hunter took a sip of his bourbon. "Okay, what do I have to do?"

"That's where our chef comes in," said Sara. "Plaster casting is old-fashioned and, at times, unreliable. It requires a simple alginate mixture but, if set too quickly, can create slight but temporary discomfort."

"I don't know. It sounds painful," Hunter shot back.

"If I may join the discussion," said Pollard, "She's overcomplicating things. All we really need to do is firmly stabilize your hand for five to ten minutes max while they set into the alginate mixture, which is soft like rubber. I messed these up enough in art school, but besides the ingredients it's really no different than the chocolate dessert and ice cube molds we make for you. With humans, it's truly only movement that ever compromises the process."

"So, you can really do this?" asked Hunter.

"Absolutely," nodded Pollard.

Hunter thought for a moment. "Okay, let's do it. Tomorrow afternoon at three o'clock. In the disco."

The group broke up. Nicole went to check on the girls.

Sara and Pollard took a walk outside, away from the house. "You find the cheese slicer?"

EVEN STEVEN

"Yes, of course," said Pollard.

"So how are we going to immobilize him?"

Pollard smirked, "Leave that to me!"

35

At 3:00 p.m. the following afternoon, Hunter, Nicole, Sara, and Pollard assembled in the disco.

"Okay, how do we do this?" commanded Hunter. "I'm beginning to have reservations."

"Step over here, sir, if you don't mind," said Pollard.

He ushered Hunter to a sort of gurney, which had been upended so that it was vertical and adjacent to a well-crafted wooden box with two hand holes.

"If you would please remove your shirt and jewelry, as they will interfere with the process, and we, of course, don't want to ruin them."

"Yes, of course," replied Hunter, who was hardly reticent about showing off his sloppy physique. He took off his shirt and jewelry and handed them to Nicole, who folded them and put them neatly on a chair. Hunter allowed Pollard to maneuver him so that his back was pressed against the mattress of the gurney.

"What's in the box?" asked Hunter.

"That's the mold setting," nodded Sara. "Nothing is in there yet. We just need to stabilize you before you insert your hands, then we'll pour in the alginate mixture."

Pollard grasped a leather strap attached to the gurney and brought it around Hunter's chest. "Just like an MRI machine, we need you to be absolutely motionless during the measuring process. So, I'll just buckle this into place like so. Is that too tight? Can you breathe all right?"

"No, it's okay," said Hunter. "I can breathe."

"I'll just go ahead and do the same for your midsection," said Pollard as he affixed a second strap. "And two more for your legs. There! Perfect! Try to wriggle your hips."

Hunter tried, but his hips were held firmly in place.

"Good," nodded Pollard. "It's important you stay absolutely motionless. Otherwise, the mold will deform."

Nicole approached Hunter, now immobilized. "You okay?" she asked.

"This is child's play compared to some of the straps I've been in," Hunter joked.

They watched as Pollard worked diligently to position the gurney to align as close to the box as possible with the appropriate height setting for Hunter's arms to enter the box.

"Now, all we need to do is get your hands in when you're ready," said Pollard.

Sara revealed a bottle of whiskey, which she put to Hunter's lips and poured a swig he was happy to imbibe.

"Should calm the nerves," she whispered.

EVEN STEVEN

"Let's get this over with," Hunter muttered.

Sara turned to Pollard. "Are you ready?"

"Ready," he nodded.

Pollard slowly poured the mixture into the box.

"This is exciting," said Nicole.

"Yes, it is," replied Pollard, focused on their task at hand as if in a trance.

The process continued with Pollard assuring Hunter that things were going smoothly while Sara gave him a few more sips of whiskey.

"Okay," said Pollard. "Two more minutes, max."

"It feels like my hands are numb. Is that normal? It's like they're in concrete," Hunter said.

Nicole eyed him quizzically.

"Does it hurt?" Sara asked Hunter.

"I don't know. I guess it's fine," he replied.

"Okay," said Sara. "Hold that position!"

Pollard chimed in, "Ten seconds," as he pulled the wood handled cheese wire from his pocket and quickly lassoed it around Hunter's wrists.

Hunter jerked but he was frozen in place.

Nicole yelled and jumped into action, "What the hell is happening?"

EVEN STEVEN

Sara stepped in front with her gun drawn, "Get back."

Pollard spoke up, "Your hands have been set in a rapid-setting concrete. Your time has come."

Sara turned to Hunter, writhing and grimacing in his bindings.

"By the way, there was a powerful anticoagulant in the whiskey you enjoyed so much. It will help you bleed out quickly. Probably take five minutes before you lose consciousness. Give you time to think about all the innocent lives you've ruined for so long as they've suffered in shame since knowing you. It's a proper death by a thousand cuts!"

"You bitch! I'll kill you!" screamed Hunter, as Pollard began to saw away at his wrists.

But he was gasping for breath. His eyes became unfocused.

Nicole clamored for her phone. "Gotta call the police!"

"Police?" sneered Sara as she snatched the phone away and held her gun at Nicole. "Sure, bring them here! They can set free all the girls in the Special House. Take you to Tutwiler Prison. I hear it's a real nice place."

"Cut me loose," muttered Hunter, as one of his handless arms flopped from the wooden box dumping a waterfall of blood onto the floor.

"Can you give Holly Givens her life back?" said Sara. "And Krissy and Mia and all the others? You're nothing but a vampire, Mr. Hunter. Well, now the tables are turned."

She looked back at Nicole. "You deserve to die also. I'll give you five seconds to get out of here or I'll kill you myself. Run! Run as far away from here as you can. And if I ever see you—anywhere, anytime—you'll be dead."

With a wild-eyed look, Nicole stumbled to the door leaving bloody handprints in her path and was gone.

Sara turned to Pollard. "You should get a head start, too. I'll take care of things here. And call your uncle, will you? He loves you despite the terrible things you've done."

Pollard looked at Hunter, whose eyes were glassy and half-closed. Then he looked back at Sara.

"Will you do the honors, or shall I?"

Sara thought for a moment. Then she said, "We'll give him a few minutes to die. Then you can do it. I'll write the letter. How's that?"

"No, I got this one, my friend," Pollard said with a grin.

While they waited, Sara wiped down the scene. The only bloody fingerprints in the room belonged to Nicole. Soon, Hunter had no pulse. Pollard took a box cutter from his pants pocket, pried open Hunter's mouth, and carved the distinctive sign of the Even Steven eye into his tongue. He pocketed the razor, peeled off the latex gloves he had been wearing, and put them in his pocket as well. He turned to Sara.

"It's been nice doing business with you," he said with a wink before darting for the door.

"Pollard!" she shouted. But it was too late. She realized she had to still deal with Hunter and her own escape route. She'd

EVEN STEVEN

have to hunt for Pollard later.

Sara grabbed the pile of clothing worn by Hunter and took the cell phone from the pocket of his trousers.

She went to her room and cleaned herself up. Then she went to find Mia, Krissy, and the other girls in the main house. "You're free to go," she told them.

"Are we going to get paid?" asked Krissy.

"I'm giving you back your life," Sara replied. "That's worth more than any money."

"How are we going to get home?" asked Mia.

"I'll make a call. The local authorities will come for you. I know you've been through a terrible experience. Just do the best you can."

Then she went to the Special House. Twelve girls were there. Most did not speak English. Many had been brutalized. She told them to stay there and that help was coming. That was all she could do for them.

The three other male guests from Nashville? They could fend for themselves.

In the garage were a Ferrari, a Cadillac, a Land Rover, and a Chevy truck. The keys were in the truck, so she took it. She backed it out and turned it around. The house looked like any other magnificent old mansion in the late afternoon sun, giving no hint of the horrors concealed within.

She drove down the driveway and, before reaching the road, she took out Hunter's phone and dialed 9-1-1.

EVEN STEVEN

"Dauphin Island Police Department," said the bored-sounding operator. "This line is recorded. What is your emergency?"

"Homicide at the estate of Wally Hunter, Bienville Boulevard. Responding officers will also find about sixteen female minors who require social services. Many are undocumented, held as sex slaves at the estate."

"What is your name, please?"

"Just a concerned citizen. I repeat, one male homicide victim and many young female victims of sex trafficking. Take good care of them."

She ended the call, wiped down the phone, and threw it out the window into the calm ocean as she crossed the Dauphin Island access bridge. As she looked ahead, the sun shined with vigor into her eyes, causing her to reach for the visor where she found a pair of sleek sunglasses. She placed them on as she drove ahead. Then with a pause, nudged them down to the bridge of her nose and turned to the rearview, catching a watchful glimpse of her own cunning eyes.

THE END